Hart of Rock and Roll Book Four

Flowers For Zoe

Mary J. Williams

ISBN-13: 978-0997616163 (Brook Publications)
ISBN-10: 0997616164

About the Author

Writing isn't easy. But I love every second. A blank screen isn't the enemy. It is the opportunity to create new friends and take them on amazing adventures and life-changing journeys. I feel blessed to spend my days weaving tales that are unique—because I made them.

Billionaires. Songwriters. Artists. Actors. Directors. Stuntmen. Football players. They fill the pages and become dear friends I hope you will want to revisit again and again.

Thank you for jumping into my books and coming along for the journey.

How to Get in Touch

Please visit me at these sites, sign up for my newsletter or leave a message.
http://www.maryjwilliams.net/
https://www.facebook.com/maryjwilliamsauthor/?ref=hl
https://twitter.com/maryjwilliams05
https://www.pinterest.com/maryj0675/
https://www.instagram.com/2015romance/
https://www.goodreads.com/author/show/5648619.Mary_J_Williams

More Books by Mary J. Williams

Contents

Flowers For Zoe

Prologue

OUR YEARS OLD. Zoe Hart was a big girl now. She could dress herself—mostly. Get her own bowl and cereal from the cupboard—with the help of a chair. And pour her own milk—the few spills that her brother Ryder quickly cleaned up didn't count. She was almost grown up. Unlike Suzy next door who was a whole year older, Zoe didn't need a nightlight, and she never wet the bed.

Pre-school was fun. Finger painting was the best because Zoe was allowed to make a mess. Ryder told her they couldn't make messes at home. She did her best—she *was* a big girl now. But sometimes she forgot. Her big brother would rush to put things right, keeping an eye on the front door. Then he would wipe away her tears—she didn't cry very often because only babies cried—holding her on his lap, telling her everything would be okay.

Ryder always made things right. He brushed Zoe's hair without pulling too hard and made the best peanut butter sandwiches ever. He knew how to tie her shoes and always held her hand when they left the apartment. He never scolded. She loved Ryder more than anything in the whole world—even her teddy bear.

It seemed like Zoe's friends were afraid of everything. Spiders. The dark. And something they called the boogeyman. She didn't know who that was, but she knew he wouldn't frighten her. Nothing scared Zoe. Except the Monster.

The music brought the Monster. Deep asleep, Zoe never heard it, but Ryder always did.

"Shh," he urged, waking her up with a gentle shake. Before she could complain, he would put a finger to Zoe's lips. "Hear that?"

Counting flowers on the wall, that don't bother me at all.

The sound was faint, but Zoe could hear the words through the thin apartment walls. When she was a little girl—a whole year ago when she was three—she thought the music sounded happy. Now that she was grown up, she had figured out that the song made Ryder sad. He was sad for a long time after it finally stopped playing. She might not understand the reasons, but Zoe knew one thing. If her big brother didn't like it, neither did she.

"Do you have your teddy?" Ryder would ask.

Zoe nodded, she always slept with teddy. Ryder would take her hand. He had her crawl under the bed, way in back to the farthest corner, before tucking a blanket around her.

"Remember the invisible game?" Ryder whispered. "You have to stay right here, Zoe. Curl up in a little ball, don't make a sound, hold on to teddy, and keep the blanket tight. The Monster can't see you if you follow the rules. He won't know you're here."

"I remember," Zoe whispered back. She knew it was part of the game. But she didn't like it. She didn't want to play by herself. "Stay with me."

"Shh." A loud thump from the other room made Ryder hurriedly look over his shoulder. "You know I'll be back."

"But—"

The bedroom door slammed open, making Zoe jump, the squeak she let out muffled by Ryder's hand.

"*I need my little boy.*" The Monster's voice was sing-songy, and though the words were slurred, they were unmistakable.

"I'll always come back for you, Zoe. Always. Now close your eyes. Please?"

Reluctantly, Zoe scrunched her eyes tight.

"There he is." Zoe knew she wasn't supposed to, but she couldn't help peeking. The Monster grabbed Ryder's arm, jerking him from under the bed. "Come keep Daddy company."

With a silent sob, Zoe shut her eyes. *Daddy.* She never thought of the Monster that way. He was rarely around. Ryder made certain Zoe had something to eat. They would play games or watch something on the television. After she brushed her teeth, her big brother would tuck her in, reading her a story. Zoe liked it when it was just the two of them.

On the few occasions when the Monster spent the evening in the apartment, Ryder made her stay in the bedroom, quietly playing by herself.

The song grew louder. Zoe pressed her hands to her ears, unable to block out the noise or the sound of Ryder crying out. She knew there would be boo boos on his arms in the morning. Dark spots he tried to hide under an old, ripped shirt that was way too big, the sleeves hanging past the ends of his fingers.

Why won't the Monster stop? Furiously, Zoe wiped the tears from her cheeks, clutching her teddy bear close. Humming a nonsensical tune, in her head she recited Ryder's words over and over, drifting into a deep but troubled sleep.

You are invisible. I'll always come back for you. You are invisible. I'll always come back for you. You are invisible. I'll always come back for you.

Chapter One

FLOWERS COVERED EVERY spare inch of Zoe Hart's dressing room.

Huge arrangements of roses on the tables. Vases overflowing with tulips littered the floor. Carnations. Orchids. Combinations of every color. Bright red. Cheery yellow. Orange. Purple. Blue. White. With only a small path between where she stood and the bathroom, the closet that held her street clothes was completely blocked.

Though she had never been to the circus—and avoided funerals like the plague—she imagined this was how a crazy-ass, mash-up version of the two would look. With a sigh, Zoe stood in the doorway, careful not to breathe in the scent of clowns and death.

"Lolli!"

"Sorry." It seemed to be Lolli's favorite word. Out of breath, the bright-eyed young woman pushed back her mop of dark, curly hair. "I was talking to one of the roadies. We come from the same hometown. If fact, our brothers—"

"*I. Don't. Care.*"

The success of *The Ryder Hart Band* left little time for things like doing laundry, answering fan mail, buying groceries, and so forth. Between recording, songwriting, touring, and the general business of being part of a very, very successful music group, the little things tended to fall by the wayside.

Ryder couldn't live without his ever-so-efficient assistant. Dalton and

Ashe felt the same about theirs. Two years ago, Zoe had given in to pressure from her bandmates and hired someone who was supposed to magically make her life easier. Instead, it had been just the opposite. Lolli Mankiewicz was a pain in the ass number five.

"Did I do something wrong?"

"For the love of God." Zoe rubbed a hand over face. "Are you crying?"

"No," Lolli sniffled.

Zoe didn't think she was an unreasonably demanding person. With each hire, she didn't ask for much. However, there were some things that were deal breakers.

"What did I tell you about flowers in my dressing room?"

"That they were bad?"

Not exactly the word Zoe used. For some reason, no matter how she tried to discourage the practice, fans deluged her with flowers. The deliveries began on the day of a concert, continuing while she was on stage, and after. As if sending a dozen roses was the key to Zoe's heart—or getting her into bed. Men. Women. Zoe had suitors of every gender thanks to a persistent rumor that she swung both ways.

That was so beside the point, Zoe mentally shook herself. As assistant after assistant fell by the wayside, Zoe was about ready to give up. She was giving it one last chance. Lolli or bust—so to speak. After a week of trying her best to ease the young woman into her duties, tonight's concert had been the big test. Zoe gave Lolli one thing to do. Just one. Keep the floral deliveries—every piece of baby's breath, every frond, every petal—far, far away from her dressing room.

If an arrangement or two had slipped by, Zoe would have looked the other way. The dressing room was packed. It looked like the flowers were multiplying on their own. This wasn't a mere slip. It was a fail of epic proportions.

"Do you have the phone number I gave you? Byron Banks?"

Lolli nodded, dabbing at her eyes with a soggy tissue.

"Call him. He will arrange to have the flowers sent to a few local hospitals. After that, you can go home."

"Am I fired?" Lolli asked.

"Take care of this. I'll talk to you in the morning."

Arms crossed, her chocolate brown eyes narrowing as she waited for Lolli to get the hint.

"Should I do it now?"

"Yes, Lolli." God, Zoe felt tired. "Now would be good."

"I'll get right on it."

"Are you going to fire her?" Quinn Abernathy asked as she watched Lolli scamper away.

"Hell, yes." Resigned, Zoe entered her dressing room. The outfit she had worn on stage was limp from the lights and the sweat that ran freely from her body during the two-and-a-half-hour concert. The drying film of sticky salt made her skin itch. If she didn't get a shower—soon—she would go crazy.

"It's only been a week."

Quinn had followed, slipping through the door before Zoe could shut it in her face.

"Look around."

"Oh." Quinn drew out the word. "I see what you mean."

"I'm going to hop in the shower. As long as you're here, make yourself useful and try to get my stuff out of the closet."

"I could do that." Quinn sent Zoe a half smile. "If you throw in a please."

"Oh, for—" Pulling her shirt over her head, Zoe tossed it on the floor. "Fine. I forgot about your delicate sensibilities. Will you please get my stuff out of the closet, Quinn?"

"My sensibilities are no more delicate than your average human being," Quinn yelled through the firmly shut bathroom door. "It's called basic manners."

Smiling despite herself, Zoe turned the faucets on full blast. Sitting on the closed toilet seat, she unzipped the long, high-heeled leather boots, flexing her feet. Making quick work of the black leggings and lacey underwear, Zoe removed the large, glittery hoops from her ears. The rings on her fingers came next.

It was all part of the show. Zoe's stage persona glittered. In real life, her style was a bit more understated. Not that she wasn't fashion forward. One of the greatest joys of money was the ability to buy a pair of shoes, or a leather jacket, or a perfectly tailored dress, without worrying about the cost. For a woman who had spent years buying everything in thrift shops and scouring eBay for the best secondhand bargains, she would never take for granted what it felt like to have a huge, walk-in closet filled with designer labels, some of the outfits made especially for her. Clothing that nobody but herself would ever wear.

"Success," Quinn called out as Zoe stepped into the shower stall. "I put everything into your suitcase, and I'm leaving it outside the door."

"Thank you."

"You're welcome. See? Mutual common courtesies. How hard was that?"

Shaking her head, there was a smile on Zoe's lips as she put her head under the hot spray of water. Quinn had taken some getting used to, but Zoe was beginning to like the woman—even think of her as a friend. That wasn't an easy admission. She didn't like a lot of people. She trusted fewer. On the fingers of one hand, she could count the ones she loved.

Quinn Abernathy was a talented photographer. That was how she and Ryder met. At first, she had her doubts that the woman was right for her brother. Time, and seeing the couple together, had eased her worries. This woman made Ryder happy. Even more, she helped him let go of the past. That dark place he sometimes fell into had been filled with light—and Quinn was the reason. There was no doubt in Zoe's mind. Quinn loved Ryder. Unconditionally. Unabashedly. Unequivocally.

Resting her hand on the shower tile, Zoe lifted her face, the water washing away the dirt and sweat. She wished it could do the same for her weary brain. It seemed that lately, she couldn't shut it down. Thoughts zipped around like an out-of-control ping pong ball—never settling in one place for long.

Zoe felt restless. For the first time since she was in her mid-teens, she didn't feel quite comfortable in her own skin. There had been a rapid succession of upheavals in the band. Mostly personal—mostly good. For a long time, her family had consisted of three other people. Her brother Ryder, Dalton Shaw, and Ashe Mathison. They were a tight unit—growing tighter as they weathered the storms of a struggling rock band. Over the years, there had been some crazy ups and some soul-searing downs—one that came close to tearing Dalton from them.

They made it through—as a group. Ryder called them battle-toughened warriors. Given the circumstances, he wasn't far from the truth. *The Ryder Hart Band* had formed ten years earlier. Three young men with a similar vision for their music and their futures. Zoe had joined three years later, on the day of her eighteenth birthday. Two years later, the band took off. Ryder, Dalton, and Ashe called her their lucky charm. Zoe knew the truth. She was the lucky one. The band had given her life purpose. The young men who welcomed her without reservation had given her a family and absolute unconditional love.

It had always been just the four of them. In the past year, that had changed. The family had expanded by three. Her brothers—and that was how she thought of them all—had found *the ones*. The love of their life.

Their other half. First Ryder and Quinn. Then Dalton and Colleen. And finally, Ashe and Belle.

There were couples to the left of Zoe, couples to the right. Even their longtime manager, Alden Christopher had a new boyfriend and seemed happier than she had ever seen him. Suddenly, Zoe felt like the lone solo traveler on *The Ryder Hart Band's* newly constructed Ark.

Zoe grabbed a towel, wrapping it around her long, blond hair turban style. It wasn't as if she expected to be thrown off the boat. Nor did she feel left out or unwanted. Just the opposite. She had never had close women friends. It was a fact. One she never thought much about. In high school, she didn't have time for the social politics of teenagers. Besides, she found out early that snarky girls (Zoe was a natural) and mean girls were a bad fit.

It hadn't occurred to Zoe that things would change simply because the men in the band added their women to the mix.

The problem—if Zoe wanted to think of it that way—was with those women. They refused to let her keep them at arm's length. Somehow—without her realizing it happened—Quinn, Colleen, and Belle had sucked her in. First, it was a few shopping trips—a weakness of Zoe's. Then lunch out with the girls. Gab sessions during which Zoe mostly sat and listened. At some point when she wasn't paying attention, they became her friends.

"Hey, Zoe. Move your fine ass. We're heading for Ashe's place in ten minutes."

Zoe's lips quirked. It was funny. For a man who was the best drummer she had ever heard, Dalton Shaw pounded on a door with the finesse of a battering ram.

"Have you ever known me to keep you guys waiting?" Zoe yelled back as she slathered lotion over her long limbs.

"Nope. But there's a first time for everything."

"Asshole." Muttered under her breath, Zoe chuckled when Dalton answered. The man had the hearing of a bat.

"I love you too."

Combing out her hair, Zoe stared at her reflection. Pretty enough, she supposed. Some called her looks classic. The high cheekbones. The oval face. A man had once said her dark eyes contained the secrets of the ages. What the hell *that* meant, she would never know.

Here were the facts as Zoe saw them. She had blond hair and brown eyes. Her body was slender but strong—not by accident. Working out every day was a must. Playing lead guitar was hard work. They toured, recorded their own music tracks, and performed at least a dozen benefit concerts in a calendar year. To maintain that kind of a schedule, Zoe had to take care of herself.

Grabbing the suitcase from the other side of the bathroom door, Zoe shook out a pair of fawn-colored, soft-as-butter, straight-leg leather pants before sliding them on. She topped it with a silk blouse the color of the richest cream. A pair of low-heeled ankle boots, some diamond-stud earrings, and the simple gold bracelet Ryder gave her for her sixteenth birthday completed the outfit.

Loving clothes and fashion didn't mean Zoe fussed over her appearance. Casual cool would be a good way to describe her everyday style. A touch of cherry-red lip gloss, a quick fluff of her thick, blond hair, and she was ready to go.

"Finally."

Zoe didn't blink to find Dalton waiting outside her dressing room. The men in her life were overprotective in a non-cloying manner. It had become second nature. When they were on tour or doing one-night gigs, they made certain she never went anywhere alone. Especially before and after a concert. The band had their share of overzealous fans. Once or twice, it had crossed over into something much more serious. They took the threat of stalkers seriously.

Though Zoe prided herself on being a strong, take-no-crap kind of woman, she wasn't a fool. Bodyguards, just like the wired security fence that circled her home, were a part of the life she had chosen. *The Ryder Hart Band* was at the top of the entertainment world. Fame and fortune came with a price. Lack of privacy being right at the top of the list.

"Where is Colleen?"

"She caught a ride with Ryder and Quinn."

Dalton took the suitcase from Zoe, swinging his free arm over her shoulders. He was one of a select few who could get away with touching Zoe without her express permission—casually or otherwise. Those who tried risked pulling back a bloody stump where their hand used to be. Call her prickly. Call her an unreasonable bitch. Zoe was fine with either.

The rules were simple. Don't crowd her. And *always* ask before you touch. Zoe didn't think it unreasonable to expect people to respect her personal space.

"You didn't have to stick around for me."

Zoe didn't say it—she never would—but deep down, she was glad Dalton cared enough to make certain she was safe. Ryder was her brother by blood. Dalton and Ashe, her brothers by choice. She didn't want to think about what her life would be like without them.

Lonely. That was a fact. The years in foster care had been torture. Zoe didn't like to think about the first few years, shuffling from home to home. Always an introvert, she turned further into herself, only coming out when Ryder came to visit. Or when she played the guitar.

One thing was certain. In a childhood filled with the worst kind of uncertainty, music had been Zoe and Ryder Hart's salvation.

"I don't get to spend enough time with my little sister lately." Dalton brushed a kiss across her temple, his blue eyes twinkling.

As they reached the exit, Jasper Frost, one of their regular bodyguards, opened the door. Signaling that all was clear, he waited for Zoe and Dalton to leave the building, walking behind at a discreet distance.

"You would if you weren't in Colleen's pocket most of the time." There was no heat to Zoe's words. Dalton knew how she felt. There was nothing she wanted more than her friend's happiness.

"Colleen *does* have mighty fine pockets." They had reached the waiting car. In a secure parking lot, they were free of fans mobbing them. The driver held the door, shutting it behind them. Serious, Dalton turned to Zoe. "I hope you aren't staying away because you think we want our privacy. You're always welcome, Zoe."

It took less than a five-minute drive between Zoe and Dalton's houses. A fact that came in handy after Colleen first moved to Los Angeles. Rather than stay with Dalton, she had lived with Zoe. It seemed reasonable at the time. Though committed to each other, the couple was still in the *getting to know you* stage of their relationship. They progressed quickly—Colleen spending more nights in Dalton's bed than in Zoe's guest room. However, it had given the women a chance to build a solid base for their friendship.

Zoe didn't stay away because she felt unwanted. It was more a case of not wanting to get in the way. She and her bandmates saw each other all the time for work. If she was left out a little more on the social side, so be it. She wasn't afraid of spending some time alone. She liked a little solitude now and then. Especially when she thought about the months to come.

The Ryder Hart Band would soon be starting a huge tour that would take them through the summer and well into next year. Before long—after weeks and weeks of concerts, travel, and little down time—Zoe would be begging for five minutes to herself.

"What are we doing tonight?" Zoe asked, pouring herself some sparkling water from the stocked limousine bar. Taking a beer from the cooler, she handed it to Dalton.

"The whole gang always meets up after a gig. When was the last time we hung out just for the hell of it?"

For the last seven years, it had been just the four of them. They struggled side by side to find a foothold in the ultra-competitive music business—developing their unique sound as they developed a following. The days of rickety tour buses and worrying about paying rent on the crappy apartment they shared in East L.A. were things of the past. They had money. Lots of it. And four had grown into seven. The days of the casual drop-by were gone. They were growing up. Getting older. Change was inevitable.

"Are you feeling sorry for me?" The very idea appalled Zoe.

"You? The most self-sufficient person on the face of the Earth?" Dalton waved off the idea. "Take it from me, pity is the last emotion I would ever feel for you, kid."

"Then what is the point of—" With a sigh, Zoe closed her eyes. "Despite what Noah and the Ark tried to teach us, two by two is not the only way to live your life."

Dalton had the grace to look uncomfortable with the subject, but that didn't keep him from sticking his foot further into his mouth. "We thought—"

"We?" Zoe's eyes flew open. "As in more than one of you? Ryder? Ashe?"

Dalton shrugged. "They may have been part of the discussion."

"Now it's a discussion. What the hell, Dalton? When have we ever trod on each other's love lives?"

"We don't. But Quinn thought…" Realizing his mistake, Dalton trailed off. "It was a group thing, Zoe."

With a shake of her head, Zoe turned toward the window, watching the lights of downtown Los Angeles sail by. She knew it wasn't fair, but of the three women who had so recently joined their ranks, Zoe found Ryder's fiancée the least easy to warm to. A psychologist would have a field day rooting out the reasons. But Zoe didn't need her head shrunk to understand the problem.

For as long as she could remember, Ryder had taken care of her—often to his detriment. When Quinn came on the scene, Zoe's biggest fear had been that the other woman would hurt her brother. Trust—for all of them—meant everything. When Zoe believed Quinn had betrayed Ryder, she acted without all the facts. Though the truth came out, and Zoe apologized, there remained a touch of coolness—mostly on Zoe's side.

Things were better and getting better all the time. However, the relationship wasn't perfect. Finding out that Quinn had initiated the conversation about Zoe's personal life didn't help.

"Quinn needs to mind her own business."

"I thought you were over the idea that Quinn is the enemy."

Hearing the disappointment—tinged with disapproval—in Dalton's voice hurt more than Zoe would care to admit. Knowing he was right made it worse.

"I like Quinn."

"But…" Dalton urged.

"Why won't happily involved people leave us singles alone?"

"Ah." Not bothering to hide his smile, Dalton nodded.

"Is it so hard to believe that I'm fine buying food for one? Or taking in a movie by myself?"

"No. But when was the last time you saw a movie that wasn't streamed? Alone or with a date?"

"That isn't the point." Zoe jabbed Dalton in the leg. "I don't need a man in my life."

"Or a woman?" Though Dalton said it with his tongue planted firmly in his cheek, Zoe wasn't amused.

"Shut up. That crack has lost you conversation privileges until we get to Ashe's place."

There had always been plenty of speculation in the press and on fan sites concerning Zoe and her sexuality. As the only woman in a hot-as-hell rock band, the speculation was natural—and completely unfair. She was under a bigger—more critical microscope. Who she dated. How long they were together. If she was seen looking friendly with a woman? Bam! They were lovers. The rumors were in a constant swirl. Bisexual. Lesbian. She hated men. She loved women. She loved men. She hated women. Though she avoided the tabloids like the plague, she knew that one of the supermarket rags once had her involved with aliens. The kind from outer space.

The days of pairing her with Dalton or Ashe—sometimes Dalton and Ashe at the same time—seemed to be a thing of the past. But every other man—and woman—was fair game.

"If you promise not to tell Ryder that I threw Quinn under the bus, I'll buy you an ice cream cone."

Zoe's lips twitched. When they first met, Zoe was fifteen. Too old to be bribed into liking her brother's new friends with promises of sugary treats. However, she and Dalton had bonded over their love of Mocha Almond Fudge Swirl. Since then, it had been their thing. That he would bring it up now, made her heart melt—just a little.

"What did I say about speaking with me?" Melting heart or not, Zoe wouldn't cave *that* easily.

"Look out the window. Ashe's condo is right there."

"Smug jerk," Zoe muttered.

"How about that ice cream?" Dalton took Zoe's hand.

"We don't rat each other out. Ever."

That could have been the unofficial motto of *The Ryder Hart Band*. There were no real secrets between them—nothing that needed to be aired out. When it came to small things like individual confidences, they had no problem keeping each other's counsel.

"Thanks, kid." Dalton helped her from the car. They nodded at the doorman, walking across the lobby to the elevator. "If it's any consolation, Ryder wasn't interested in discussing your love life."

"You mean my brother would rather not hear about the men I date? Shocking."

"None of us want the details." Dalton shuddered at the thought. "We want you to be happy."

"I am."

"Then end of discussion. I will pass the word."

Satisfied, Zoe leaned back as the elevator soared to the top floor. Happy was a relative term, but for the most part, it was accurate. But she wished she could drop the feeling of restlessness that continued to creep into her subconscious at the oddest times. Zoe knew the reason—not that it helped. And if asked, she would have denied it to her dying breath.

The doors opened to the living room of Ashe's condominium. There was music—naturally. Laughter greeted them. *This* made her happy. Friends. Family. A small group of people. They were important. Vital.

"Hello, Zoe."

Zoe felt her shoulders stiffen. The reaction was automatic. Every time, without fail. No matter how loose and relaxed she might be, one word, one look, and she tensed up, ready to take flight.

Though her insides began to heat, Zoe calmly turned her head, her gaze meeting a pair of deep, emerald-colored eyes. Restless? No, it was more than that. It was a feeling she couldn't put her finger on. But she knew the source. Six feet three inches of dark-haired annoyance.

"Hello, Smith."

Chapter Two

SMITH CARSON. ZOE gritted her teeth. Why couldn't she shake this man? It seemed wherever she turned, there he was. If not in person, then on billboards, or the radio, or television, or on the cover of a magazine. Talk about overexposure. By now, the public should be sick of him—Zoe certainly was.

"Why are you here?" Zoe deliberately made the question accusatory and rude.

Smith smiled. He actually smiled. *What was wrong with this man?*

The flash of his strong, white teeth emphasized the creases in his cheeks. Dimples. Those were supposed to be cute—associated with innocent little boys. But there was nothing little—or innocent about Smith Carson. He was fully grown. A man, top to bottom.

When Zoe looked into Smith's eyes, she had the uncomfortable feeling he knew things. About her. Secrets. Intimate details she had never shared with another human being.

"I was invited," Smith said with a slight Southern drawl that sent an unwanted shiver down Zoe's spine.

"Not by me." Nose slightly in the air—as though Smith was beneath her interest—Zoe tried to move past him. When he took her arm, her eyes dropped to his hand. "*That* is a mistake."

"You don't like to be touched?"

Smith worded it as a question, though it was obvious he knew the answer. His grip loosened. Not letting go, Smith's thumb lightly caressed Zoe's skin through the silk of her blouse. Later, she would tell herself that she let him—just for a moment—because the audacity of his move made her freeze. It wasn't that Smith's touch felt good or made her heart race. That would be crazy. She disliked the man. Intensely.

Too handsome for anybody's good, Smith Carson was one of those people who photographed like a dream—then had the nerve to look even better in person. Zoe wasn't above admitting that he had a certain appeal. Fangirls certainly agreed. However, he was not her type. She preferred less obvious looks. Subtle. Smith had an in-your-face vibe that put Zoe off. Until they were in the same room. Then...

Taking back her arm with a firm jerk, Zoe gave herself a mental shake. *Do not go down that road.* Smith Carson, for all his smooth charm and sexy smile, was the last man she wanted to encourage. And if his reputation were even halfway accurate, it wouldn't take much.

"Zoe—"

Zoe cut Smith off with a sharp glance. When she spoke, her words dripped with ice. "Never touch me again. Understood?"

"Understood." Smith gave her a considering look. "Unless you ask."

"That will never happen."

"We'll see."

They could have stayed like that all night. Trading one-liners, neither willing to let the other get the last word. *The hell with that.* With a half smile and slight shake of her head—Zoe's way of telling Smith that he wasn't worth the effort—she turned and walked away. It was tempting to glance over her shoulder to see Smith's reaction. But she knew it would lessen the impact of what she considered a damn fine exit. Instead, she continued into the room, stopping—with her back to him—where Ryder, Quinn, and Ashe stood by the fireplace.

"There you are." Ryder gave Zoe a warm, brotherly hug, keeping his arm around her shoulders. "I was beginning to wonder if you decided to blow us off in favor of a good night's sleep."

"Zoe doesn't need much sleep." Ashe Mathison leaned over, greeting her with a kiss on the cheek. "I'm the same way. We have superior metablolisms."

"*You* are a freak of nature." Ashe's girlfriend, Belle Richards, took his hand as she joined the circle. "Lucky for me."

"No, sweetheart. I'm the lucky one," Ashe whispered near Belle's ear, but it was easy for everybody to hear.

"What about me?" Zoe asked, raising an eyebrow. "Do my sleeping patterns make me a freak as well?"

"I remember when you were a little girl. You never wanted to go to bed and were up with the chickens."

"We lived in Chicago," Zoe reminded her brother.

"Pigeons, then," Ryder chuckled. "Either way, it was hard to keep up with you. Still is."

Zoe smiled at Ryder's lighthearted comment. But she felt a sting of tears she would never shed behind her eyes. There had been a time—not so long ago—when he never spoke of their childhood. Not even the good times. One mention of Chicago would have had him close down, seeking out his guitar. If Zoe never again had to listen to Ryder's mournful rendition of *Flowers on the Wall*, she would be happy.

Meeting Quinn's gaze, Zoe blinked, mouthing a belated *thank you*. The surprise she saw in the other woman's eyes—followed by a warm smile—made her feel a burst of guilt. Quinn was the reason Ryder found peace with his past. Her love and support finally healed the wounds that had festered for years—coming to the surface from time to time.

"Am I the only one who was surprised when Smith showed up at the concert alone?"

"He was at the concert?" Why hadn't Zoe known that? And what had Quinn said about a girlfriend?

"Word has it the actress is history," Belle lowered her voice, her tone conspiratorial. "My assistant is friends with Thea Davidson's assistant. Smith dumped Thea. I guess it was pretty messy."

"You get the best gossip." Quinn checked over her shoulder. Following the direction of her gaze, Zoe saw that Smith was across the room, deep in conversation with Dalton and Colleen. "What's the dirt?"

"You're okay with this?" Zoe asked Ryder before Belle could answer.

The Ryder Hart Band were a notoriously close-mouthed group. Nothing leaked unless they wanted it to. And then only if it had to do with business. Their personal lives were off limits to the press. When they first started out, it seemed like a strategy that could backfire. To get ahead, unknown artists relied on the public's interest. The more their fans knew about them, the better the chance that interest would translate into record sales and filled concert venues.

For whatever reason, *The Ryder Hart Band* didn't put people off with their reticence. It was intriguing. Different. The mystery drew fans in. Ten years later, they could count themselves one of the biggest acts in music.

"Gossiping amongst ourselves isn't a crime, Zoe." Ryder winked at Belle. "Go on. Tell us about the pretty boy and the actress."

Zoe told herself that she wasn't interested in anything about Smith Carson. However, it didn't hurt to listen.

"With that kind of buildup, I wish I had more information." Shrugging, Belle smiled. "It seems Smith was tired of Thea using his celebrity to increase her own. He ended it at her apartment."

"Smart," Ashe said. "It gives him an escape route."

"Did he need one?" Quinn asked.

Belle nodded. "From what I hear, Thea went ballistic. If it was breakable, she smashed it. If it was heavy—aka a metal paperweight—she threw it at Smith's head. Short story shorter, Thea has a lousy arm, and Smith hightailed it after the first missile was launched. *That* is why he is now flying solo."

"A man like that? He won't be alone for long."

"Excuse me?" Ryder pulled Quinn to his side, his deep blue eyes holding a teasing glint. "You think Smith is attractive?"

"Weren't you the one who just called him a pretty boy?" Quinn touched the ends of Ryder's hair. He wore it longer than usual because she liked the way it curled around her fingers when she ran them through the dark locks. "Our admiration seems to be mutual."

"Oh, for the love of—" The couple was so cloyingly cute, Zoe had to laugh. It was either that or gag. "Do you talk like this when you're alone?"

"Sometimes." Deliberately, Ryder met his sister's gaze. "Most of the time, we don't talk at all. We're too busy—"

"No, no, no!" Zoe put her hands over her ears. "What is the rule? Never share details about our love lives. *Never.*"

"I was going to say that we were too busy binge watching *Game of Thrones*. You are the one with the dirty mind, Zoe." Tapping Zoe on the chin before she could make a retort, Ryder asked, "Can I get you something to drink?"

"Water. Sparkling. Jerk." Zoe muttered the last word under her breath. She knew that Ryder heard, but he let it go.

"Quinn? Belle?"

"I'm good." Belle held up her glass of wine.

"I could use a refill," Quinn said, draining the last of her drink.

"What about me?" Ashe held out his empty beer bottle.

"I could tell you where to shove that, but you've heard it before, and I hate to be redundant."

Ashe laughed. "God forbid. I guess that means I have to serve myself. Come on." He slung his arm companionably around Ryder's neck. "Pretty boy."

"Ruggedly handsome," Ryder insisted as the friends walked toward the kitchen.

"I've fallen in love with a man whose sense of humor sometimes borders on the juvenile." Belle shook her head, dark eyes shining with good will. "Why doesn't that bother me?"

"You said it yourself. You're in love." As a woman who knew how that felt, Quinn could speak with authority. "Besides, Ashe is a sweetheart. Through and through."

"No argument here." Belle's skin seemed to glow with happiness.

Was that what love looked like, Zoe wondered. Wandering a few steps away to look out the window at the downtown lights, she pondered the question. Suddenly—after years of thinking love was an overrated emotion—it was all around her. She should have a better grasp on what it meant. But it seemed a person had to experience it first hand, or it remained a mystery. The closest Zoe had come had been a teenage crush. One that turned out to be nothing but an illusion. Since then, Zoe's heart had been locked away. Not surrounded by ice. More like an impenetrable fortress. She hadn't met anybody willing to attempt swimming the moat or scaling the walls. Nor had any man interested her enough for her to consider giving him the key.

Zoe knew that twenty-five was too young for her to give up. However, she had to wonder if she was capable of that kind of passion. Love for her brother. Her friends. That was easy—natural. What she saw between Ryder, Quinn, and all the rest? Somehow, Zoe couldn't see it happening for her.

Was it genetic? Outside of her brother, Zoe didn't think her family knew what love was. Her parents had been all kinds of messed up in that department. A monster of a father and a mother who abandoned her children to him.

Zoe and Ryder had survived. If money, fame, and happiness were the best revenge, the Hart siblings definitely had the last laugh. They had so much. Not more than they dreamed of. If there was one thing they had in that rat hole of an apartment, it was dreams. Big ones. And they weren't done yet. There were always new horizons to explore. The world was changing. Fast and furious. *The Ryder Hart Band* would never be left behind.

No matter what people said, Zoe didn't believe love waited around every corner or that there was enough to go around. That everybody had a soulmate. But if only one of them would find it, thank God it had been Ryder. More than anybody she knew—after all he had suffered—her big brother deserved what he had found with Quinn. She hoped it was what it seemed. True love. Deep. Abiding. Forever.

Zoe knew one thing for certain. If Quinn did anything to break Ryder's heart, there would be no place the woman could run where Zoe wouldn't find her and kick her ass.

"Who pissed you off and should I be worried about the repercussions?"

"You know me better than that. I never leave a trail." Zoe took the glass of bubble-filled liquid from Ryder, smiling as she took a sip. When he gave her a steady, unblinking look, she bumped him with her arm. "Relax. I'm not contemplating anything but the view."

"I thought you might be stewing over Smith Carson."

"Why would you think that?" Zoe refused to squirm. She had a perfect poker face. Unfortunately, Ryder knew her almost better than she knew herself. If anybody could tell something was bothering her, it was her brother.

"You never liked the idea of combining tours with Smith. Now that the time is getting closer, I wondered how you were feeling."

With a nonchalant shrug she was damned proud of herself for pulling it off, Zoe glanced at Ryder. "Like you said, it's only a few dates scattered throughout the summer and fall. Besides, we voted. You guys won."

"Stop pouting."

"Pouting?" Zoe felt the blood rush to her face, the heat making her dark eyes flash. "I never pout. Not when I was a child and certainly not now. And stop grinning." Stomping her foot was not what a mature woman would do. But, oh how Zoe wanted to do exactly that. Ryder had purposefully goaded her. Like the typical little sister, she had fallen for it.

"If there is a reason you don't want Smith around, you would tell me. Right?"

Gone was the teasing brother; in his place, her protector. It made Zoe think of all the times he had kept her safe. When Ryder had pushed her as far under the bed as possible before the Monster would drag him from the bedroom. Her finger's gripped her glass until her knuckles turned white, chastising herself for dredging up the past. Why was she traveling down that old dark and winding path of horrors? Ryder had let it go, why couldn't she?

"Zoe?"

The worry in Ryder's voice snapped Zoe back to the present. Taking a deep breath, she gave him a smile—one that almost reached her eyes.

"I have no problem with Smith Carson." Because she planned to stay as far away from him as possible. "If you think it will benefit the band to join up, consider me on board."

"That's my girl." Ryder winked, his blue eyes filled with affection. "Or should I say woman. Is girl politically incorrect?"

"Yes. But for you, I'll make an exception."

Resting her head on Ryder's shoulder, Zoe stood with his arm around her waist. She no longer needed her big brother to protect her from monsters—real or imagined. But it felt good—just for a little while—to relax and pretend that everything would be fine as long as Ryder was near.

Chapter Three

HERE WERE TIMES when Smith Carson wondered at his success. Not often. He wasn't the kind of man who wasted time pondering the whys and wherefores of life. He preferred to live in the moment. If things were good, he let himself enjoy. If things were bad, he decided on a course of action, plowing ahead until he had his world back on track.

It was only human to occasionally think about the turns that brought him to where he was. Smith was nothing if not human—down to his core.

Taking a cup of coffee from the outrageously expensive machine his assistant insisted he needed, Smith leaned against the poured-concrete counter. Growing up, his mama cooked for a husband, six kids, and three grandparents in a kitchen that—compared to the massive one he currently stood in—was the size of a small postage stamp. She did it all on a two-burner cooktop and an oven that dated back to the Second World War.

Somehow, Nellie Carson turned out the tastiest meals in three counties. On a minuscule budget, she filled the stomachs of her large brood—and any of their neighbors who were temporarily down on their luck. In South Ridge, Alabama, that wasn't an unusual occurrence. The Carsons had almost nothing. Some of their neighbors even less.

Mostly rural, South Ridge was little more than a blip. Blink and one missed it. The countryside was littered with farmers who barely scraped by—and that was a good year. They knew nothing about depressions or recessions. Booms or busts. Things didn't change. Nobody was getting rich.

The abandoned fallow fields that flanked the Carson farm were proof of that. They represented the tiniest bit of hope that bloomed from time to time, but never materialized.

The best way to survive was to keep your head down. Work from sun up to sundown. Day after day. Month after month. Year after year. On the day a man died, if he could say he kept his family fed, he considered his life a success. It had been the same for generations.

Dreams were a dangerous thing in South Ridge. It didn't pay to encourage a child to think there was more to be had than dirt under his fingernails and tired muscles at the end of the day. For all their problems. The lack of money. The lack of rain. The lack of... everything. With all that, Smith had a childhood filled with love, laughter, and endless encouragement from both of his parents.

Smith moved from the kitchen to the open living room, his bare feet grateful for the heated hardwood floors. Dropping into an overstuffed chair, he laughed remembering the expression on his father's face the first time he visited. *Heat? In the floor?* Ben Carson shook his head. *What will they think of next?*

The best thing about making more money than he ever imagined, was lavishing it on his family. His parents had been reluctant at first. Not because they objected to a few luxuries. Practical to the bone, they worried that Smith would spend it all on them and have nothing left. It took awhile, but he finally convinced them that wouldn't happen. If something happened and he could never perform again, the royalties from the songs he wrote would keep his bank account fat for the rest of his life and beyond.

The sun was just beginning to rise. Smith loved this time of the day. There were times when his body was so exhausted from touring, recording, and just the crap that came with building a music empire, that he should have been collapsed in bed—dead to the world for a good eight hours. Instead—no matter where in the world he was at the time—Smith would find himself watching the day break.

It came from years of joining his father and his siblings in the field. The three Ps. Plowing. Planting. Picking. On a working farm, there was no time to sleep in. Smith yawned, stretching his long arms over his head. He didn't have to worry about any of that now, but that didn't change his sleeping patterns. Some habits—no matter how he tried—were impossible to break.

As Smith rested his head against the back of the chair, his mind drifted. There was another habit he would like to pick up, yet he had no way to tell if it would be good or bad for him. But damn, he would like to find out. The problem—and it was a big one—was his potential habit wasn't cooperating.

Zoe Hart. Just thinking her name brought a speculative smile to Smith's lips. When was the first time they met? Six? No, seven years ago. He remembered thinking Ryder Hart's kid sister was pretty. A bit introverted. Zoe hadn't had much to say for herself in those days—except with her guitar. Damn. That woman could play like nobody he had ever known. That hadn't changed. Smith laughed. But she was no longer shy about speaking her mind. Though it surprised him, it seemed Smith had a soft spot for sharp-tongued women. Or rather *one* woman in particular. It didn't hurt that she had deep, chocolate-colored eyes, shiny blond hair, and legs that went on for days.

To say that Smith no longer thought of Zoe Hart as somebody's cute kid sister was putting it mildly.

Realizing he wanted to make a move on Zoe was easier than actually doing it. She was all prickles. Yet for some reason that went beyond his hefty male ego, Smith couldn't let go of the notion of a spark when she looked at him. If he could get her to exchange more than a few snarky comments, perhaps he could find out.

A grudging attraction—at least on her part? He could work with that. Smith was all in. He would like nothing more than to spend several nights exploring Zoe Hart. From top to bottom and back again. She was a challenge, that was for sure.

Smith had asked himself if that was the real attraction. Did he want Zoe so much because she was so cool to him? Had the unthinkable happened? Was Smith so jaded by the years of women throwing themselves at his feet that he was looking for something in Zoe that wasn't there?

The situation wasn't cut and dried. But if cornered, Smith would say the answer was no. Whether she fell into his arms or he had to work for it, he wanted Zoe Hart. Now was his time to find out if that was going to happen. Through the summer and fall, he would play select dates with *The Ryder Hart Band*. It was business. Period. Smith didn't make career decisions based on his libido. Time to work his charm on Zoe was simply a nice bonus.

The sun had broken over the horizon and a new day had officially dawned. Smith got to his feet. Rinsing out his cup, he set it in the dishwasher. His morning schedule was tight. A hard workout was first on the agenda. Meetings with his lawyer, his manager, and his agent were next. There had been a time—back when he was a foolishly naïve novice—when Smith thought that to be a success, all he had to do was play his music. There was so much more. He refused to give anybody power over his finances.

The horror stories were endless about business managers making bad investments or absconding with their client's money. Smith worked hard. The easiest way to make sure he was around for a long time was to keep an eagle eye on his career—and his finances. He was not going to become a punchline in a joke that began *whatever happened to Smith Carson.*

The money and fame were great. But if Smith had to, he could live without both. Look at his parents. They lived most of their lives on practically nothing while managing to stay married, stay in love, and raise six fairly well-adjusted children. In the end, it was the music that mattered most. As long as he could write, play, and sing, he would be just fine.

As for Zoe Hart? Smith's green eyes heated. Maybe she would get away, maybe she wouldn't. But something told him—either way—he was going to have a good time finding out.

"WHO TOLD YOU to change the beat?" Zoe stopped the song mid-verse.

"Nobody told me," Dalton said with an arrogant tilt of his head. "I'm the drummer. I set the rhythm."

"It's my song. I wrote it." Zoe pushed her hair behind her ear. She had learned early on to push back when one of the guys tried to exert their will over her music. "This one needs a driving beat. Soft at the beginning. Building. Harder and harder. You're treating it like one of your sappy love songs."

"Sappy—" Dalton's eyes narrowed. "I beg your pardon? I do not write sap."

They had known each other a long time. Zoe knew how to push the right buttons when she wanted a rise. "Since you met Colleen, sticky and gooey have become your specialty."

"Did you hear that?" Dalton turned to Ryder and Ashe for support. "Me? Tough as nails ex-con? Gooey, my ass. Back me up here, guys."

"I've noticed a bit of goo." Ryder shrugged, straight-faced. "How about you, Ashe?"

"More than a bit." Looking thoughtful, Ashe removed the mouthpiece from his saxophone. "I fell in love, and my writing turned sultry. Ryder's is more... what's the word, Zoe?"

"Heartfelt?"

"That sounds right." With a wink in her direction, Ashe set the instrument in its case. "On the other hand, Dalton's hard edges have melted to—"

"Goo." Zoe, happy with the support from her friends, kept her gaze locked with Dalton's.

"Tell me again why I like you?" After a good thirty-second stare off, Dalton gave in, laughing. "Fine. We'll try it your way. You can apologize later."

It turned out that Dalton was the one eating humble pie. They ran through the song—Zoe's way—without stopping. The build was subtle at first. Zoe's guitar. Ashe sounding a bit mournful on the horn. Dalton's backbeat. Ryder waited for his moment to join in, his voice— his instrument—blending perfectly. Then it grew. Slowly. Each of them building the intensity with Dalton driving the action. When the last note had been played, Zoe closed her eyes, the tips of her fingers tingling.

"Where the hell did that come from?"

"I bow down in awe, kid." Dalton shook his head, wiping the sweat from his face with the towel he always kept near his drum set. "You've always played world-class lead guitar. And your songwriting has gotten better and better. But I have to ask. Where the hell did that one come from?"

"I was wondering that myself." Ryder sent his sister a speculative look. "Is there something going on you want to tell me about?"

"Sometimes a song is just a song." Zoe shrugged. Since Ashe hadn't chimed in, she turned to him for support. "Right?"

"Sure." But Ashe's eyes narrowed. "Who's the guy?"

The conversation had taken a turn Zoe didn't like. Too close to home was the term she was looking for. Deciding to deflect speculation, she went for casual instead of defensive.

"You know me. There's always a guy."

"Forgettable wankers." Ryder dismissed Zoe's constantly expanding and contracting stable of admirers. "This sounds different. More personal."

"There is no man—or woman," Zoe added, shooting Dalton a warning look before he could make a joke at her expense. "In case none of you have noticed, I've grown up. I'll turn twenty-six on my next birthday."

"The hell you say." Ashe looked genuinely stunned. "The last time I looked, you were a gangly sixteen-year-old girl. Bam!" He snapped his fingers. "I blinked and ten years flew by."

"It's been a good ten years." Zoe smiled at Dalton. "For the most part."

"If you are referring to my unfortunate incarceration, I've come to terms with that. I survived. Hell," Dalton winked, "I thrived. And ultimately, it brought Colleen into my life. Only a fool would complain."

"You're the biggest fool I know. Colleen, on the other hand, is a saint. I don't know what she sees in you."

"Funny. I was wondering the same thing about Belle." Dalton threw his sweaty towel. It landed—a perfect strike—right on Ashe's face. "She could have done a lot better."

Ashe growled, pulling off the towel. "You better run. When I catch you, I'm shoving this thing where the sun don't shine."

Watching with satisfaction as Ashe chased Dalton from the room, Zoe began to hum. The tune died on her lips when she spied Ryder—arms crossed over his chest—watching her closely.

"It isn't going to be that easy with me, Zoe."

"Ryder—"

"Don't worry. I won't push." Ryder laid a gentle hand on Zoe's shoulder, his blue eyes filled with love and affection. "You *have* grown up. You don't need me like you used to."

Yes, I do, Zoe wanted to shout. *This is all a cover. An illusion.* Instead, she pushed back her insecurities, giving Ryder's hand a reassuring squeeze.

"Isn't that a good thing? You took care of me when I needed it. Now, I can take care of myself." *Most of the time.*

"I'm not going anywhere." Zoe went into Ryder's open arms. Even when her emotions weren't in turmoil, she never turned away a hug from her brother. "Until my last breath, I will watch over you."

"Aren't you sick of me by now?"

"Never." Ryder kissed Zoe's forehead. "It's never been a chore or duty. From the moment you were born, Zoe, you held my heart in your hands."

"I love you, too."

"And you'll come to me if something is bothering you?"

Zoe couldn't tell Ryder about Smith Carson. For so many reasons. Mostly because she didn't understand it herself. Moving away, she met his gaze.

"I was eleven years old the first time—and last time—I asked you about sex."

"Don't remind me." Ryder shudder was exaggerated—but sincere. "I gave you a book. The one I read when I needed answers. I never want to—" Ryder groaned. "Hell. Is that what this is about? Jesus, Zoe."

The look of sheer panic on Ryder's face lightened Zoe's mood considerably. "Relax. I don't need instructions. I know how everything works."

"Somehow, that doesn't make me feel any better." Rubbing a hand over his face, Ryder sighed. "Tell me one thing. Do I need to kick some dickwad's ass?"

"No," Zoe assured him. "I'm good."

Ryder smiled. "Yes, you are."

Zoe had a sobering thought, one that sometimes kept her awake at night. "Do you ever worry that our blood is bad?"

"The Monster?" Zoe and Ryder rarely referred to their father any other way.

"And a mother who left us with him."

"I couldn't give a shit about either of them. The only blood I share is yours, Zoe. As far as I'm concerned, they were a sperm donor and an incubator."

There was heat in Ryder's words, but Zoe knew he meant what he said. He was in a good place where the past wasn't forgotten, but it no longer colored his present or future. Zoe wished she could say the same.

"I sometimes wonder about her." When she was little, Zoe used to ask Ryder about their mother. She soon learned that Ryder had no more idea than she did. The woman left soon after Zoe was born. His memories— what there were of them—were vague and hazy at best. "What kind of person could walk away from two vulnerable children? She had to know what he was like."

"I've told you how I feel about it." Ryder held Zoe's jacket for her to slide into. "For me, the woman no longer exists. But if you need to find her—for whatever reason—I'm fine with that."

They walked from the rehearsal room, down the hall, and to the parking lot. Ryder opened the passenger side of his brand new Lamborghini. Wanting to show off the dark blue beauty, that morning he had given Zoe a ride to the studio. Tapping her fingers on the roof, she hesitated before getting in.

"I don't need a mother or want a mother." Zoe was certain of that. "Most of the time, I happily forget all about her. Then there are times when I…"

"When you what?"

"Questions swirl around in my head. Usually around three in the morning. There are too many whys, Ryder." Unseeing, Zoe stared at the passing traffic. "I think I need the answers."

Taking a deep breath, Ryder nodded. "I know a private investigator."

"You do?" That was news to Zoe.

"We dated. Briefly."

Zoe's lips curved upward. She should have known.

"There's a possibility that she's dead, Zoe. Or that she fried her brains on drugs."

Nodding, Zoe got into the car. She had thought of all the possibilities. If somehow she was able to track down their mother, she might not find any satisfaction when she heard the answers to her questions.

"Closure," Zoe whispered, almost to herself.

"What?" Ryder frowned, buckling his seatbelt.

"Isn't that what the last year has been about? First you, then Dalton and finally Ashe. The three of you have found a way to put the past in the rearview mirror. More than that. You've found peace."

"I feel like an idiot."

"Why?" Zoe hadn't brought this up to make Ryder feel bad. That was the last thing she wanted.

"You are the most together young woman I know. I didn't realize you were struggling with this. I'm sorry."

Frustrated, Zoe leaned over, punching her brother in the arm. She could have hit him harder—her slight frame belied a surprisingly brutal right cross. But her purpose was to wake Ryder up to a few home truths, not hurt him.

"You aren't a mind reader. Thank the Lord. Besides, you have a life of your own. Remember Quinn? The annoyingly perceptive woman you seem intent on making my sister-in-law?"

Rubbing his arm, Ryder smiled. "I have a vague recollection."

"She's been taking up a lot of your time lately. As it should be," Zoe hurriedly added. "I don't feel left out or neglected."

"Good." Ryder started the car. "Quinn wants to be your friend, Zoe."

"We're getting there." Slowly. But to Zoe's surprise, it was happening. "She makes you happy. How could I not like her?"

Pulling into traffic, Ryder shot Zoe a thoughtful look. "When you find what you need to know? One way or the other?"

"Yes?"

"I hope it gives you the peace you deserve."

"So do I."

Zoe hadn't expected more. Ryder had made it clear that he didn't care why their mother left. For him, knowing wouldn't change anything. She understood her brother. He meant what he said, and she doubted he would ever ask what she found out.

Zoe envied him. She wished she could find a small room in the back of her mind, shove her questions inside, lock the door, and throw away the key. She had tried. But for reasons she couldn't explain, recently the need to track down the answers had grown to the point that she couldn't ignore it. No longer a mere niggling annoyance, it had gotten to the point that—for her sanity—something had to be done.

"What about the man?"

Zoe had been certain he had forgotten about that. She should have known better. Sometimes Ryder was worse than a dog with a bone. He just couldn't let it go.

"If I told you there was no man, would you believe me?"

"No."

In spite of herself, Zoe chuckled. She loved her brother with all her heart, but he could be a major pain in her ass.

"Right now, there isn't anything to tell." Zoe held up her hand. "God's truth. Nothing has happened. I doubt anything will. Right now, I'm annoyed and a little restless."

When Ryder's only response was to let out a long breath, Zoe frowned.

"What?" she demanded.

"Nothing. It's just…"

"Yes?" Ryder rarely minced words. The fact that he hesitated had Zoe worried.

"Quinn annoyed me—at first. And restless doesn't begin to describe the way she made me feel."

"I don't like where this is going." For the first time since she was a little girl, Zoe was tempted to put her fingers in her ears and hum—loudly. Anything to block out Ryder's words.

"How do you think I feel?" Ryder squeezed the steering wheel until his knuckles turned white. "I don't even know this idiot's name."

"You don't need to. You're making too much out of a few sleepless nights."

"You can't sleep? Great." Ryder turned off the highway, taking the street that would eventually lead them to Zoe's house. "Restless. Annoyed. Sleepless. And don't forget that song. Sounds like trouble to me."

Ryder had no idea how right he was. Zoe hadn't realized how much *trouble* one little song would cause. It had started out to be a throwaway. A way to exercise the demon that was Smith Carson. However, when she was done, it turned out to be so much more. It wasn't the best thing she had ever written; it was pretty damn close.

It had been foolish to think she could slip it into the band's playlist without it raising a red flag or two. Zoe closed her eyes, kicking herself. She could insist on pulling the song. That was her right. But the truth was, it was too good to go unheard.

Zoe had made her bed—or in this case, written her song. Now, she had to live with it. With a sigh, she relaxed in her seat. At least there was one saving grace. No matter how many times they played, *It's Out of My Control* while on tour, Smith Carson would never know that she wrote it about him.

Chapter Four

THERE WAS NO feeling quite like the thrill of stepping in front of a stadium packed with screaming fans. It never got old—not for Smith. The day it did, he knew it would be time to hang up his guitar. Playing to one or one hundred thousand. The inspiration was the same. To touch somebody's emotions. Happy. Sad. Tears. Laughter. It didn't matter. As long as Smith could feel the connection, he knew he would never get tired of what he did.

Smith walked down the hall of the empty stadium. Tomorrow at this time, the backstage would be too busy for him to think. Right now, before the controlled chaos of last-minute sound checks and set changes, he liked to take a few minutes to get his bearings. He had been to Houston many times, but Breakfield Stadium was a new venue. The huge billboard across from his hotel said it all.

One Night Only. The Ryder Hart Band
with Special Guest Smith Carson.

That billing would alternate from city to city. Their next collaborative gig would be in St. Louis where Smith would play host. It seemed like a silly detail, but there was more involved than his ego. There were sponsors to appease. Agents. Managers. They all had a say. At this point, *Smith Carson* and *The Ryder Hart Band* were not just musical acts. They were corporations. They had signed enough contracts for this single tour to gut a small forest. When that much paperwork was involved, nothing was simple.

Stopping at the edge of the darkened stage, Smith closed his eyes. Every place was different yet somehow the same. It was a far cry from the crap dives he played when his backup band consisted of a cocaine-addicted bass player who more often than not was a no show. God, he had been young. Every day was a struggle, but the belief in himself had never wavered. Back then, he believed that talent was all it took. The truth was, talent made a difference, but without a hell of a lot of luck, he would never have seen the inside of a place like this unless he bought a ticket.

The sound of a chair scraping across the surface of the stage pulled Smith from his musings. *What the hell?* Smith squinted into the dark, barely making out a slim figure. *So much for getting some alone time.* About to leave, chalking it up to bad timing, he stopped when the first notes of a familiar song drifted his way. But it was a version of the song he had never heard. In Smith's estimation, Kris Kristofferson was a freaking genius. But not even the man himself could have envisioned *Help Me Make It Through the Night* played like that.

Achingly bluesy. Infinitely haunting. Smith took shallow breaths, afraid to make the slightest sound for fear of interrupting. Each pluck of a guitar string made him hope it would continue. And made him wish—just once—that he could make an instrument sound half that good. Whoever was on that stage, he wasn't letting them get away. Talent like that needed the chance to shine, and he would make certain it happened.

Leaning against the wall, his arms crossed, Smith waited, certain it couldn't get any better. Then he heard the voice and knew he had never been more wrong in his entire life. The second she sang, *Take the ribbon from my hair*, he was a goner. Lost. Somehow, she breathed new life into the old standard. Though everybody from Janis Joplin to Martina McBride had performed the classic, at that moment, Smith would have sworn he had never heard the song until now.

That was a voice. The range was impressive. But it was the subtle nuances she brought to every word that made Smith's insides quake. Knowing the device could never do the singer justice, he quickly took out his phone, hitting record. If the playback caught even a fraction of what he heard live, it would be magic—something Smith knew he would listen to over and over again.

It ended too soon. When the last note faded, Smith waited, hoping for an encore. He wanted to call out in protest. *Play me another. And another.* But it seemed his wish would not be fulfilled. Not today. But soon, he promised himself. This woman had to be heard. By him. By the world.

Cautiously, Smith eased onto the stage. The last thing he wanted was to frighten her. But he wasn't letting her get away without seeing her face and getting her name. His eyes had adjusted to the darkness, making it easier to maneuver around the amps and speakers that littered the area. Smith could see her movements as she bent over to return her guitar to its case. Long hair swirled around her shoulders, obscuring her face. Intent on seeing behind that silky veil, his foot caught on a piece of equipment, tripping him up. His curse echoed through the empty stadium, alerting his quarry. Her head flew up, startled eyes met his.

"Zoe?"

"What the—" Zoe pushed her hair behind her ear. Even in the dark, Smith could tell she wasn't happy to see him. Pissed would be a mild way of putting it. "Are you following me?"

"You caught me. I waited for you to leave the hotel. Grabbed a taxi that was waiting for me—around the corner so you wouldn't see. Then trailed you here." Smith hoped Zoe heard the sneer in his voice, since he couldn't be certain she could read it on his face. "What the hell, Zoe? I have better things to do than trail around after you."

"And yet here you are."

Zoe stood, holding her guitar case as a shield. She was tall, but even in heels, only hit Smith at chin level. The air crackled between them. It was so dark, he was surprised the sparks weren't visible.

"I don't need to explain my movements to you." Smith took a step closer. Not to crowd Zoe, but to gauge her reaction. Would she shy away? Stand her ground? When she did neither, inching closer with a step of her own, Smith couldn't hide his smile.

"What do you want, Smith?"

"That's a leading question." Smith's gaze settled on Zoe's lips. "Do you really want an answer?"

"What I don't want is to play games."

Zoe pushed past him. She was halfway across the stage when he called out.

"I want to know why you don't sing in public."

Zoe stopped, slowly turning. "I do. Every time we take the stage, I sing."

"Not lead." Smith skirted an amplifier, catching up to her in two long strides. "You belong out front, not playing second fiddle to your brother."

"I'm where I want to be."

"Are you?" Perplexed, Smith shook his head. "I don't get it. You aren't shy on stage. Under the spotlight, when you have a guitar solo, you mesmerize the audience. I've never seen anybody better."

"You noticed?" Zoe's lip curled. "Thank God you didn't pull the old, *nobody puts Baby in the corner,* crap. I get all the attention I want or need. And trust me, I'm nobody's baby."

"Good. The last thing I want is a baby."

"Say it," Zoe taunted.

Smith knew what she was asking. Say the words. Stop avoiding the elephant in the room.

"I want you."

Zoe lowered her guitar case, moving until barely a breeze could squeeze between them. She tilted her head, meeting his gaze, then slowly lowered her eyes to his mouth. Smith stifled a groan as her tongue ran along her bottom lip. He knew what she was doing. Teasing him until he made the first move. She wanted him to grab her arms. Pull her close. *Take* the kiss he longed for. Hands fisted, Smith held them at his sides so he wouldn't reach for her. *Damn, she smelled good.* Warm, cinnamon-flavored apples. More than his next breath, he wanted a taste.

However, Smith was nothing if not disciplined. Zoe said she didn't want to play games? Neither did he. Cursing himself as all kinds of a fool, he stepped back before he gave in. The look of surprise in Zoe's eyes was some consolation. A very small one.

"Chicken," Zoe said, shaking her head.

"Smart." Smith did himself a favor, he put some space between them. "You're dying to shoot me down, aren't you?"

"I don't know what you mean?" Zoe blinked innocently, not quite pulling it off.

"Sure, you do. There is nothing you would like more than to have me make the first move only to shoot me down."

"I might have kissed you back." With a shrug, Zoe picked up the black leather guitar case. "Now you'll never know."

"You would have kissed me back," Smith told Zoe's retreating back. "No doubt about it."

"You're wrong."

"I'm right." Smith trailed behind, easily keeping up. His mama would skin him alive if he ever let a lady walk to her car alone—no matter the time of day. Besides, he had a few more jabs to make at Zoe Hart's well-placed personal armor. "The kiss would have been hot. Not incendiary because our first time together is not going to be on stage—even if the seats are empty."

"Our first time?" Zoe pushed through the side door, the bright Houston sunlight making her squint. Not stopping, she took a pair of sunglasses from her bag. She was parked on the other side of the lot, far from the entrance. No wonder he hadn't noticed the sleek silver Mercedes when he arrived. "There won't be a first time, Smith. I was going to give you one kiss. Since you chose not to take it, your window has closed."

"Bullshit."

"You're a good-looking man, Smith. Hardly irresistible."

"That's not what the fan magazines say."

To Smith's surprise, his tongue-in-cheek comment elicited a low, husky chuckle. *Damn. What do you know?* Gorgeous and she had a laugh that sent a shot of heat straight through his bloodstream. If she kept this up, he might end up liking her as well as wanting her.

"I never read them," Zoe quipped.

When she took out her keys, Smith scooted ahead, opening the driver's side door. From the look she gave him, it seemed that for the second time in less than an hour, he managed to surprise her. Then, before he could blink, she returned the favor.

The kiss wasn't out-of-control hot. It was sweet, yet unbelievably erotic. Zoe slid her hand around Smith's neck, her fingers threading through his hair until her palm cupped the back of his head. Going on tiptoe, she lightly brushed her lips against his, then pressed firmly. Smith's mouth parted, first to gasp, then to taste. He was right. Spicy-sweet. Zoe touched her tongue to his, slanting her head to gain a better angle.

Resting his hands on Zoe's hips, Smith would have deepened the kiss. Instead, Zoe moved away.

"Come to my hotel room."

"No." She put her guitar and bag on the passenger seat, then slid into the car.

"After the show?"

"No, Smith."

"But—"

"Smith." Zoe paused, gaining his full attention. "No."

Zoe shut the door, starting the car. Smith stepped back, watching as she drove onto the street. No meant no. But that didn't mean he was going away. The regret in Zoe's eyes told him there would be more between them than one kiss. Smith was a patient man.

Smiling, Smith jogged to his car. When was the last time he had to woo a woman? Maybe never? He was used to getting what he wanted as soon as he wanted it. That was one of the perks—and pitfalls—of fame. Zoe Hart didn't know it, but she had issued a challenge that he couldn't resist.

Smith licked his lips. Mm. Spicy sweet. Friendship first, he decided, with anticipation. That wouldn't be difficult. He liked Zoe. And whether she wanted to or not, she liked him.

They lived in a world where everybody expected instant gratification. Not this time. Not with this lady. Slow and steady would be the secret to winning the race. Smith's reward? The pleasure of Zoe Hart in his bed.

Chapter Five

AFTER HOUSTON, SMITH, and *The Ryder Hart Band* parted ways for the next week. He made a three-night stop in Chicago—for some reason, Zoe and her bandmates weren't hitting the Windy City during their tour. That was fine. The separation gave Smith time to plot and plan. Not that he let Zoe forget about him. Seven days wasn't long, but in the seduction game, it could be an eternity.

Smith racked his brain for how to go about his mission. He had plenty of time since these days, he wasn't in the mood for after-hours company. The choice was simple. Toss and turn, wishing Zoe were with him. Or figure out a way to make it happen.

Expensive gifts? Smith quickly threw that idea on the scrap heap. What could he buy for Zoe that she hadn't already gotten for herself? Candy was too cliché. He had heard about the great flower debacle. No. He needed something unique.

Or perhaps, the answer was to go old school.

Rolling over, Smith grabbed his phone, typing in a text to his assistant. It wasn't his usual request, but he knew from experience that Randy wouldn't blink an eye. He started out as the perfect employee. Now—six years later—he was also a friend. Efficient, but most of all, discreet. Smith never had to worry about his personal business becoming a tabloid headline.

Smith had barely set the phone down when Randy sent an answer. Not surprising. Even at three in the morning, the man was on top of things. Plus, after all this time, he was used to Smith's erratic hours.

Stationery? Did you check the desk?

Smith fired back. *That has the hotel logo. I want it to look like I put some thought into it.*

Randy didn't hesitate. *There's a drugstore down the street. If you want something more high-end, it might take a little longer.*

Fancy wasn't necessary. Smith typed. *As long as there are no kittens—or flowers. Get it to me ASAP.*

A man of few words, Randy answered. *On it.*

That was that. Smith knew from experience that he would just have time for a quick shower. Jumping from the bed, he didn't bother to put on a pot of coffee. After the drugstore, Randy would make a stop at the nearest drive thru for a cup of cappuccino for him and a plain, no-frills, black-as-ink brew for Smith.

With perfect timing, the knock on the door came just as Smith exited the bedroom, hair damp, dressed in loose-fitting sweats and an old Alabama State Fair t-shirt. Letting Randy in, he took the coffee and the box of stationery.

"You are a lifesaver." Smith took the lid off the cup, breathing deeply. "Sometimes I think it smells even better than it tastes."

"The way you drink it? I concur."

Randy Stapleton was a big, burly man. In his late thirties, with dark hair and eyes, he looked more like a linebacker than a personal assistant. Something that had come in handy a time or two when Smith's fans would get overly enthusiastic.

"Concur." Smith chuckled. "You're showing off that college education again."

It was a running joke between the two men. Randy Stapleton had attended a community college for two years, majoring in computer science. Smith finished high school—just barely.

"It's more about what I read." Randy nudged the copy of *A Brief History of Time* that sat on the coffee table. "You do pretty well yourself."

"Shh." Winking, Smith opened the bag from the drugstore. "You'll ruin my reputation."

The truth was, Smith made certain his fans knew he was a big proponent of improving one's mind. His parents had encouraged their children to read. His father built shelves to store the secondhand books that his mother always brought home. Smith had started *The Nellie Carson Foundation* in her honor. The charity had raised almost five million dollars last year to provide reading material to children from low-income families.

"I hope that's what you had in mind." Nodding toward the stationery, Randy sighed with pleasure as he sipped his steaming cappuccino. "The selection wasn't great. Especially since you banned kittens. God, there was a shitload of kittens."

"The world loves a cute pussy."

Snorting, Randy almost spit his mouthful of liquid onto the floor, swallowing at the last second. "Jesus, Smith," he wiped his chin, chuckling. "Save the one-liners for when I'm not drinking a hot liquid."

At best, Smith's pun had been mediocre, but Randy was an easy audience. The other man loved lowbrow humor. The lower, the better. Examining the plain blue paper with a small embossed diamond in the top, right-hand corner, Smith decided it would do.

"Thanks, Randy. This is great."

"Any chance I'll get an explanation as to why you needed stationery at this time of night? Or anytime, for that matter. Who writes letters anymore?"

"Nobody. That, my friend, is exactly the point."

Smith took a seat at the desk, pen in hand. The world zipped by at an eye-popping rate. He and Zoe zipped from city to city, concert date to concert date. When they weren't playing live, they had recording sessions, personal appearances. It never seemed to stop. How better to get her attention than with a good old-fashioned letter. Something that made her sit down and take the time to read. If Zoe wrote back, Smith would know he stood a chance with her.

This wasn't about the instant gratification of an email or a hastily sent text. It was about taking the time—and care—to share his thoughts and feelings. Hopefully, Zoe would understand what he was trying to say— beyond the words that were on the blue pieces of paper.

Dear Zoe. Looking at his scrawled greeting, Smith grinned. *Seduction by letter.* If it didn't work, at least he had a damn good title for a new song.

"I NEED A shower. And hamburger. In that order."

Zoe wiped her face. Whoever thought of giving an open-air concert in Atlanta—in the middle of summer—must have had a screw loose.

"You signed off on the schedule," Ryder reminded her as she grumbled her way to her dressing room.

"That was in November—when we were in the mountains skiing. It's impossible to think about how I'll feel in August when there is snow everywhere."

"Fair enough." The towel around Ryder's neck was soaked through with sweat. "Next time, our first consideration is the time of year and the heat index. Or whatever the hell it is weather people talk about." He tore the lid off a bottle of water, downing the entire contents in a few gulps.

"It isn't the heat, it's the humidity," Dalton informed them, bare chest glistening.

Around the middle of the first set, the drummer had disposed of his shirt. Unfortunately, Zoe hadn't had that luxury. She stripped down to a boldly embroidered tank top, but that was as far as she was willing to go. Thank goodness she had the foresight to wear leg-baring shorts, though the suede knee-high boots hadn't been the best choice. Unwilling to walk another step, she dropped onto a wooden crate. Lifting her right leg, she tugged—unsuccessfully—at the offending footwear.

"Here, let me." Ashe grabbed Zoe's foot. "Jesus. These babies are soaked through."

It took some effort, but with one foot pushing on Ashe's butt, and him tugging on the other, the boot finally came off.

"Thank God," Zoe sighed as Ashe worked on the other. "I've been standing in a pool of my own sweat for two hours."

"Why do you put yourself through the torture?" Triumphantly, Ashe held up the long piece of damp leather. "Put on a pair of flip-flops. Nobody will care. And with those long legs on display, nobody will notice what you wear on your feet."

"I care," Zoe exclaimed, rubbing her right foot with a relieved sigh. "As for nobody noticing? Good luck with that. According to our in-the-know manager, what I wear is the first thing fans notice. After all the man candy."

Dalton struck an exaggerated bodybuilder's pose, flexing his considerable biceps. "It's true. The ladies come to see my guns."

"Get over yourself. Did you hear the screams whenever I moved to the front of the stage?" Ashe winked at Zoe. "They love their Asheman."

"*Asheman*? Ugh." Zoe turned to Ryder who had been unusually quiet. "What about you, brother dear? Aren't you going to chime in about how much the fans adore your curly hair and blue eyes?"

"No need." Ryder shrugged off the suggestion. "I know what fills the seats."

"Do tell," Dalton crossed his arms, waiting.

"Why, my swoon-inducing, honey-laced vocals, of course."

"Oh, for Christ's sake." Ashe rolled his eyes. "Get over yourself. It's my backup vocals that make you sound good."

"Hey, what about my harmonies?" Dalton chimed in.

Chuckling, Zoe left them to their good-natured argument. Though they had been fully-grown men for years now, there were times when they could quickly devolve into teenage boys. She found it highly amusing and normally would have stuck around for the show. But she desperately needed to get to her dressing room where she could divest herself of her clothing. And a shower. Lordy, Lordy, thank goodness for indoor plumbing.

Most backstage dressing rooms were barebones at best. This one was an exception. The Atlanta venue had recently been renovated. There was a large, lushly covered sofa lining one wall and two matching chairs. The dressing table had drool-worthy lighting, rivaling the one in Zoe's bathroom at home. Then there was the shower. A huge, rainfall head that she couldn't wait to try out.

Shimmying out of her shorts, Zoe removed her silk panties at the same time. Her top and bra quickly followed. Leaving the heap of sweaty clothing where they dropped, she padded to the bathroom, shivering. *Why was the air conditioner turned to frostbite?* It was one thing to cool off after a long concert. It was another to deal with potential pneumonia. Too hot then too cold. That couldn't be good.

Instead of the bracing shower Zoe had planned, she set the water to a moderate temperature. *Oh, yes*, she hummed as she stepped into the stall, lifting her face. If this wasn't heaven, she didn't want to go. It took fifteen minutes, but when she left the bathroom, Zoe felt human again. She stood in the middle of the blissfully flower-free room, stretching her arms over her head. The satin of the bright red robe felt wonderful against her freshly washed and moisturized skin.

Instead of changing into her street clothes, Zoe flopped onto the sofa, taking a minute to relax. They were at the beginning of their tour, and she knew from experience that taking care of herself now was the key to staying healthy and energetic for the next six months. It didn't take much. Moments like this—alone without interruptions—could make a world of difference.

As Zoe rested her head against the plush cushion, something on the dressing table caught her eye. Certain the blue paper hadn't been there before she went to take her shower, she frowned. Intrigued, she snatched up the envelope.

It was a letter addressed to her in care of the Atlanta stadium. In all the time she had been working as a professional musician, this was the first time Zoe had ever received a piece of mail before or after a performance. It seemed to be a letter. From? She checked the envelope's upper left-hand corner. Smith Carson! His return address was listed as a downtown Chicago hotel. She knew the place well, having stayed there on more than one occasion.

Returning to the sofa, Zoe stared at the envelope as if she had suddenly been bestowed with the power to read the unopened contents. Why would Smith write her a letter? A text or an email, maybe. Maybe a phone call. Though to be fair, she hadn't given him her number. Or email address. However, she imagined Smith to be a resourceful man. If he wanted the information, it wouldn't be that difficult for him to get it.

For whatever reason, Smith had chosen a letter. Thoughtfully, Zoe tapped the envelope against her leg. This was ridiculous. It was a piece of paper. Presumably with a few parts of the alphabet strung together into words that formed sentences. After the way she left things with him, it was hard to imagine what he would have to say. What could be important enough to make him take the time?

Curiosity, and consideration for Smith's efforts, meant Zoe had no choice. With a sigh, she carefully tore open the blue envelope. Her first thought was what nice handwriting Smith had. Masculine. Strong. And wonderfully easy to read.

Dear Zoe,

If you find it strange that I'm writing to you—finding a stamp took some effort—try putting yourself in my place. The last time I put pen to paper was to write my mother, assuring her I was in good health. That was ten years ago, about a month after I left home to pursue my dreams. I didn't have the money to make a phone call. Can you imagine? Pay phones were still readily available back then. I scraped together enough change to send the letter—just barely. Can you remember the days when a few quarters seemed like a lot of money?

Luckily, I started getting work. Nothing major, but I made a few bucks and called home every few weeks. I think my mother would have enjoyed a letter now and then, but it was easier to pick up a phone. Sorry if I'm rambling. This is a first for me, and I admit, my thoughts aren't as focused as I would like. Maybe next time.

Zoe lowered the paper. Next time? Did that mean Smith planned to send her more letters? For some reason she didn't want to think about, the idea made her smile.

It is almost four o'clock. In the morning. Finding myself awake at this hour isn't that unusual. I grew up on a farm. My father didn't know the meaning of sleeping in. To my sorrow, I've been afflicted with the same malady. Late nights and early mornings aren't supposed to mix. Someday it might catch up with me. So far, so good.

I have given a lot of thought to what you said. "No." That one word has been haunting me. I realize you meant it. Right this minute, you don't want to see me naked.

Zoe laughed. Smith had no idea just how wrong he was.

I've been told that I'm not too hard on the eyes. I exercise regularly, and there is no unsightly hair growing in odd places. Rather than take my word for it, I would be happy to send you a list of recommendations.

All joking aside, while I respect your decision, forgive me if I don't agree with it. No. I take that back. I don't want your forgiveness. I simply want you to change your mind. Consider this the first volley in what I hope will be a short and bloodless battle.

Sincerely,

Smith

It was a straightforward letter. However, that didn't stop Zoe from rereading it—twice. If Smith's purpose was to pique her interest, he had succeeded. The thought of more to come, had her thinking ahead, wondering what he would have to say. Hoping the next one was on the way. Wishing it was in her hands, waiting to be read.

Smith wasn't giving up. Of course, Zoe was flattered that he wanted her. She was only human. Wasn't that a laugh? How many men had accused her of just the opposite? Cool, unemotional, unfeeling, Zoe Hart. It was a reputation she knew she had earned. It wasn't that she wanted to come off as an ice queen. But how could she pretend to feel passion when none existed? That one little kiss that she shared with Smith had been the best she'd ever experienced. Zoe had spent the days since trying to decide if she should be encouraged—or terrified. She was still trying to make up her mind, and Smith's letter hadn't helped.

Thoughtfully, Zoe returned the sheets of paper to the envelope. She was a strong, independent woman. Her body was hers to do with as she chose. She didn't have a husband, fiancé, or boyfriend standing in her way. Nor did she have any moral objections. The reasons she hesitated to take Smith as a lover were nobody else's business.

Whatever Zoe decided, it wasn't something she could take lightly. When she told Smith no, that was what she meant. However, she had the prerogative to change her mind. Luckily, it appeared that Smith wasn't going to push. She needed time, and he was giving her exactly that.

Smith didn't know it yet—maybe never would—but the letter was a great big plus in his favor.

Suddenly, Zoe felt energized. Hopping to her feet, she stashed the envelope in the side pocket of her bag before pulling on clean underwear. It was after midnight, but she knew the heat and humidity of Atlanta wouldn't have waned. A sleeveless, knee-length summery dress was the perfect solution. Slipping it on, she did a twirl in front of the mirror. The color of ripe raspberries, it complimented Zoe's pale skin. Pinning her long, blond hair on top of her head, she slid her feet into a comfortable—ever stylish—pair of sandals.

Not bad, Zoe decided. She added a touch of color to her lips, and she was finished, the sharp rap on the dressing room door coinciding perfectly.

"Hustle it up, Zoe. We're dying to get something to eat."

"I want a hamburger," Zoe told Ryder as she opened the door. She handed him her guitar case, slinging the strap of her bag over her shoulder. "And French fries. Plus, a chocolate milkshake."

"Is that all?" Ryder chuckled. Zoe always had a healthy appetite. However, after a long show, she tended to eat light.

"It will do. For a start." When they reached the end of the long corridor, Ryder reached to open the door. "Before we join the others at the restaurant, I need to make a stop."

"Where?"

Zoe frowned, suddenly perplexed. "I have no idea." She looked at her brother. "Do you know where I can buy some stationery?"

THERE WERE TWO things Smith never missed when he was in St. Louis. Barbecue and a Cardinals game. If baseball was out of season—or the team was on the road—he was happy to settle for a plate of the best ribs money could buy.

If Zoe agreed, he would take her to the best joint in town. The thought brought a smile to Smith's mouth. The letter he received the other day put the odds decidedly in his favor. Short, but Smith thought it was wonderfully sweet, he had read it so many times that he had it memorized.

Smith,

Not, dear Smith. He could live with that—for now.

I don't want to talk about the word no—or yes.

After reading that Zoe included a yes, Smith did a fist pump.

For now, let's put that on the back burner. I'm interested in the revelation that smooth, sophisticated Smith Carson is really a farm boy at heart. I never would have guessed. Do you come from a large family? It was always just Ryder and me.

Early to rise? I understand that, though my reasons have nothing to do with… slopping hogs? Sorry if that's way off base, I'm a city girl, through and through. I would love to hear more about your childhood.

Zoe

Zoe might not know it, but that short note had given Smith two important bits of information. He already knew that she and Ryder were close. The fact that she said it had been just the two of them was telling. No mother or father? He resisted the urge to look her up on Google. That would defeat the purpose. *Slow and steady*, he reminded himself.

The second thing he learned was that Zoe didn't like to sleep in. Was that an old habit or a new one? One day, she would tell him. Hopefully while lying in bed, wrapped in his arms.

Smith had mailed his second letter just before leaving Chicago. He had been tempted to send it FedEx, but that would be breaking the rules he set for himself. Snail mail or nothing. It should arrive today—tomorrow at the latest. Filled with details of growing up on a farm, he wondered what Zoe's reaction would be to his graphic description of when he had to deliver a calf all by himself. It might not be the most romantic passage, but Smith would bet the income from a week's worth of concert dates that she would find humor in his words—just as he intended.

The sound check for tonight's show had been smooth as glass. By now, Smith's crew had things down to a science. There wasn't a lot of flash or fireworks to his concerts. There was a green screen behind him that flashed pictures and home movies—the crowds loved seeing him as a little boy. Other than that, Smith relied on his talent. So far, that had worked just fine for him.

"You have an interview with one of the local television stations scheduled for two-thirty. After that, you're free until the concert. The car will be out front to pick you up at seven o'clock."

Technically, *The Ryder Hart Band* was his opening act this time around. Smith wouldn't go on until almost ten o'clock. There was no need for him to be at the arena until nine. Nine-thirty at the latest. But the chance to watch Zoe perform was too much of a temptation. He still believed she should be out in front, sharing that spectacular voice with the world. It bothered him to think that she was holding back—for whatever reason. Knowing it was none of his business didn't stop Smith from wanting to find the answer. A solution was another matter altogether. It was out there, and he was determined to find it.

"Have a sandwich sent to my room at noon, Randy. Turkey, light on the mayo. You know how I like it."

"Beer?"

Smith nodded. "Something local. Otherwise, I'll stick with bottled water. Any luck with the Cardinals tickets?"

"There's a private box at your disposal on Sunday afternoon."

"Perfect." Now all Smith had to do was convince Zoe to go with him. "I want to get in some writing, so unless it's an emergency, I am officially incognito."

"You got it, boss."

Alone, Smith took a moment to enjoy the silence. These moments were few and far between—especially when he was in the middle of a tour. Some men relaxed by turning on ESPN. Others went to their local bar and threw back a few while visiting with friends. For Smith, it was a guitar and an empty room. From the time he had learned to pick his first chord, there was nothing he liked better than finding a new melody. The words came later. As always, everything started with the music.

Taking the vintage Gibson from its case, Smith took a seat. He fiddled with the tuning pegs, getting the sound he wanted. Inspiration was more often than not an ephemeral bitch. When he was looking, it rarely came. One of the best songs Smith had written came to him when he was in an airport, waiting to catch his flight. There was a woman, laughing with her friends while they shared a bag of caramel corn. *Sweet on the Lips* was born. Before his plane touched down in New York, Smith had a multi-platinum-selling record—and a standard that had been recorded by more artists than he could remember.

The first notes Smith played were merely a warm up for his fingers. When the melody started, he wasn't certain, but the tingle that ran up his spine told him there was something to it. Grabbing a piece of paper, Smith jotted down the notes. The opening had a catch to it, something that would stay with the listener.

In his mind, Smith saw an image as clear as day. Dark brown eyes filled with attitude, humor, and a touch of sadness. It was a combination that hit him in the gut every time. Honey-blond hair, thick and silky. And a pair of soft, full lips whose taste was burned into his memory.

Hello, Zoe Hart. Considering how much she had dominated his

waking hours—and a few very explicit dreams—it was a wonder she hadn't inspired him before now. The more he played, the more complex the melody became. It made sense. Complex woman, complex song.

There was nothing better in Smith's world than a moment like this. Some tweaking would be done, but not much. This song was a gift— delivered fully formed. He wondered what Zoe's reaction would be. Then it hit him. The solution he had been looking for.

Energized, Smith hit record on his phone. The sooner he finished, the sooner he could put his plan in motion.

Chapter Six

ZOE LOOKED AT the private investigator's report. When they had spoken on the phone, Riesa Frost had seemed like she knew what she was doing—not that Zoe had anything with which to compare. Ryder promised she was good at her job. That was good enough for Zoe.

It had only been a few days. Zoe wasn't expecting miracles. However, since she had decided that she wanted to find her mother, she was impatient to have it done. For so long, the woman had been a shadow from Zoe's past. Tired of wondering, it was time to shine a light on the bad so she could let it go and move forward.

According to Riesa Frost, the trail of April Hart had come to a screeching halt a few months after Zoe's birth. It was as if she had dropped off the face of the Earth. Riesa assured Zoe that nobody was untraceable. It would take a bit more time, but the detective was confident she could do the job for which she had been hired. As soon as she knew anything—even the slightest thing—she promised to be in touch.

Frustrated, Zoe snapped her laptop shut. It was too late to go back—even if she wanted to. The path to finding her mother might not be a straight one, but she was determined to follow all the twists and turns to the bitter end. Some odd premonition told her that is what it would be. Bitter. There would be no happy reunion. Good or bad, at least she would know.

The hard part was not talking to Ryder. Zoe knew he wouldn't stop her if she insisted on keeping him up to date on her search. If she really needed somebody to listen, he was always there. But this wasn't like most problems. In his mind, April Hart had ceased to exist. He wasn't curious why she left. He wasn't filled with sadness, hatred, or bitterness. Ryder simply didn't care.

Zoe envied Ryder. She wished it was that simple for her. The biggest question—the one she could never share with her brother—had haunted her for as long as she could remember. Her father wasn't around to ask. After years of neglect and abuse, fifteen years ago, he set his children free by taking his own life. Zoe didn't feel an ounce of guilt. She believed it had been a gift—the only one he had ever given them.

With her father died the answer to Zoe's question. All those years when he abused Ryder, why had he never raised a hand to her?

As a little girl, Zoe thought it was Ryder who kept her safe. When he would tuck her under the bed and tell her she was invisible, she believed with all her heart that it was magic—Ryder's magic—keeping the Monster from hurting her. Of course, that wasn't true. A little boy had no power over a full-grown man. There had been nothing stopping him from doing anything his twisted mind wanted. Why beat Ryder with his fists, kick him black and blue, smash his son's knee with a baseball bat? Why not take some of that sick, disgusting rage out on Zoe?

Guilt dogged Zoe. It wasn't fair that Ryder had suffered. For whatever reason, their father had acted as if Zoe didn't exist. He never looked at her. Never said a word. Never raised a hand.

Through it all, Ryder did his best to take care of her. Always. When they were put into foster care, Zoe's greatest fear had been that she would never see her brother again. Ryder could have left Chicago. Los Angeles was warmer. New York filled with more opportunities. Getting out would have made sense. Instead, he stayed in the city that he hated—keeping his word to Zoe that he would always come back for her.

There were no guarantees that her mother—if the detective found her—could tell Zoe anything she didn't already know. Her only hope was that whatever the outcome, she would find some peace of mind.

"Fifteen minutes, Ms. Hart." The knock on the door from one of the stagehands made Zoe jump.

"Thank you," Zoe called out.

"I have a letter for you."

With a bounce in her step, Zoe rushed to open the door, snatching the envelope before the young man could hand it to her.

"Sorry I didn't get it to you sooner. We don't get personal snail-mail very often."

"That's all right." Zoe flashed him a megawatt grin. "Thank you," she said, shutting the door as quickly as she had opened it, unaware that the voltage of her smile had left a lasting impression on the stagehand who was barely out of his teens. He had been a fan before coming face to face with the beautiful Zoe Hart. Now, with that brief encounter, he fancied himself a little bit in love.

Christmas and birthdays were never given any fanfare when Zoe was a little girl. But holding Smith's letter, she felt the kind of giddy anticipation she imagined normal children experienced on those days.

Smith would be headlining with *The Ryder Hart Band* for the next few days. Because Zoe would see him, she hadn't expected him to send another letter until next week. It was a surprise. Normally, she wasn't a big fan of the unexpected, but in this case, she was happy to make an exception.

Glancing at the clock, Zoe debated whether to give the letter a quick read or save it until after the show. She was ready to go on stage. Dramatic eyes, the dark eyeliner, and smoky shadow making them look even larger than usual. Her hair hung in a straight line down her back like a trail of liquid gold. Since they were performing inside, she had chosen a long-sleeved silver lame dress that hugged her body, the hem ending at mid-thigh, met by a pair of black thigh-high leather boots.

It wasn't the outfit of a wallflower. Zoe liked the attention she received when performing. She had worked damn hard to be the best guitar player she could be so that when she joined the band, nobody could say she was merely there as window dressing. There wasn't a shy bone in her body. Zoe had her reasons for not wanting to sing lead—ones that were private and personal. However, they had nothing to do with wanting to hide her talent.

Ten minutes. It was plenty of time, Zoe decided, ripping the envelope open with none of the trepidation she felt before reading Smith's first letter. Better a quick perusal now. That way she wouldn't have it in the back of her mind while on stage.

Dear Zoe,

Why a letter now, you may be asking yourself? At this moment, we are undoubtedly in the same city. Perhaps in the same building. Why not say these words to your face instead of writing them on a few thin pieces of paper? Good question, gorgeous.

Zoe smiled. Compliments tended to go right over her head. Smith's started a warm glow in the pit of her stomach that slowly spread through her body.

I've always found it easier to express deep emotions through the written word. Though this is the first time music did not accompany them. These thoughts are for you alone, Zoe. An audience of one. Too corny? Sorry, I'm new at this letter-writing thing.

Where was I? Oh, that's right. You wanted to know if I had ever slopped a hog. Hell, yes. We had hogs, chickens, goats, a milk cow, and a rooster that believed he was the center of the universe. A true cock of the walk.

What I miss the most is having a dog. When I left home, I left behind my best friend, Clyde. His breed was indeterminate—a mutt of the first order. He had been my constant companion since I was nine years old. My folks had to put him down several years back. I'm not ashamed to admit that I cried. It seemed disloyal to consider getting another dog. Though, unlike when I started out, I have the resources to bring one with me on the road. At times, the life of a traveling troubadour can be damn lonely. A dog has no hidden agenda, only unabashed love, and loyalty. One day soon. I think Clyde would understand.

Zoe had always wanted a dog. When she was a little girl, the closest thing she had to a pet was her teddy bear. He was retired to a place of honor in her home office right next to her Grammys and other awards. Maybe soon. Like Smith's Clyde, she was certain her teddy would understand.

I need to wrap this up. The crowd sounds particularly rowdy tonight, so I better not keep them waiting. Just one thing before I go. You have been on my mind—more than I should admit. One kiss. That's all we've shared. Brief, but memorable. I don't think I'm giving anything away if I tell you that I want more.

When we meet in St. Louis, the ball will be in your court, Zoe. A touch. A kiss. Or nothing at all. The choice will be yours. You know how I feel.

Always hopeful,

Smith

"Time to go on, Ms. Hart."

"I'll be right there."

Zoe didn't have time to do more than trace Smith's name with her finger. Folding the papers, she returned them to the envelope, rushing to put it away. She checked her reflection one last time, adjusting her silver and diamond earrings. Later, she would read Smith's words again before composing a letter of her own. If he could keep up their correspondence while in the same city, so could she.

"All set?" Dalton fell in step with Zoe as she exited her dressing room.

"Aren't I always?"

"There was that one time in Madrid. Five minutes late."

"I had the flu, jerk." Zoe bumped him with her hip. She remembered that night with a grimace. She had been late because she was throwing up what she swore was the lining of her stomach. "I still outplayed you for almost two hours."

"Then spent the next day flat on your back with an I.V. needle stuck in your right arm." Dalton shook his head. "Never again, kid. If you miss one show, it won't be the end of the world."

"Says the man who played for the last two weeks of a tour with a sprained wrist."

"I know. All of us have gone on stage a time or two when we shouldn't have. Whoever said the show must go on was a masochist."

"Or a sadist," Coming up behind them, Ashe slung an arm over Zoe's shoulders. "It depends on which side of the curtain he was on."

They stood where they would make their entrance, waiting for the lights to finish dimming.

"If I recall, you like a little pain with your pleasure." Dalton laughed when Ashe gave him a narrowed look of warning.

"Really?" Zoe found that fascinating. They had shared some tight quarters over the years—crappy tour buses and crappier accommodations—during which the guys talked about everything, rarely worrying about Zoe overhearing. But the particulars of their love lives were seldom mentioned. "How kinky do you get? And is Belle onboard?"

"Remind me to kick your ass, Shaw." There wasn't much heat in Ashe's threat. It appeared to Zoe that he was trying hard not to laugh. "Belle has no complaints."

"But—"

"That's the last word on the subject." Ashe lightly flicked the end of Zoe's nose. "Understood?"

Ryder, dressed in black leather pants and a black silk shirt arrived, stopping beside Zoe. "What is Zoe supposed to understand?" he asked as he ran a hand through his dark, wavy hair.

"That Ashe's freaky sex life is not a topic for conversation."

"Jesus." Ryder cast his eyes to the rafters as if asking for guidance from above. "If this keeps up, I'm telling Belle." Dalton snorted. "And Colleen."

"Hey," Dalton protested. "I'm not the one who kept a riding crop stashed in his—"

"*Are you ready, St. Louis?*" the announcer interrupted.

"There is a God." Ryder sighed. Without needing to be told, the other three gathered around him for their pre-concert ritual. "Are you with me?" he asked.

"Always," Zoe answered.

"Hell, yes," Dalton nodded.

Ashe slapped Ryder on the back. "To the end, brother."

"Then let's give them our best." Ryder met their gazes one by one. "This is what we do. This is who we are."

Nodding as one, they waited for a beat, then ran onto the stage.

"Give a big welcome for the greatest rock band in the world. Ladies and gentleman, The Ryder Hart Band."

SMITH WATCHED WITH increasing admiration as Zoe moved around the stage, playing her guitar, singing harmony, and somehow staying upright in spiked heels that must have been at least five inches high. Walking in those things had to be a balancing act. Zoe did a hell of a lot more. She hopped, danced, ran, hit her knees, and popped back up again, doing it with the grace of a long-legged gazelle. All the while exuding a blistering sex appeal that made Smith's mouth water. Why she didn't leave a trail of singed hardwood behind her was a mind-boggling mystery.

The band finished with a hard-driving rendition of their current number one hit, *Lost Until You.* Then the stage went black. Naturally, the audience wasn't having any of it. Immediately, they began clapping their hands and pounding their feet. They knew there was at least one more song in their future, probably two.

"Smith." Ryder, face glistening, his smile wide, held out his hand. "We've warmed them up. Are you ready to take over?"

"We're a tough act to follow. Maybe you should call it a night rather than embarrass yourself." Dalton winked, his blue eyes filled with good-natured teasing. "The audience won't complain. They got their money's worth."

"Get your ass out there for the encore." Laughing, Smith tossed Dalton a bottle of water from the craft services table. "Once I'm into my first song, they won't be able to remember your name."

"Is that right?"

Zoe. Smith turned. After the workout she'd been through, the woman should have looked a mess. Instead, all he could think about was finding an empty room so he could rub her sweat-slickened body all over his—tasting every salty inch along the way.

Instead, Smith gave Zoe a slow smile, lowering his voice so only she could hear over the roar of the ever-increasingly impatient crowd. "Not you. As I'm quickly learning, Zoe Hart is damn hard to forget."

"Zoe!" Ryder grabbed her arm. His mind on the next song, he missed the electric sizzle popping between his sister and Smith. "Time to put the cherry on top."

The band was back on stage, the audience rocking. Smith took a deep breath, exhaling slowly. There had been a definite change in Zoe's attitude toward him. Gone was the icy glare, her eyes looking like warm chocolate. The moment had been necessarily brief, but when her mouth parted, Smith could have sworn he saw a glimpse of Zoe's tongue running along the inside curve of her bottom lip. Damn. Good thing he was starting his first set with something up tempo. It would be the perfect way to burn off a case of sexual frustration.

Fine with that—for now—Smith crossed his arms and followed the audience's lead. Tapping his leather-clad foot, he enjoyed the rest of the show.

Chapter Seven

ZOE STRETCHED HER arms over her head, bending to the right, then the left. Because of her travel schedule and crazy working hours, maintaining a regular workout routine was a challenge. She found early morning worked the best. Most hotels had adequate facilities. This morning she enjoyed a well-equipped exercise room. With one of the band's hulking roadies along to watch her back, Zoe had run five miles on the treadmill, done the circuit of weight machines and was about ready to head back to her room for a dip in her bathroom's enormous jetted tub. Not bad considering the day was still five minutes shy of seven o'clock.

"I missed you after the show. Now it looks like I'm too late again."

Bent at the waist, her hands flat on the floor, Zoe looked between her legs as Smith entered the room. Unconcerned by her less-than-flattering pose, she continued her cool down routine. It was crazy to feel a surge of nervous energy, but Zoe recognized the feeling for what it was. Last night, she had been all set to surge ahead, guns blazing. She had been a hairsbreadth away from inviting him to her room. If their meeting backstage had happened after the concert instead of in the middle, she might have done just that.

The look Smith had given her, the words he whispered for her ears only. They had infused Zoe's body with heat that had nothing to do with the performance she had just given. The reason she hadn't followed through was simple. She had too much time to think.

The second Zoe was alone in her dressing room—doubt quickly

replaced desire. Once she had showered and dressed, all she could think about was getting as far away from Smith as possible. She wasn't proud of taking the chicken's way out. She tried to convince herself that things were moving too quickly. She needed to step back and think. It was a lie. However, she wasn't ready to face the truth. So, she slunk back to her hotel room and spent the night brooding.

"I told you I was an early riser." Zoe stood up. Not knowing what to do with her hands, she reached back, tightening the band that held her hair out of her face.

"So, you did."

Smith set his towel and bottled water on the floor. The green t-shirt he wore was a few shades darker than his eyes, the short sleeves brushing against his well-defined arms. When Zoe caught herself staring, she shifted her gaze to his face, relieved that he was busy adjusting one of the machines.

Walk out the door. It was the easiest solution. Smith had put the ball in her court. Her decision. Her move. If Zoe left, they could leave it at that. A minor flirtation that sputtered out with little fanfare. Except that—no matter the stumbling blocks she had placed in her path—she didn't want to lose her tenuous grasp on what could turn out to be a special relationship.

"Tank?"

The roadie who had accompanied Zoe that morning paused in the middle of his forty-pound bicep curl.

"Problems, Zoe?" Fixed on Smith, Tank's gaze narrowed.

"Everything is fine," Zoe assured the big man. "Would you mind giving us a few minutes alone?"

"Are you sure?" Though Tank and his cohorts had accepted the addition of Smith's crew, the bunch that worked for *The Ryder Hart Band* were leery of the other tour members. They were protective of their turf and the talent they worked for. Smith belonged to the other camp. Tank's body language made it clear he wasn't thrilled with leaving Zoe alone with a man he didn't know.

"I'll be fine."

"Okay. I'll be right outside if you need me."

"Sorry about that." Zoe took a bottle of water from her bag, then instead of drinking it, proceeded to fiddle nervously with the label. "Tank can be a bit overprotective."

"If he's watching out for you, there is no such thing."

The words were a good sign, but Smith delivered them with little inflection, his expression deadpan. Zoe searched the deep green eyes for a flicker of emotion. She thought she detected something, but it might have been nothing but her own wishful thinking.

"Are you mad at me?"

"I don't know what to feel. Last night, when you looked at me, I thought something had changed. Then you disappeared." Smith shrugged. "Was I wrong, Zoe? Are my feelings one sided? Because it would be better to tell me now before I make a bigger fool of myself than I already have."

"You wrote me two letters. How does that make you a fool?"

"My brothers would laugh their asses off if they—" Smith's eyes sharpened, the green taking on a definite glint. "*Two* letters? When did the second one arrive?"

"Just before I went on stage."

"Jesus," Smith muttered, briskly rubbing at the stubble on his cheeks. "Now I feel like twice the fool."

"Do you want to know how I felt when I read it?"

"Did you laugh? No." With a huff, Smith's head dropped back. "Let me save a bit of my dignity."

Zoe sat on the padded bench, trying to find the right words. Long ago, she had learned to keep her emotions in check. Ryder could read her better than anybody. But after they were put into foster care, she stopped sharing with him her every fear and doubt. He had his own problems; the last thing he needed was his little sister whining every time her feelings were hurt or something didn't go her way.

More and more, Zoe learned to rely on herself. That was a good thing. To survive, she went from easily cowed, introverted little girl to a strong, independent woman. Refusing to take shit from anybody, Zoe learned how to stand up to bullies and shoot down mean girls with a precision Annie Oakley would have envied.

As Zoe's edges toughened, so did her heart. Not to solid stone. There were cracks that a few select people had slipped through. The list of those she held dear had doubled in the past year—much to her surprise. Friends were one thing. Romantically, Zoe hadn't let her guard down since she was fifteen years old. Until now.

"Your letter made me feel special."

Smith straddled the bench. For a second, Zoe thought he would touch her. Instead, he rested his elbows on his long legs, clasping his hands together. "You know how special you are. The audience tells you every night."

Zoe felt a surge of disappointment. She thought Smith of all people would get what she meant. He said it himself in his letter. The life they had chosen could be lonely. Watching her friends fall in love—finding that one person with whom they wanted to share their lives—had brought home to her just how alone she really was.

"Tens of thousands of screaming fans is a rush, Smith. But—"

"Connecting with all those people is easier than connecting with just one."

Nodding, Zoe smiled. Smith *did* understand.

"It's hard to know if the men I meet are interested in me or my celebrity." When Smith's mouth quirked, Zoe remembered the rumors about him and Thea Davidson. "Been there, done that?"

"More often than I care to think about." Smith laid his hand on the bench, a few inches from Zoe's. "I'm not after you for the publicity."

"What are you after?" Zoe hadn't meant to ask, but the question had been zipping around her brain for weeks. She couldn't it keep inside any longer. "Sex?"

"Yes," Smith nodded, his hand inching closer, stopping before his fingers could brush against Zoe's. "That was the original plan. It still is. However, I find the longer we circle the inevitable, the more complicated it becomes."

"Inevitable?" Where Zoe was concerned, there was no such thing. She knew how to put on the brakes. As tempting as Smith was, that hadn't changed.

"Don't forget complicated."

"You've got that right." Making the final move, Zoe laid her hand over Smith's. "Too complicated?"

Smith turned his hand until they were palm to palm, adjusting the position of his longer fingers, the tips pressed against Zoe's. Matching callouses met, built up from years of playing the guitar.

"Are you secretly married?"

Startled by the question, Zoe's gaze zipped to Smith's face. The twinkle in his green eyes letting her know his intent was to tease.

"No lurking husband," Zoe assured him, her lips twitching.

"Are you planning on having a sex change operation in the near future?"

"Nope. I'm comfortable in my woman's body."

"That's good," Smith nodded, tracing the line of Zoe's index finger. "Mind you, I support LGBT rights."

"Good to know. Me, too."

"Another fact in the plus column." Smith's gaze turned serious. "I can deal with complicated, Zoe. As long as I know what the complications are."

"Are you sure you want to know?" Zoe asked.

"Tell me."

"At the moment, the most complicated thing in my life is you."

"Well, damn." Smith grinned. "That's the best compliment I've had in a long time."

Shaking her head, Zoe laughed. "It wasn't meant that way." Not exactly. Smith had shaken up her life. Time would tell if that were a good thing or not.

"Zoe?" Smith leaned close, his eyes on her lips.

"What are you doing?"

"I'm going to kiss you."

"But—"

"Remember," Smith's fingers tightened over hers. "You touched me first."

Zoe could have stopped him. Smith gave her plenty of time to pull away. However, at this point, any protest would have been cutting off her nose to spite her face. Keeping her eyes open, locked with his, Zoe tipped her head to the side.

Smith cupped the side of Zoe's neck. "I'll take that as a yes," he breathed into her ear.

Zoe's pulse spiked. "I'm all sweaty."

"Last night when you came off stage, I fantasized about tasting your skin." Smith spoke with his lips pressed against Zoe's neck. The quick swipe of his tongue made her gasp. "Better than I imagined."

With a growl of pleasure, Smith claimed Zoe's mouth with his. It was nothing like their first kiss. Within seconds, banked fires Zoe hadn't known existed went off like trees in a drought-stricken forest. Whoosh. Crackle. Pop. There was no time to prepare for the desire that scorched through her body. Smith was in the driver's seat. All she could do was wrap herself around him and enjoy the ride

"So delicate." Smith's hand slid under her shirt, his fingers running up her spine. "Yet so fiercely strong. Do you have any idea how sexy that is?"

Was she supposed to answer? Zoe's brain was turning to mush. How did Smith expect her to connect two coherent words together, let alone carry on a conversation? She pulled her mouth away, her tongue dipping into that sexy as hell crease in the middle of his chin.

"Stop talking."

"Okay."

Already dizzy, Zoe closed her eyes as Smith rolled to the floor, taking her with him. Landing on his back, Zoe sprawled on top, he quickly reversed their positions until he was lying over her, his eyes the darkest shade of emerald green she had ever seen.

"Just one thing. I—"

Whatever Smith had been about to say would remain forever a mystery, interrupted by a loud pounding on the door.

"Hello! There are some people out here who want in. I told them you were busy, but they are pretty insistent."

"Give me one minute, Tank." Mortified, Zoe shoved at Smith. "Are you laughing?" she demanded.

Smith collapsed onto his back, an arm over his eyes. "It's either that or let out a string of curse words a mile long." He peeked as Zoe jumped to her feet. "I would suggest that we take this back to your room—or mine. But something tells me the moment has passed."

"The moment never should have started." Zoe jammed her arms into a red warm-up jacket. "What if Tank hadn't been out there?"

"Relax. Nobody saw anything. Hey. Are you angry?" Smith grabbed Zoe's ankle when she would have stalked past him. "We got carried away. That isn't the end of the world."

"I'm not angry, Smith." More like stunned. Zoe never let passion override common sense. It had never been a possibility—until Smith. "I have to go." Zoe paused, her hand on the doorknob. "I wrote you a letter."

That perked him up. "You did?"

"Should be here this afternoon. I didn't think it was cheating if I sent it express mail as long as I used the U.S. Postal Service." Zoe tossed Smith her towel.

"What's this for?" he asked with a puzzled smile.

"Cover yourself up," Zoe nodded toward the bulge between Smith's legs. "The people out there might have a good idea what we were doing. No need to give them visual confirmation."

Laughing as Smith scrambled to his feet, his back to the door, Zoe pulled a Seattle Mariners cap low over her eyes and exited the room.

"Zoe Hart?" A woman wearing vivid pink yoga pants exclaimed. "Marion. That's Zoe Hart."

"Don't be ridiculous, Tawny. What would Zoe Hart be doing working out here in the hotel?"

"I say it was her," Tawny insisted.

Hurrying down the corridor, Zoe felt an impulse come over her that she couldn't resist. Besides, she didn't like the snotty tone in Marion's voice.

"Tawny's right," Zoe called out as the elevator opened. Stepping into the car, she pulled off her hat. To her satisfaction, Marion gaped, and Tawny squealed. "Have a good workout, ladies."

Totally worth it, Zoe decided. Maybe she should give into her impulses more often, especially if they involved Smith's big, hard body lying on top of hers. A sudden thought had Zoe chuckling.

"What's the joke?" Tank asked, always ready for a good laugh.

"If *I* surprised Tawny and Marion, wait until they get an eyeful of Smith."

"Maybe we should have warned him."

Still smiling, Zoe shook her head. "Trust me, Mr. Carson is one man who can take care of himself."

Chapter Eight

THE BEST LAID plans of mice and men. Smith had never been a big proponent of well-worn idioms, but hell, if the shoe fit—so to speak. The weekend had not gone as planned. After their brief but steamy encounter in the workout room, finding a single moment alone with her had proved impossible.

The business of touring didn't begin and end on stage. There were meetings and interviews and personal appearances. Smith was more of a media person than the members of *The Ryder Hart Band*, but that didn't mean Zoe's time was her own. Like him, she had obligations that couldn't be ignored.

"Lunch?" Smith called Zoe once he was back in his room, showered, and his erection under control. Though that problem waned as soon as Zoe pointed it out. Thankfully, it was gone by the time his two *biggest fans* entered the workout room.

"Sorry. I have plans. We are adding a couple of new songs tonight. There are still some kinks that need smoothing out." Zoe didn't try to hide the laughter in her voice when she asked, "How was your workout?"

"Great. I took a long run around the city."

"You didn't keep Marion and Tawny company? They must have been disappointed."

"They were fine. I exchanged pleasantries. And posed for a dozen pictures or so. When I left, Marion and Tawny were a couple of beaming little fans."

"You're a good man, Smith."

"I can't tell. Was that statement tinged with irony?"

"Nope," Zoe said. "Straight-up serious. You care about your fans. You care about people. That isn't something you can fake."

"I care about you, Zoe."

Smith didn't know which of them had been more surprised by his spontaneous declaration. Zoe had quickly ended the call without acknowledging his words. Caring was a long way from something stronger. However, he knew that Zoe was skittish. As for Smith, he didn't know what was happening. He wanted her. Found her surprisingly funny and likable. But after that? He cared. That was as much as he was willing to commit to.

Saturday's concert flew by without a hitch. Ryder Hart invited Smith to join them back at the hotel. They were having one of their post-show get-togethers in Dalton's room.

"Consider it a standing invitation," Ryder said, accepting Smith's offered beer.

Ryder was dressed in street clothes, his hair damp, looking mussed as though he hadn't combed it after his shower. Smith had ten minutes before he was due on stage, plenty of time for a visit. Relaxed, he sipped from a cup of hot tea—his pre-performance beverage of choice.

"I appreciate it, Ryder. But I just got off the phone with my dad. He decided at the last minute to catch a few days of the St. Louis Farm Expo. He got into town this afternoon, caught up with some old friends, *then* got in touch with me." Smith chuckled. "Typical. Dad didn't want to bother me. Can you imagine? There's nothing I like better than spending time with my old man."

"That's how it should be." Ryder set his almost untouched beer aside, getting to his feet. "If you want, bring your dad along. He's more than welcome."

Alone, Smith frowned. Ryder's exit had been abrupt. They had known each other for a long time. More casual acquaintances than friends, but unlike his more reticent sister, Ryder was always genial and ready to laugh. Something had happened. The withdrawn man who left his dressing room was not the same smiling one who had entered.

"Are you ready?" Randy asked, sticking his head in the door.

"Did you get my dad settled in his seat?"

"I did." Randy walked with Smith toward the stage. "Your dad is a hoot. He wasn't there a second before he had introduced himself to half the crowd, telling jokes and laughing like he'd known them forever. That man makes friends easier than anybody I've ever met. You sure hit the jackpot in the dad department."

Smith nodded with pride. He knew how lucky he was. Not everybody had parents as loving and supportive as his.

"Well, shit," Smith muttered.

"Did you say something?" Randy leaned closer. The closer they got to the stage the harder it was to hear over the sound of the expectant crowd.

Smith shook his head. "It wasn't important."

Except it was. The mystery of what happened with Ryder was solved.

Kicking himself, Smith wondered why he hadn't remembered sooner about Ryder's childhood. Ryder's *and* Zoe's. They didn't talk about it to the press—to anybody. But some of the circumstances were public knowledge. Abuse. Neglect. Suicide. Those details were public record. It had been a long time since Smith had heard the story. He couldn't remember from whom. Not that it mattered at this late date.

Smith took a deep breath. He was sorry that he had upset Ryder—it had been unintentional. It was Zoe that concerned him. Was he going about this all wrong? She came across as one of the most together women he had ever known. Strong. Independent. The epitome of standing on her own two feet. But nobody lived through a childhood like hers without some scars. Smith didn't know all the details—she and Ryder had managed to keep those to themselves.

Was he pushing Zoe too hard? Was that why she seemed to take one step toward him only to stop and take two in reverse? Or was he not pushing her hard enough? Kid gloves or no gloves at all? He doubted that Zoe would appreciate him rooting around in her past. It wasn't a subject he could see her bring up on her own and couldn't ask without worrying about alienating her.

Smith had told Zoe that he didn't mind complicated. It was true. But this was way out of his wheelhouse.

"That's your cue," Randy yelled.

The second Smith stepped into the spotlight, everything else faded away. The search for answers to his Zoe questions could wait. Right now, he had a show to give and an audience that had paid good money to be here. They deserved his undivided attention.

Smith moved to the microphone. "Hello, St. Louis. Are you ready to rock?"

"I DON'T KNOW how you do it. Much of this nightlife would send me to an early grave." Ben Carson, his green eyes holding the same emerald glint as those of his famous son, patted his stomach with a satisfied smile. "However, it's hard to argue with a stomach full of tender, sauce-slathered ribs—even at two in the morning."

"Dessert?" Smith asked. Knowing his father, Smith motioned for the waitress.

Ben glanced at the menu. "Cheesecake. Don't tell your mama."

"Mom won't ask. She lets you run wild when you're on a road trip."

"True." Ben patted his flat stomach. He naturally ran to tall and slender—had all his life. A young fifty-five, his metabolism and lifestyle hadn't changed. It would take more than a late-night meal or two for him to turn to flab. "My Nellie is a saint."

It gave Smith a warm feeling to hear the love in his father's voice. His parents had married young. The youthful passion they shared as teenagers had matured. Grown. Strengthened. The depth of their feelings were beyond Smith's understanding because he had never felt anything even close. Ben and Nellie Carson had set the bar high.

Smith aspired to the standard set by his parents. Someday. If he could be half as happy, he would consider himself a success.

"If Mom asked, would you tell her about the late-night ribs? And the cheesecake?" Smith thanked the waitress as she set down the dessert. He noticed the way the pretty brunette batted her eyelashes. Instead of shooting her down, he chose to pretend he hadn't.

"Of course, I would tell her." Ben took a healthy bite, sighing with pleasure. "I never lie to your mama. I may keep a few things to myself—nothing important. But straight out lie to her face? Never."

"There must have been bumps. You've been together since you were little more than kids."

"I fell for Nellie the first time I saw. She was the new girl in town. Thirteen and so pretty it made my throat ache. You know that feeling you get when you're so emotional you can't swallow?"

Smith nodded. He had heard the story a hundred times. At telling one hundred and one, it had never grown old.

"I still feel it. All my Nellie has to do is walk into a room. She's the brightest light in my life. Always was. Always will be." Thoughtfully, Ben tapped his fork on the side of his plate. "Who's the woman?"

"Woman? What do you mean?" Smith hoped to convey a casual,

nonchalant tone. His father's knowing smile told him he had failed miserably.

"Smith." With a sigh, Ben shook his head. "Before you could talk, you flirted with the ladies. You had them eating out of your hand with a smile and gurgle. It didn't matter that there was drool running down your chin. I can't remember the last time you passed up the chance to charm a woman. That waitress was all primed to be your latest conquest, but the best she got was a bland smile, and a thank you."

"I'm a little tired. In case you've forgotten, I just did a full show."

"And could do another without breaking a sweat." Ben raised an eyebrow, a smile on his lips. "That excuse might fly with somebody else. This is your father. So, I repeat. Who is the woman?"

"You don't know her."

"I assumed. You have never brought one of your ladies home to meet your mama and me. The day you do, I will know it's serious."

"There isn't much to tell." Smith grasped his coffee cup between his hands, his gaze locked on the black liquid inside. "She's—" He racked his brain for a better word, but only one seemed to tell the story. "Complicated."

"Any woman worth her salt is."

"This is different." Frowning, Smith raised his eyes. "I need your advice."

Ben smiled, his chest puffing out. "That's what I was waiting to hear. Go on. What's the problem, son?"

"First? Her name is Zoe."

"Zoe Hart?" When he saw Smith's surprised look, Ben shrugged. "It isn't a name I hear every day. Your mama and sisters are big fans."

"It seems to run in the family."

Smith spent the better part of the next hour telling his father about Zoe. How they had met years ago, but it was only recently that his interest had become personal.

"Letters? Nice touch."

"It started as a way to make Zoe more comfortable with me. Sort of catch her attention. But now…"

"You're the one who's been caught in the trap? Hoisted on your own petard?"

"There's that tenth-grade education talking again." Smith laughed despite himself. "Even without a high school diploma, you are the smartest man I've ever known."

"Now, isn't that a nice thing for a father to hear from his son?"

"I'm damned lucky to have you." Smith noticed the trace of moisture in his father's eyes. "Zoe wasn't as lucky."

The story wasn't long. Smith had few details. But the ones he did have were bad enough to make his hands bunch into fists as he spoke, every muscle in his body tensing.

"Son of a bitch." His appetite gone, Ben pushed aside the rest of his dessert. "In a just world, some people wouldn't be allowed to father children. Then again, if some enterprising soul had castrated Zoe's father—and justifiably so—she wouldn't be here. It's the worst kind of catch twenty-two."

"You see my dilemma?"

"Not really. Hear me out." Ben raised a hand when Smith would have protested. "You say that Zoe is a fierce, strong-willed young woman. Do you think she would want you to treat her like a victim?"

"No." If he tried, Zoe would kick him in the balls. "It's hard to think of her that way."

"Then don't. If Zoe has found peace with what happened to her, let her keep it."

"That's it?" His father made it sound so simple. But that was one of Ben Carson's gifts. He knew how to skim the crap off a subject, leaving only the bits that really mattered. "What if Zoe brings it up?"

"Simple. Listen, son. Just listen. If Zoe talks to you, it's because she needs somebody to listen. Be there for her, and you'll never go wrong."

It was amazing how a few hours with his father—and some sage advice—had put Smith's situation with Zoe into perspective.

"Are you sure you don't want to stay with me? I have a suite. The extra bedroom is sitting empty."

"I'm happy at the Marriott. It's walking distance to the place where they're holding the Expo. Get some sleep. Have a good breakfast—with Zoe if you can swing it. I'll catch you up with all the goings-on at home tomorrow afternoon."

Smith had invited his father to the Cardinals game. Zoe wouldn't know the difference, and his dad was a big baseball fan. Since St. Louis was playing Atlanta, and the Braves were Ben Carson's team, it was the perfect father/son outing.

The game had been a rout. Ten to one in Atlanta's favor. After saying goodbye to his happy father and wishing him a safe trip home, Smith returned to his hotel room, contemplating a nap before that night's show. All thoughts of sleep left his head when he found Zoe's letter waiting for him. He had looked for it the day before, calling the desk to check if it had arrived or been misplaced. To his disappointment, he was assured there had been nothing delivered for him.

Smith hadn't exactly forgotten Zoe's letter. But with his father's visit, it had been pushed to the back of his mind. Kicking off his shoes, he fell onto the bed, fluffing a couple of pillows and stretching out his long legs. Tearing open the envelope, he settled back, Zoe's opening words sending a shot of pleasure through his blood.

Dear Smith,

He had been elevated from simply *Smith*, to *Dear Smith*. Progress indeed. Smiling, he resumed reading.

Dear Smith,

Where to begin? I'm hiding in my hotel room. There. I admit it. Though if you ask, I'll swear you must have read it in somebody else's letter. I know we got our flirt on before you went on stage. Did you look for me afterward? Obviously, you wouldn't have found me. Don't ask why I'm locked in a lonely room when I could be with friends—with you. I don't have the answer. If you leave it at that—at least for now—I will be eternally grateful.

Zoe's eternal gratitude? Smith would be a fool not to grab hold for dear life.

I've been giving a lot of thought about what to tell you about myself. You've given me little glimpses into your childhood and the things that helped shape you into the man you are today. Who am I? That's easy. I'm a sister. A friend. A songwriter.

And, a guitar player. Would you like to know how that came about? If not, skip the rest of the letter. I'm afraid I'm about to ramble a bit.

Smith laughed. Right. Like he would miss a chance to find out how the guitar goddess got her start.

When we weren't in school, I went everywhere Ryder went. He was my idol—still is. If he tried something, I was right behind, doing my best to keep up. When he was eight, he started taking guitar lessons from Mrs. Finch—a woman in the neighborhood—in exchange for doing chores. Eight years old and Ryder knew what he wanted. I was five. What did I know? I was happy to sit and watch.

Smith bet himself that watching wouldn't have satisfied Zoe for long. Five years old? She must have been adorable.

Ryder told me to sit still, be good, and not make any noise. Mrs. Finch was a bit of a tyrant. She would make him practice the same chords over and over again. I sat. I watched. And I guess I learned. One day, they left me alone while Mrs. Finch showed Ryder the flower bed she wanted him to weed. Though I wasn't supposed to touch anything, I couldn't resist. When Mrs. Finch found me, I was playing. Not a song. I had no idea how that worked. But I could play the different chords. And I got them right the first time without any help.

After that, Mrs. Finch had two students. I would say the rest is history, but it sounds a bit pretentious. So, I will leave it at this. I learned the guitar. I play for a living. End of story.

One thing before I go. If you get yourself a dog—which I think you should—please don't give it a music-related name like Banjo or something equally cringe worthy. Just my opinion. Do with it what you will. About the name Clyde? Perfect.

Zoe

Smith gave himself a moment to absorb, before reading the letter again. There was so much packed into a few paragraphs. It was easy for him to picture a little, blond-haired girl, who had at the center of her chaotic world, a brother she adored. Smith wanted to play the guitar, so naturally, Zoe wanted the same thing. She had turned out to be a prodigy. That was Smith's interpretation, but he thought it accurate.

Zoe hadn't given a reason for why she had spent all her free time with her brother. Smith frowned. There were pieces to the puzzle, but they didn't fit together in a cohesive manner. He could speculate, using what he knew. However, his conclusions might be way off base. It was better to wait, hoping that Zoe would eventually fill in the blanks.

Looking over the last passage, Smith chuckled, making a mental note to himself. Banjo was off the list of potential names—not that it had ever been a possibility.

Tucking the letter into his suitcase, Smith glanced at the clock. His pre-concert meal would be arriving any minute. Then a quick shower and it would be time to leave. The weekend hadn't gone as planned—his time alone with Zoe had been almost non-existent. Yet Smith felt that real progress had been made. The ice had melted—at least on the surface. Little by little, he was peeling away Zoe's layers, though they were turning out to be more than he could have imagined.

Zoe was complicated. Also, fiercely loyal, staunchly independent, and wildly passionate. Smith could personally attest to that. Then there was that touch of vulnerability she tried so hard to mask with her tough persona. Zoe wasn't a marshmallow, but there was a softness that now and then she couldn't hide. It made for a fascinating—and for Smith—irresistible combination.

Three weeks. That's how long it would be until Smith saw Zoe again. He would be going west, *The Ryder Hart Band's* schedule had them traveling north. Eventually, their tours would meet up again in New York for five sold-out shows.

Under different circumstances, Smith would consider the time apart to be a major stumbling block. He did not prescribe to the belief that absence made the heart grow fonder. However, when a man was wooing a woman with the written word, twenty-one days was an opportunity more than a liability.

The letters they had exchanged so far were a good start. A beginning. A way of feeling each other out. Smith was ready to delve deeper. Was Zoe of the same mind? One thing was for certain, by the time they met up in New York, things between them would be different. The question was, would it be better or worse? Only time—and the efficiency of the U.S. Postal Service—would tell.

Chapter Nine

USICIANS WERE ODD creatures. To make a living, they had to travel from place to place, city to city. They lived out of a suitcase, slept in strange beds, and kept odd hours, often missing the sun's light because most of the work they did was done at night.

"Do you ever think that we would have made good vampires?" Zoe asked,

Ryder laughed. "The sparkly kind. Emo types or the savage ones who rip off people's heads and drain their innards?"

"Obviously, you've given this some prior thought." Zoe settled into her seat on the plane. "Mine was just a random musing."

"Quinn got me hooked on *True Blood*. I admit that I identified more with the tall, sardonic Viking than the whiney, self-hating Southern gentleman."

"I have no idea what you're talking about."

"Come on. Eric versus Bill? Sookie Stackhouse?" Dalton, the biggest binge watcher of the group, gave Zoe an exasperated shake of the head when she shrugged. "The show went off the rails around season four, but it was great campy fun. I'm team Eric, by the way."

Ashe joined Dalton who was rooting around in the mini-fridge. When he offered Zoe a beer, she shook her head. "Ryder?"

"Hell, yes." Ryder twisted off the cap, tipping the bottle for a long drink.

"The hell with that television crap." Ashe chimed in his opinion. "I would go old school. Nosferatu. That S.O.B. was hardcore scary."

"This isn't about badassery," Dalton argued. "It's about the way you would want to live."

"In that case, I pick one of those Vampire Diary dudes. They get to walk in the sunlight. Plus, they have great hair."

Zoe threw up her hands. "I made an off-hand remark concerning the hours we keep, and suddenly we're debating the merits of fictional bloodsuckers?"

"The major difference is that we can eat anything we want. Can you imagine a steady diet of a warm, iron-based liquid?" Ashe shuddered.

"Oh, for the love of… Forget I said anything."

The fact that she opted out didn't stop Dalton and Ashe from continuing their less than heated exchange. They were a couple of idiots. They were also loyal and protective and unfailingly supportive. Zoe wouldn't have traded them—and their ridiculous ramblings—for anything.

They were in their private plane, waiting to be cleared for takeoff. The fact that Zoe didn't find anything unusual about that sentence spoke volumes about how far they had come.

Zoe had never imagined the kind of success they enjoyed. The fame and fortune were nice. Better than nice. She had no desire to go back to barely scraping by. They had paid their dues and then some. But private jets, hobnobbing with kings, queens, and presidents? If she took a moment to reflect, it was all a bit much for a girl who, until she was fourteen, had never owned more than one pair of shoes at a time. Now, she had more than she could count. There were things in her huge, walk-in closet that she had never worn and didn't remember buying.

Nothing had been handed to Zoe on a silver platter. She worked hard and had earned every perk, pleasure, and spiked stiletto.

"Did you ever think that flying in our own plane would become a common occurrence?" Zoe asked Ryder when he took the seat next to her. The pilot had just announced that they would be taking off soon.

"Yes." Matter-of-factly, Ryder buckled his seatbelt. Seeing Zoe's surprised expression, he smiled. "Not when I was a green-as-grass sixteen-year-old hustling for a paying gig. Then it was all about filling my belly and scraping together enough to buy a second-hand winter coat."

"And sending me a few dollars that you couldn't really spare."

At thirteen, Zoe had been clueless. She was so worried that Ryder would forget about her that she hadn't considered the sacrifices he made to keep his promise. *I'll always come back for you.* And he had. Every time.

"It was only a few dollars." Ryder always shrugged it off.

"I had a warm place to sleep and regular meals. You were lucky if you ate once a day."

"That's old news, Zoe." Frowning, Ryder laid a comforting hand on her arm. "What's with the trip into the past? Or do I already know the answer?"

"It's nothing. Really."

"Did you hear from Riesa?"

Zoe frowned. She loved her brother, but there were times when she wished he couldn't read her so well. While in her dressing room before the concert, she had received a message from the private detective in her pocket. There had been some progress. Riesa finally had a lead on April Hart. It was thin, and there was no telling where it would lead or if it would end after a turn or two. But it was more than she had a week ago. That was progress, Zoe supposed.

"I don't want to bother you with this, Ryder."

"It isn't a bother. Honestly." Ryder sighed. "Here's the truth. God's honest—whatever that means. I don't want you to be hurt by what you find. Or don't find."

"I'm not the one who suffered because of her."

"Aren't you? That's not the way I remember it." Ryder shrugged it off before Zoe could respond. "I've been through the fire and come out the other side. You know better than anybody how I struggled."

"It killed me that I couldn't help."

Ryder met her gaze, his eyes a deep, intense blue. "I wouldn't have survived if it weren't for you."

"Me? I was always in your way. You had to feed me and dress me and hold my hand."

"You think I minded?" Ryder's words were spoken with a fierceness that tore at Zoe's heart. "It wasn't an obligation. It was love. There were a few times when the thought of you was the only thing that kept me alive."

Was Ryder saying he had considered taking his own life? Zoe couldn't wrap her head around it.

"No! You wouldn't have—" Zoe grasped at Ryder's hand, unable to speak the unthinkable.

"I wouldn't have," Ryder assured her. "Because I had you."

Stunned, Zoe stared at Ryder for several moments. Then she did something she hadn't done since she was a little girl. She threw herself into her brother's arms and cried. Hard, gut-wrenching sobs. There was no controlling it. No stopping the flow of tears.

"It's okay," Ryder soothed, holding her close. "I've got you."

"Hey. What happened?" Concerned, Dalton dropped to his knees next to Zoe, his hand going to her back.

"Is something wrong?" Ashe joined Dalton, adding his support.

"This is something she has needed to get out for a long time." Ryder handed Zoe a tissue.

"Have I told you guys how much I love you?" Zoe hiccupped as the tears slowed.

"Not recently," Dalton said, exchanging looks with an equally puzzled Ashe. "But it's always nice to hear."

"You're my family." Zoe sat up with a watery laugh. "From now on, you'll be hearing it more often. So be prepared."

"No more calling me an asshole or jerkwad?" Ashe teased.

"Let's not get carried away. When you act like an asshole, I will respond appropriately."

"Thank God." With the back of his hand, Ashe made an exaggerated swipe across his brow. "For a second there, I thought we had lost our girl. I'm all for the occasional helping of mush, but I need my snarky Zoe."

It felt good to laugh. Much better than crying. Though Ryder was right, she had needed that kind of purge for a long time. What brought it about was another matter altogether. She swallowed the catch in her throat. A world without Ryder in it? Zoe shook off the thought. It hadn't happened. That was all that mattered.

Zoe looked out the window as the plane taxied to the runway. Life was so unpredictable. She didn't know what tomorrow would bring. Happiness or heartache. She had no way of predicting.

However, as unpredictable as it could be, there were some things that Zoe had control over. Professionally, her life was full-steam ahead. It was time to treat her personal life the same way. For too long, she had kept that part of herself on hold. For the first time in a very long time—maybe in forever—she had met a man who made her forget to think about the consequences.

Smith Carson and his crazy, wonderful, improbable letters.

For the last three weeks, hundreds of miles had separated them. Yet, through his words, Zoe had gotten to know Smith better than if they had gone out on dozens of dates. His willingness to open up had given her the freedom to do the same.

It was the little things. Smith's favorite food. Or Zoe's love of reading historical biographies. She knew that he hated getting his hair cut. There was something about sitting in a chair, putting himself at the mercy of a scissor-wielding stranger that gave him the willies. In return, Zoe shared that she kept her bedroom freakishly neat. Not the rest of the house—just her bedroom.

By some kind of silent, mutual agreement, Zoe and Smith had kept the tone of their letters light. Some things were too intimate for the printed word. They were meant to be said face to face. Zoe didn't know if that was where they were headed. She wasn't there yet.

For the next week, they would be in New York. Together. Smith and Zoe. Zoe and Smith. Friends. Lovers. Zoe ran the words through her head. Not bad, not bad at all, she decided. Whatever the combination, there was a very nice ring to it.

It wasn't often Zoe had an afternoon all to herself. When the band was on tour, they ate together, worked together, and for the most part lived in each other's pockets. It was a good thing their personalities meshed. The ties that bound groups together could be strained to the limits at times like these. Even the closest friends needed a break now and then.

"This is New York City. It would be criminal if we didn't shop our asses off."

"You go ahead," Zoe said to Quinn who had stopped on her way out of the hotel. "I'm going to take a long, hot bath."

Another advantage of staying in one place for a week—at least for her bandmates—it meant Quinn, Colleen, and Belle could join them. These were working women with flourishing careers of their own. It was difficult to be separated from their men, but they knew what they were getting when they fell in love with rock stars.

"It's about compromise and trust," Quinn had told Zoe when she questioned how they made it work. "I love Ryder. Whatever it takes, I'm in. One hundred percent. All the way. Ryder feels the same way. *That* is the key."

Zoe couldn't argue. There was no doubt that Ryder and Quinn's relationship was tighter than ever.

"Are you feeling okay?" Quinn placed a hand to Zoe's forehead. "You never turn down a chance to shop."

"I made a vow not to buy another thing until I clean out my closet. When I had it built, I didn't think I would be able to fill half of it. Four years later, it's bursting at the seams."

"You don't have to buy anything. Colleen wants to get some seriously sexy nighties. Belle is on the hunt for the perfect pair of gray leather boots. I feel like a walk along Madison Avenue. Come on. Four women on the hunt for lace and footwear? How can you resist?"

"It's easier than you might think," Zoe said sardonically. Quinn had a way of drawing her in, like it or not.

"We'll be stopping for something to eat. Wherever you want."

Zoe sighed. She understood what Quinn was doing.

"You want to bond with your boyfriend's little sister?"

"Too pushy? A little desperate?" Quinn sighed. "I want us to be friends."

"Like I told Ryder not too long ago. We're getting there."

"Really?" That seemed to perk Quinn up. "Good to know. I like you, Zoe."

"And?" It sounded like there was going to be a qualifier attached.

"That's it. No ifs, ands, or buts. Enjoy your bath. Would you like us to bring you back something ooey and gooey from that pastry shop around the corner?"

"Sounds good. Thanks." Quinn was almost out the door when Zoe made a sudden decision. "I need some advice."

Surprise—and delight—didn't begin to describe the look on Quinn's face. "Are you sure?"

"I asked, didn't I?"

"Don't get me wrong. I'm thrilled that you want to confide in me." Retracing her steps, Quinn tossed her purse onto a chair, before taking a seat on the sofa. "Tell me your problem."

Where to start? Zoe hadn't planned this conversation. But the closer she came to seeing Smith, the less certain she was about how she should proceed.

"There's this man."

"Okay." Quinn kicked off her shoes, drawing her feet under her. "That sounds promising."

"It is. At least I think it is. Honestly, at this point, I don't know what it is."

"Wow."

Zoe stopped pacing, sending Quinn a frown. "What?"

"It's just that I've never seen you so… unsettled. Whoever he is, this guy must be something. Does he have a name, or are you keeping that to yourself?"

"Of course, he has a name," Zoe huffed. She wasn't frustrated with Quinn's question as much as her own muddled thoughts.

"If you're worried about Ryder, don't be. I won't tell him. Unless you've gotten involved with a gangster or a gangster's hitman." Quinn joked, but when Zoe didn't answer, she grew pensive. "If this man is trouble, all bets are off. Ryder would never forgive me if I kept that from him."

"Relax. I haven't fallen into the clutches of a dangerous degenerate." For some reason, Quinn's agitation calmed Zoe. "It's Smith. Smith Carson," she qualified.

"I assumed. How many Smiths are there?" Quinn slowly smiled. "I'll be damned. So, all that furor over combining the tours? Was that a smoke screen to cover your relationship?"

"It isn't a relationship—exactly. And no, it wasn't a smoke screen." Zoe resumed pacing. Great, now she was back to agitated. "Smith has a way of making me…"

"Uncomfortable?"

"That's as good a word as any." Taking a seat, Zoe spread her hands on the armrest, her fingers tapping. "Smith has a way of invading my space. Even when he's across the room, it feels like he's breathing down my neck. Does that make any sense?"

"I have a good idea what you mean," Quinn nodded. "Your brother has the same ability."

"This isn't like you and Ryder. I'm attracted to Smith. And he has turned out to be surprisingly likable. And funny. And kind of sweet."

"But it's nothing like Ryder and me."

"This isn't funny, Quinn."

Zoe's narrowed gaze didn't deter Quinn's grin. "I'm not laughing. I'm happy for you. Smith seems to be one of the good guys. You like him. He likes you?" Zoe nodded. "So, what's the problem?"

Here was where the conversation got sticky. Zoe felt torn between her innate need for privacy and wanting another woman's advice. She had come this far. With a sigh, Zoe went to the closet.

"We've been exchanging letters." Zoe took the ribbon-bound stack of envelopes from her suitcase.

"Actual letters." Quinn's eyes lit up when Zoe handed her the pile. "How lovely. Nobody does that anymore."

"That's what I thought. Smith's first letter arrived when we were in Atlanta. I wrote back. And," Zoe shrugged. "You can see the results."

"Smith has been seducing you with the written word." Eyes glowing, Quinn touched the letters almost reverently. "That is the stuff of legend, Zoe."

"Don't get carried away." Zoe's first instinct was to sneer, but how could she when Quinn's reaction was so like her own.

"You haven't slept together?"

"No."

"And this has been going on for close to two months? Did I say legend? Smith Carson is approaching sainthood."

"Come on," Zoe scoffed.

"Zoe. It's clear that Smith isn't looking for a pen pal. Or a quick wham bam roll in the hay." Quinn handed back the letters. "Those took time and a lot of thought. From both of you."

"It's been nice." That seemed like such an insipid word, but not in this case. "The anticipation of when Smith's next letter would arrive. Before I open it, my heart pounds like I've run a marathon. I find myself grinning as I devour every word."

"Oh, Zoe." Quinn sighed, her smile beaming. "I've never heard you speak that way."

"Sugar sweet?"

"There's nothing wrong with a little romance."

"I suppose you're right." Opening the mini-bar, Zoe removed two little bottles, then poured their contents into a couple of glasses. Walking across the room, she handed one to Quinn.

"Whiskey?" Puzzled, Quinn looked at the amber liquid. "Am I going to need this?"

"No, but I hate to drink alone. Here's the deal." Zoe took a sip. In one great gush, she continued. "The logical conclusion to those letters is for me to have sex with Smith. It's going to happen. But I've never done it before, and I want to know if I should tell him or keep it to myself. What do you think?"

Wide-eyed, Quinn opened her mouth, closed it, and then tossed back the shot of whiskey in one gulp. With a small cough, she wiped her bottom lip, carefully setting aside the glass.

"That was a lot of information to take in." Quinn cleared her throat. "Let me get this straight. Did you just tell me that you're a virgin?"

"Yes. If you want to be technical."

"How is that possible?" When Zoe simply stared, Quinn tossed her hands up. "Come on, Zoe. You know what I mean. You date. A lot."

"Since you've been keeping track, you must have noticed that I rarely go out with those men more than once. Twice at the most."

"Is there a reason?"

"They bore me. Or slobber on me. Or paw at me. Or want to show me off like a trophy."

"I meant, is there a reason you haven't had sex?"

"You mean was I assaulted? Or am I saving myself for marriage?" Zoe shook her head. "No and no. I didn't plan on living a celibate life. It just worked out that way."

"Virginity isn't a crime."

"I'm aware." Zoe finished off her whiskey. "When I was fifteen, there was this boy that I was crazy about. We started dating and—"

When Quinn's phone rang, she snatched it up. "Go without me," she said without preamble. Hitting a button, she tossed it into her purse. "It's off. Go on."

"Who was that?"

"Belle. She and Colleen were waiting in the lobby." Quinn waved it off. "They won't bother us again. You were saying? There was a boy…?"

Amused by Quinn's eagerness, Zoe rubbed her neck. "His name was Norman. He had this smile that put butterflies in my stomach."

"First love," Quinn nodded.

"Probably. At the time, I would have agreed."

"And now?"

"He turned out to be an asshole." Zoe's lips quirked. "Or a teenage boy. Maybe they're one and the same. The point is, I had decided that Norman was going to be *the one*. In a year or so. When I was ready. Norman was very understanding when I told him I wanted to wait."

"But?" Quinn grabbed two more whiskeys, filling their glasses. "I assume Norman morphed from Prince Charming? Into what?"

"A braggart." Zoe swirled her drink, watching it with a frown. "There were quite a few girls like me in my high school. Foster kids," she explained when she saw the question in Quinn's eyes. "I knew of seven others in my class alone. I don't know why there was such a stigma attached to it, but other kids tended to look down on us. You can't blame teenage girls for wanting to fit in and be liked."

"It's natural."

"Earned or not, foster kids—girls specifically—had reputations for putting out on the first date. One of my classmates *kindly* informed me that was the reason Norman asked me out. He had been bragging about our sexual exploits for weeks."

"The little bastard."

"I called him worse. To his face."

"Good." Quinn looked fierce. "Did you add a kick to his nuts?"

"No. My revenge was more diabolical. I dated Norman's friends. All of them. Just once. Nothing happened. I didn't give them as much as a kiss. I knew they would lie—just as Norman had."

"And Norman—who didn't get what he wanted— would never know if you had put out for his friends. Brilliant."

Zoe had enjoyed her revenge. But the choice she made had been a lonely one. Never terribly social, she spent the last two years of high school pretty much on her own with her guitar as her main companion.

"I'm sorry, Zoe."

"It wasn't the end of the world." If living well was the best revenge, Zoe had hers in spades.

"What about later? After you graduated?"

"Why didn't I jump the first attractive man I met?"

"Something like that," Quinn chuckled.

"It was the plan." Closing her eyes, Zoe let her head fall back. "I wasn't waiting for hearts and flowers. Just good old-fashioned lust. But it didn't happen. Months passed. Then years. I figured I wasn't the lustful type."

"Until Smith."

"He came as a bit of a surprise."

"A good one?" Quinn asked.

"It took me a while to decide. Hence the initial pissy attitude."

"But you do pissy so well."

"I do." Zoe said it with undisguised pride. "Back to my original question. Do I announce to Smith that he is about to deflower a twenty-five-year-old virgin, or would that be the buzz-kill to end all buzz-kills?"

"I doubt Smith would lose his ability to perform, but that isn't the issue."

"It's isn't?" Zoe raised her eyebrows. "I've waited a long time. A limp response would be a huge letdown."

"Was that pun intentional?"

"No. Just got lucky."

"Good one." After a laugh, Quinn turned serious. "It isn't any of Smith's business unless you want it to be."

"So, I shouldn't tell him?"

"Are you in love with Smith?"

"No." Zoe answered before she could give herself time to think. At this point, she didn't know what she felt. Love wasn't on the table. Or in the same building.

"You answered awfully fast, but I will let it pass."

"It doesn't count as letting it pass when you preface it with *you answered awfully fast.*"

"Fair enough," Quinn conceded. "Forgive me. This conversation is a first for me."

"We're talking about *my* first. Not yours."

Quinn rolled her eyes. "My empathy is quickly fading, Zoe. If fact, I'm starting to worry about Smith."

"Let's wrap this up, shall we?"

"With pleasure." Quinn reached for her glass, frowning when she realized it was empty.

"Do you want another?" Zoe started to rise.

"No. I haven't eaten today. I don't want to go from a pleasant buzz to flat on my ass drunk. The way I see it, you don't have to tell Smith, but it might be a good idea."

"Why?"

"Blood." Zoe grimaced. "Exactly. There are all kinds of myths out there about women and their hymens."

"You can write a book. *The Hymen Games.* Just leave my name out of it."

"My point, smartass, is that even though you have an active lifestyle, there could be a considerable amount of blood during your first time. Unless you've taken care of it?"

"Taken care of it?" For a second, Zoe had no idea what Quinn was talking about. Then the light turned on. She groaned. "No. I have not used artificial methods to rid myself of my virginity."

"How was I supposed to know?" Quinn cried out, rubbing her temples.

"This is quickly veering toward a really bad farce. Thank you for listening and your input. Subject closed."

"Good." Quinn got to her feet. She swayed but corrected the problem quickly before walking a straight line to the door. Before leaving she turned, her expression hesitant. "Zoe?"

"You were so close." Zoe made a shooing motion with her hands. "Do us both a favor and keep your question to yourself."

"Is there anything you want to know?"

"About?"

"What to expect."

"Oh, for the love of God. I have spent the last seven years in the company of three sexually active men. They don't brag it up in front of me, but occasionally details slip out." Zoe pushed Quinn through the door with more consideration than she was feeling. "And I read. A lot."

"You know where to find me if anything comes up." Quinn snorted. "So to speak."

Lips twitching, Zoe firmly shut the door. Collapsing onto the sofa, she broke out laughing. Considering how much she dreaded talking about it, Quinn had made the experience relatively painless. Embarrassing as hell. But there shouldn't be any lasting scars.

That bath she had thought about taking sounded good. And something to eat. Zoe was just deciding in what order to put them when there was a knock on the door. Know it couldn't be Quinn, Zoe checked the peephole. The woman didn't look familiar, but she was wearing a uniform with the hotel's insignia emblazoned on the left shoulder and a silver name tag.

"Ms. Hart. My name Lana. This was just delivered with today's mail."

There it was. That surge of anticipation. Zoe wondered if she was becoming like one of Pavlov's dogs. Show a blue envelope, and she began to drool.

"Thank you, Lana."

"Ms. Hart," Lana said hesitantly. "I'm not really supposed to ask."

"Would you like an autograph?"

"You wouldn't mind?" The young woman, hardly out of her teens if Zoe's guess was correct, handed over a pad and paper.

Zoe scribbled a personalized note. "Do you have your phone with you?"

Mouth agape, Lana nodded. Excited, she fumbled to find the right setting.

"Here." Gently, Zoe took the phone. Pushing right buttons, she draped her arm around Lana's shoulders. "What's your favorite one of our songs?"

"*The Road Back.*"

Ryder had written it for Quinn, but his fans didn't care about that. It was the ultimate love song and from the blush staining her cheeks, Lana probably imagined that Ryder sang it just for her.

Zoe snapped the picture

"Thank you so much, Ms. Hart."

"It was my pleasure. And call me Zoe."

"Zoe." Lana backed away, clutching her camera to her chest. "I'll never forget this."

That was Zoe's favorite kind of fan interaction. One on one. She hoped she never reached the point where such moments felt commonplace. That would be sad indeed.

The letter. Zoe did a private happy dance. She hadn't expected number ten to arrive today. She should have known better. It was Smith's turn, and a little thing like them being in the same city wouldn't stop him from fulfilling his part of their ongoing snail-mail foreplay.

Lovely Zoe,

Lovely Zoe? That was different.

I thought it was time to mix things up. I know. Lovely Zoe isn't exactly groundbreaking, but it's certainly accurate. I have a confession. I have become a bit of a Google fanatic. I'm following The Ryder Hart Band's tour. Or rather one particular member of the band. Nashville. Minneapolis. Cleveland. Baltimore. That little number you wore in New Orleans? Bright blue leather suits you. Then again, what doesn't?

Hello, New York. I love that town, but I can't remember anticipating my arrival quite as much as during this tour. I have a proposition. Many, many propositions. They fill my head when I'm in my bed thinking of a certain blonde with the longest, sexiest legs it has ever been my pleasure to drool over.

Smith's comments had grown more personal in his last few letters. Not graphic or salacious. Small things. The softness of her skin. The silkiness of her hair. And her legs. Smith was very fond of mentioning Zoe's legs.

But I digress. I propose that we meet for dinner after tonight's show. There is a private place in the hotel that very few people know about. I will leave a note in your dressing room with directions—if your answer is yes. A nod. A wink. Even a twitch as I leave the stage. No. I need something more definitive. Say yes, Zoe. Please.

Hopefully,

Smith

Alone with Smith. Zoe hadn't expected to see him alone tonight. It was silly, but she had expected a settling-in period. Laughing at herself, she set the letter next to the bed. Unbuttoning her blouse, she walked into the bathroom. Dinner didn't have to be followed by sex, she thought as she turned the taps on full blast. As the tub filled, she finished undressing.

With a sigh of pleasure, Zoe slipped into the water, breathing in the scent of lemons. She filled her hand with body wash, thinking of Smith as she lathered her leg with the silky gel. He had made it clear that she had to make the first move. She wanted to. Would tonight be the night?

Humming, Zoe sank lower until her shoulders were completely submerged. Play it by ear. Why not? It had worked so far.

Chapter Ten

NERVES WERE PART of the game. Smith had never suffered from the debilitating anxiety that plagued some performers. However, before every show, his adrenalin spiked while his butterfly-filled stomach informed him that it was time to earn his supper. Once he stepped on stage, he was in his element, giving his all to a sold-out crowd and loving every second. It was that first step that was the hardest.

Tonight, when Smith played the last note and the lights dimmed, he felt the butterflies return—something they had never done in the past. The unknown was waiting for him in the shadows.

Yes or no? Had there ever been a question with so few words that held so much meaning? Certainly, not as far as Smith was concerned. There could be a dozen reasons for Zoe to answer one way or the other. It wouldn't be the end of the world—or their budding relationship—if she had to bow out of his proposed date.

Jesus. Smith paused at the edge of the stage. The sweat that coated his palms had nothing to do with the draining performance he had just completed. Fucking butterflies. Zoe had done this to him. Somewhere between a mild flirtation and several thousand words written on a few scraps of paper, she had become important. Bordering on vital.

Zoe Hart was the train engine he never saw coming. Wham! Blindsided by his own machinations.

Which didn't make any sense. Zoe hadn't snuck up on him. No shrinking violet, she was a force of nature. Right in his face from the very beginning with a punch to the gut that belied her deceptively delicate build. Smith had gone into this with his eyes wide open. He saw a beautiful woman, and he wanted her. Nothing new in that. The problem was, there had been no way to anticipate what would happen. Write a few letters, he told himself. Break down her resistance. No big deal. Except that is exactly what it had turned out to be. A big, life-changing, stomach-roiling, palm-sweating deal.

"Great show." Randy waited—as always—greeting Smith as he left the stage with a fresh towel and a bottle of water.

"There is something about a New York crowd. The energy level is different." Absently, Smith wiped his face—and his palms. Trying to look nonchalant, he scoured the area. Zoe wasn't anywhere to be seen. Nor were her bandmates. "Where are the headliners?"

Randy chuckled. "It sounds so weird when you say that. You're supposed to be the main draw."

"As long as we're in New York, that honor goes to *The Ryder Hart Band*."

"I know the deal, it's just not what I'm used to."

Join the club, Smith thought. He was in the middle of *not what I'm used to*. Where was Zoe?

"There was some kind of last-minute glitch with their equipment. Ryder and his gang are checking it out before they go on."

"Right. It's a bitch when that happens." It figured that it had to happen tonight.

Disappointed, Smith listened with half an ear as Randy chattered on about an interview he was scheduled to give with a national entertainment program.

"Tonight? I don't remember signing off on that."

Smith tried to keep the time after a show to himself. He didn't do the party scene—he had gotten that out of his system in his early twenties. A good meal, maybe a few drinks with friends. That was the exciting post-performance life of *this* rock star.

"I reminded you this morning."

"Did you?" Smith vaguely recalled. He had no reason to doubt Randy. The man was a computer when it came to keeping Smith's schedule straight. "Where and when?"

"In your dressing room. You have forty-five minutes to decompress."

"I screwed up, Randy. Not your fault. But in the future, keep me from agreeing to this shit."

"It's Melody Royce."

"Well, fuck me," Smith muttered, pausing at his dressing room door. "Did I know she was the reporter when we set this up?" If he had, Smith needed his head examined. Immediately.

"Nope. She was a last-minute substitution. Extremely last minute. As in I got word while you were on stage. Sorry, boss." Randy took out his phone. "Give me the word, and I'll cancel. They know better than to drop that kind of change on you."

"It's too late." Under his breath, Smith cursed a blue streak. "This has Melody's fingerprint all over it. She knew the only way to get within a mile of interviewing me would be to play dirty."

Melody Royce had been one of those mistakes Smith wished he could attribute to the idiocy of youth. Unfortunately, he was twenty-five and a battle-hardened superstar when he let her slither into his bed. It started out as good fun and good sex. Then Melody began using him to further her career. Smith could have lived with that. It happened all the time. But when she reported unfounded gossip and innuendo about him and his friends? Then claimed that he was her source? Nobody's life had been destroyed. If that were the case, Smith would have sued the ass off her and the rag she had worked for at the time. Instead, he cut her from his life with surgical precision. She had been trying for the last five years to wrangle an interview. Through trickery, she finally got her way.

"Fifteen minutes. Understand?" Shutting the door, Smith took a seat. As he pulled off his boots, he pinned Randy with his *serious as death* look. "From the minute the camera rolls, that viper has fifteen minutes of my time. Not a second longer. Make it clear to her. When you give me the signal, I'm out of here."

When Smith was alone, he shucked off his sweaty clothes. Naked, he stood in the middle of the room, stretching his arms over his head. It wasn't a big deal. Melody was an annoyance, nothing more. But Smith hated that she had found a way to wheedle an interview. It was what it was. As satisfying as it would be to cancel, he wasn't going to inconvenience a television show and the people working with her on the story. She could have her moment. But he would make it clear that this was a one-off. Next time? Well, for the sake of Melody's career, there better not be a next time.

The sound of the crowd practically had the walls vibrating as the announcer introduced *The Ryder Hart Band*. That's what it was all about. Smith enjoyed the recording process. He had gotten into the producing end, finding another outlet for his creative juices. But it was performing live that gave him the kind of rush he craved. It had been that way when he was ten, playing for his hometown on the Fourth of July. It was the same today.

Smith checked his phone. No message from Zoe. Maybe that *was* the message. Silence said it all. If she didn't want to meet him for dinner, he wished she would have said so to his face. He was about to toss his phone onto the dressing table when a flash of color caught his eye.

On the mirror, written in fire-engine red lipstick, was one word. *YES*, followed by the letter Z. Smith grinned. Unless Zorro had broken into his dressing room, Zoe had left her answer. He had to hand it to her. The lady had style.

Raising his phone, Smith took a picture before grabbing a handful of tissues. He smeared the lipstick, obliterating the message. With Melody Royce on the prowl, he didn't want to give the gossip hound any material to run with. When he was finished, all that was left was a red blob. With renewed energy, Smith began to whistle, not the least bit surprised when the tune turned out to be *Help Me Make It Through the Night*. In his mind, the song would forever mean Zoe.

Knowing he had something special to look forward to, Smith rushed through his shower, anxious to get the interview over with. Dressed in a pair of faded jeans and a button-down cotton shirt a shade lighter than the green of his eyes, he wiped the steam from the bathroom mirror, checking his reflection. Knowing he would be on television, Smith had taken the time to dry his dark hair. The ends brushed the base of his neck. There was a stylist in mid-town Manhattan who cut his hair exactly the way he liked—wielding a controlled pair of scissors. No matter how busy, she always worked Smith into her schedule. The big tip he always left might have had something to do with it. He would have Randy make an appointment for tomorrow afternoon.

There was a knock on the door just as Smith exited the bathroom.

"Randy?"

"Melody Royce and her crew are in the building. She's getting some filler shots, or whatever they're called. Ready for the makeup guy to do what he can with that hideous face of yours?"

"Send him in. Let's get this farce of a dog-and-pony show on the road."

"My word, your hair is thick." The man who had introduced himself as Paulo—no last name—fluffed Smith's hair for the sixth time, sighing as his fingers lingered over the strands. "And so healthy."

Smith didn't get a vibe that Paulo was hitting on him. He was safe from unwanted advances, but he wasn't so sure about his hair.

"Clean living and good genes." Smith patted Paolo's hand, gently extracting his follicles before standing and moving several feet away. "Great job, man. Thanks."

"If you ever need a personal hair and makeup man, don't hesitate to give me a call." Paolo handed Smith his card. "I freelance all the time. Beyoncé *loves* my work."

"Enough of the self-promotion, Paulo. I'm ready for a touch-up."

That was the woman Smith remembered. Melody Royce always entered a room talking, figuring it was the best way to draw everybody's attention. After that, it was almost impossible to get her to shut up.

"Hello, Melody." Always the Southern gentleman, Smith held out his hand. "Congratulations on your new gig."

"Not so new. I've had this job for almost two years."

"Is that right? I guess I wasn't paying attention." Gentleman or not, Smith couldn't resist the small dig.

Melody's mouth tightened, but she recovered quickly.

"I couldn't help but keep up with you, Smith. You career keeps going higher and higher with no end in sight. And now this tour with The Ryder Hart Band? It's really quite amazing."

"I've been very lucky."

"Talented," Melody corrected with a flip of her coal-black hair. The deep blue eyes were the result of contact lenses. She shooed Paulo away, smoothing her hands over her hips while simultaneously pushing her considerable cleavage in Smith's direction. At one time, that particularly practiced move had worked on him. Now, he found it uninspiring—to say the least. He gave Melody points for the attempt. Realizing that Smith was immune to her charms, Melody got down to business.

"I understand we are under some time constraints."

Smith didn't call Melody out on her subterfuge. He just wanted to get this over. "It's been a long night. I can give you fifteen minutes."

"So your P.A. told me. Ready to go?"

The cameraman and lighting operator were set up and ready to roll. A gum-chomping technician fit Smith with a microphone.

"Anytime."

"How is the sound?" Melody asked, adjusting her blouse so the lights hit her just right, highlighting her breasts.

"Good to go."

Melody began with the usual introductions, sucking up to Smith hard with a long list of his accomplishments. If she thought she was softening him up so he would let down his guard, she would be disappointed. Smith had been smiling his way through these interviews for a decade. There was nothing Melody could toss at him that could rattle his cage.

"Any new women in your life since Thea Davidson?"

"I'm a busy man, Melody. There isn't time for romance these days, especially when I'm on tour."

The look in Melody's eyes told Smith that she wasn't finished with the subject. "The rumor mill has linked you and Zoe Hart. Since you're on tour together, you have plenty of time for romance."

Smith's expression didn't change, his smile staying firmly in place. So, that was Melody's endgame. She couldn't know a damn thing, but she had no scruples about throwing around unfounded speculation.

"*The Ryder Hart Band* and I are sharing several concert venues. I wouldn't say we were on tour together."

"The way the tour is mapped out, it puts you and Zoe Hart in close proximity a lot of the time. Four shows in New York for instance."

"My personal life is always under a microscope. If I ever feel like talking, I'll be sure and let the press know."

"That doesn't answer my question, Smith." Smith could almost feel the heat as Melody's frustration level rose higher and higher. "Zoe Hart has been linked with a myriad of suitors. Can we add your name to the list?"

Smith paused, just to give Melody a little hope. Then dashed them with an icy bucket of water. "I believe I did answer your question, Melody. Was there anything else you wanted to know?"

"No. I believe that's all."

Smith removed his microphone, leaving it in his seat. The door was his destination, but Melody was faster, blocking his way.

"It's been a long time, Smith."

"Time flies." Smith tried to move past her, but she grabbed his arm, her long red nails digging in. She didn't anger him, she simply tired him out. "What are you trying to prove, Melody?"

"That I can always get what I want. Including you." Melody served up a smug smile. "Even if it is only for an interview."

"Do you have any idea how sad that is? Get a life, Melody."

"Fuck you, Smith."

Prying her nails loose, Smith shook his head. Thank God his taste in women had improved.

"Gentlemen?" Shaking each crew member's hand, he thanked them for their service and professionalism.

"You won't lose that card?" Paulo asked.

Smith patted his pocket. "Goodbye, Paulo."

"That woman is scary," Randy said when they were outside the dressing room. He picked up Smith's case which he had packed before the television crew arrived.

Smith sent a quick text to the restaurant that was catering his dinner with Zoe, letting them know that everything was a go. They had all the details. All Smith had to do was escort Zoe to the location.

"Melody Royce is pathetic. But she has a massive amount of ambition and just enough brains to be dangerous." Smith tucked his phone into his pocket. "She can't hurt me, but I don't want any of this unpleasantness to touch Zoe."

The car was waiting for them at the side entrance. Smith waved at some screaming fans, stopping to sign a few autographs. When they were finally on their way back to the hotel, Randy gave Smith a puzzled look.

"Ms. Hart seems like a woman who can take care of herself. Why are you worried about a little gossip?"

"Zoe doesn't need me to look out for her." Smith stared out the window. The set of his mouth was determined as was his resolve. "But that doesn't mean I won't do my holy best to do exactly that."

Chapter Eleven

RESSY OR CASUAL? Zoe stood in front of the closet unsure of which way to jump. The last time she had this much stress about what to wear, she was going to her first dance. Back then, her problem was understandable. There hadn't been much to choose from. That was when she found eBay. Secondhand clothes were the beginning of her fashion journey. Not an obsession—but close. Zoe liked pretty things. The way they made her feel even more than the way they made her look.

Tonight, her problem wasn't about not having a selection of options. When she was on the road, Zoe didn't pack light. She had an outfit for every occasion. Except one for a date with a man who made her blood heat and her skin tingle. What color was that? Deep red? Electric blue. Sunshine yellow? Or maybe hot pink? Texting Smith was out of the question. *What should I wear?* It was not a question Zoe Hart asked anybody. When it came to fashion, she was an island unto herself.

Maybe she should have gone shopping with Quinn. Zoe groaned. *Just pick something!* Tired of standing there like an addlepated twit, she closed her eyes, stuck out her hand, grabbing the first thing she touched.

Not bad. Zoe moved to the mirror. Not bad at all. Dropping her robe, she stepped into the dress. Pale peach—almost the color of her skin—the flowy material brushed her body in a flirty manner, just skimming her knees. Sexy, but not overtly so. A pair of strappy sandals with four-inch heels, stud earrings that glittered when the light hit them, and an intricately woven silver ring completed her look.

Hair. Zoe turned her head from side to side. Up or down? The thought of Smith releasing the clips, his fingers smoothing out the long, blond tresses. It was a heady thought and too tempting to resist. With a couple of expert twists, Zoe's hair was set in an artfully disheveled bun, held in place by a set of glittery hair ornaments that Ashe had given her for her last birthday. This was the first time she had worn them.

Zoe had to remember to thank her friend again—without mentioning the reason. If Ashe knew, Ryder and Dalton would soon follow. It was nobody's business what was going on between her and Smith. Especially her overprotective, buttinski bandmates. And her brother? No! Absolutely not! Dabbing on a bit of wild berry lip gloss, Zoe shuddered at the thought.

"Perfect timing," Zoe told her reflection when she heard the knock at the door. She rushed across the room, her hand encouragingly steady as it turned the brass knob. What was waiting in the hall had her dark eyes widening and a whistle slipping past her lips. "Aren't you pretty."

Smith smile was slow, his drawl heavier than usual. "You stole my line."

Zoe stood back so Smith could enter. Pretty didn't begin to describe the way he looked. He wore a dark gray suit that somehow made his eyes a brighter green than usual. She approved of his choice of tie. Emerald would have been too obvious. Silk. The solid sapphire blue was exactly what Zoe would have picked.

"Are those dress shoes?" Zoe couldn't remember seeing Smith in anything but boots—or sneakers when he worked out. Unless she was mistaken, the ultra-shiny black leather that peeked from beneath the cuff of his trousers were Italian leather. And when it came to shoes, she rarely was.

"Impressed?" Smith made a slow, showy turn.

"You clean up nicely."

Smith straightened his already impeccably knotted tie. "I thought the occasion called for some special effort. It seems we were of the same mind."

"This old thing?"

Smith chuckled. "Sorry. You are gorgeous. Always. It's just when you said this old thing, Carol Burnett popped into my head."

"I saw it in the window, and I just couldn't resist?"

"*Went with the Wind.*" Smith smile widened. "One of the top five comedy skits ever."

Zoe picked up her purse, making certain it contained the essentials. Her phone. Her wallet. Lipstick. And a box of condoms she had purchased online the first time she seriously considered having sex with Smith. She had been carrying them from city to city for almost two months.

Slipping her arm through Smith's, they left the hotel room. "Name four other skits."

To Zoe's surprise, Smith rattled off three without hesitation. "It wasn't technically a skit, but the Thanksgiving episode of *The Bob Newhart Show* where Bob and his friends get drunk while watching football? It goes on the list because it is hands down one of the funniest things I have ever watched."

"I don't remember that show. Though I love Bob Newhart when he guest stars on *The Big Bang Theory*."

"I'll send you the *YouTube* link."

They veered to the right, stopping in front of the service elevator. When they entered, Zoe was surprised when Smith opened a panel, punching a series of numbers that sent the car up instead of down.

"Aren't we going out?"

"We're having dinner. The location is *very* exclusive."

"Smith?"

"Zoe?"

"I've missed you."

Zoe threaded her fingers through Smith's hair. It didn't take much of a tug to bring his lips to hers. His resistance—caused by surprise, not reluctance—melted quickly under the heat of her kiss. The spark quickly turned into a fire. Hot. Passionate. Bone-melting.

She couldn't help herself. She had to wind her arms around Smith's neck—holding on for dear life—or her legs would have collapsed under her. His tongue was doing crazy things to her system. Flames shot through her blood stream. When his hand slid under the hem of her skirt, his fingers barely grazing the back of her thigh, Zoe saw stars. Actual, sparkling orbs that danced wildly behind her closed eyelids.

"What have you started?" Smith breathed the words against her neck, taking a nip with his teeth, soothing it with his tongue.

"It was my way of saying hello. I'm glad to see you."

"If that's the way you always say hello—"

"No." Fiercely, Zoe took Smith's face in her hands. "There is no *always*. Only now. I don't care about the women who have come before me. Or the ones who will come after."

"I was kidding. But you're right." Smith traced the line of Zoe's jaw with his finger. "This is all that matters."

The light brush of Smith's lips across her forehead made Zoe sigh. From sensuous to sweet in the blink of an eye. It made her head swim. And her heart swell. Neither was a very comfortable feeling.

"The elevator doors are open." Zoe frowned. When had that happened?

"They have been that way for some time." Smith took her hand. "I was enjoying myself too much to mention it."

"But you noticed." Unlike Zoe.

"After you ended the kiss. I was just as affected as you, Zoe." Leading her into the night air, Smith's thumb rubbed the backs of her fingers.

"Okay." Satisfied, Zoe looked around. "Are we on the roof?"

"It's pretty spectacular, isn't it?"

That was putting it mildly. From where they stood, the view of New York was panoramic. Lights as far as the eye could see. To her right, Zoe could see the harbor and the Statue of Liberty. To her right, earlier that evening Broadway's best and brightest had entertained thousands of theater goers.

Enchanted, Zoe walked around, looking at everything. "I didn't know they let people up here."

"They don't. Except for special guests." Smith grinned. "I know the owner of the hotel."

"One of the perks of fame. Or did you know this person—man, woman— before you hit it big?"

"Woman." Smith guided Zoe to a table set with lit tapered candles, gleaming white china, and silver. In the background, music played low and smooth. Taking a bottle of champagne from the ice bucket, he popped the cork with little fanfare. "And no, I didn't know her in my previous life. Eleven years ago, I didn't know anybody with more than a penny or two to rub together."

"Thank you." Zoe accepted a filled glass.

"I had a great childhood. Loving parents. Siblings I actually like and enjoy spending time with. But we were dirt-ass poor. Money—and all the perks—is better."

"We had one thing in common." When Smith waited, Zoe shrugged. "I was poor."

"Not happy?"

The last thing Zoe wanted was to talk about her childhood. Even if she had wanted to share the details with Smith, now was not the time. Until a few seconds ago, she felt as effervescent as the bubbles in her glass. Taking a sip of the wine, she let it roll down her throat. That was it. She refused to let go again.

"You said in one of your letters that your parents started their family early." Zoe held out her glass. Smith followed her lead, topping it off and shifting away from her family to his.

"They fell in love at thirteen. Married the summer Mom turned sixteen, and Charity was born the next spring."

"I—" Zoe had to take another drink while she processed the information. "Wow, Smith."

"It's not that unusual where I come from. Not common—not anymore—but not unheard of."

"Where do you fall in the baby sequence?"

Holding out a chair, Smith waited until Zoe was seated. The table was small. When he sat, it was easy for him to keep her hand in his. Enjoying the way it felt, Zoe was happy to oblige.

"After Charity came the twins, Ethan and Tim. Next was Margot, me, and finally, Petula. I know. She isn't a fan either. That's why we call her Tula. It doesn't seem like much of a difference to me, but it makes her happy."

Zoe understood. "Names are funny. I never thought about my name until a girl in junior high decided to torment me by finding as many things to rhyme with it as possible."

"And?"

"She wasn't very creative. But she did accomplish one thing. I embraced my name. Became fiercely protective of it."

"You don't back down from bullies, do you?"

"Do *you*?"

Smith gave Zoe a thoughtful look. "It isn't always easy. The ones that I can handle directly? Absolutely. I use my money and celebrity to back the politicians I believe in. A bully with power is never a good thing." He smiled. "And now I will step off my soapbox."

"I like what you said." Zoe had strong beliefs. It was nice to find out that Smith shared some of them. "Too many people sit back and do nothing. We must try. Even if it doesn't always work out the way we hoped."

"God," Smith stared at her with wonder in his eyes. "Your soul is as beautiful as the rest of you."

Zoe blinked. What was she supposed to say to such an unexpected statement? That it took her breath away? That nobody had ever looked at her the way Smith did? That he seemed to understand there were times when *she* had trouble with that? To her relief, the arrival of their food saved her from having to respond.

"Are you ready, Mr. Carson?"

"Your timing is excellent, Jacob." Smith stood, shaking hands with the short, rather squat man wearing a starched white chef's coat. "Zoe Hart, meet, Jacob Cree. He is one of the best chefs—sorry," Smith laughed when Jacob cleared his throat. "*The* best chef in the country."

"I would have said the world, but Smith barely knows the difference between gazpacho and bouillabaisse. And only because I taught him." Jacob took Zoe's hand, raising it to his lips. "You, lovely lady, need no introduction. I'm a huge fan."

"I'm addicted to your Food Network show." Zoe didn't say that Jacob looked taller on television. "I binge watch whenever I'm home."

"Do you cook?" To Zoe's amusement, Jacob insinuated himself between her and Smith. Smith simply rolled his eyes.

"Does toast count? Because a perfectly browned piece of bread is my one claim to culinary greatness. Of course, most of the credit goes to the appliance. I simply push the button."

"I could give you private lessons." Jacob winked, letting her know that his offer wasn't a clumsy attempt at a pass, but his way of a friendly jab at Smith. Since it was all in good fun, Zoe was happy to play along.

"Really? Could you teach me how to make the salmon dish with mustard sauce? It made my mouth water."

"For you? Anything."

"Okay, Romeo." With a good-natured laugh, Smith shoved Jacob in the direction of the food his assistants were currently unpacking. "Stop flirting."

"Such a beautiful, talented woman. How can I help myself?" Jacob let out a hearty sigh. "It's the story of my life. If only I had met you first, lovely Zoe."

"I can't fault Jacob. Any man would envy me."

"I think that's a bit of an exaggeration, Smith." Zoe hoped to God she wasn't blushing. She fielded compliments all the time—it was part and parcel of the world she traveled in. But it was different with Smith. *Everything* was different with Smith.

"Take the compliment, Zoe." Smith leaned closer, his green eyes bright in the candlelight. "I will never say anything to you that I don't mean."

"Lies—even white ones—are easy," Zoe warned, not wanting Smith to make a promise he couldn't keep. "Telling the truth is much harder."

"I agree. Nobody tells the absolute truth all the time. But when it matters, I don't lie."

Zoe believed him. She and Smith were on an even playing field. Professionally, each had wildly successful careers. They had money, influence. There was little they couldn't obtain with the snap of their fingers. Was it all about seduction for him? If so, she couldn't fault his efforts. Nor did she have any problem with it. She had her eyes wide open.

"Smith left the menu up to me. Which was smart of him considering he has the palate of a twelve-year-old." Jacob set a beautifully composed beet and goat cheese salad in front of Zoe."

"One time I refused to eat something Jacob prepared. He's never let me forget."

"What was it?" Zoe took a bite, the tart dressing making her taste buds sigh with pleasure.

"Escargot."

"Snails," Smith corrected. "For as long as I can remember, my mama battled those slimy suckers in her garden. The solution was never to serve the critters to her family for dinner."

Jacob shook his head, his eyes sad. "Help with this, Zoe."

"Sorry. I'm with Smith. If it leaves a trail of goo, I'm out."

"You're forgiven. What do you think of my salad?"

"Sublime."

"Hey," Smith protested. "Why does Zoe get an escargot get-out-jail-free card?"

"She's prettier than you."

"I don't know about that," Zoe laughed, spearing the perfect bite of beet and cheese. "Smith has eyelashes any woman would envy. And those cheekbones?"

"Not my type," Jacob said over his shoulder, making his way back toward his helpers.

"Thank God for huge favors." Smith tapped his glass against Zoe's. "Though if I were gay, I might consider taking up with Jacob for his omelets alone. I could muddle my way through the sex if I knew one of those babies was waiting for me the next morning."

"That must be some omelet," Zoe laughed.

"Believe me, it could make the angels weep."

"I have to get back to the restaurant," Jacob told them as a waiter removed their salad plates. Another replaced them with cloche-covered dishes.

"At this hour?" Zoe was surprised, assuming it would be closed.

"No rest for the wicked—or the owner. There are things that can only be done when the doors are locked for the night." He sent Smith a dubious look. "Are you sure you can handle the rest of the meal? I can spare Rick to stick around through dessert."

"We'll be fine." Smith stood. He and Jacob exchanged a brisk hug. "Thanks. I owe you one."

"I would agree, but you introduced me to Zoe Hart. I am now in your debt."

"It was a pleasure, Jacob." Zoe smiled. She wasn't comfortable with random acts of affection. A brief kiss on the hand was one thing, full body contact, another. In case Jacob had any plans to pull her in for a hug, she stayed in her seat.

"If you decide to take me up on those cooking lessons, let me know."

"The man is incorrigible," Smith said when they were alone. "But he's a hell of a chef."

"That smells amazing." Zoe breathed deeply as Smith uncovered their plates. "It's beef. And asparagus. After that, I'm stumped."

"Short ribs in a Bordeaux reduction with potatoes a la Jacob—creamy insides, crispy out—and oven-roasted asparagus. Eat up."

The dinner conversation was light. Zoe was already comfortable around Smith. Between his letters and easy manner, any nerves she might have felt melted away like a bite of Jacob's amazing potatoes. Dessert was a lemon tart. Zoe assured Smith that she couldn't eat another bite, then proceeded to *share* his, consuming most of it herself.

"That may be the best meal I've ever eaten."

"Dare I hope that part of the reason was the company?" Smith took a tiny remote from his pocket. With one push, the background music grew louder. "Dance with me?"

It felt natural to move into Smith's arms. He held Zoe close, his hand on the small of her back guiding her steps.

"You've done this before."

"A time or two," Smith admitted, a smile playing around his mouth. "The last time was at my sister Charity's wedding. That was... almost eight years ago. Wow. I can't believe it was that long ago. My oldest niece is almost seven, and her brother is five. The next generation is growing up fast. Makes me feel old."

"You don't move like an old man." Zoe laughed when Smith dipped her low. "On or off the stage."

Smith caressed Zoe's cheek, his hand lingering, his gaze locking with hers. "There are times, like right now, when I wish the world didn't turn so quickly."

Zoe knew what he meant. She didn't want tonight to end. "The good times seem to go by in a blink of the eye, don't they?"

"We can't do anything about the seconds ticking by. It's up to us to fill them with as many meaningful memories as possible."

The kiss was a sigh. A whisper. Zoe's lips parted, ready to ask for more, but Smith was ahead of her. Cupping the back of her neck, he took her mouth with his. Searching. Hungry. Passionate. Zoe gripped his wrist—not to pull him away, but to anchor him to her—wanting more. Hoping it would never end.

"That time in St. Louis? In the hotel's workout room? I told myself it was only a kiss." Smith's lips brushed Zoe's ear, causing shivers to run down her spine. "I would wake up in the middle of the night, your taste on my tongue. Not the memory. Your actual taste. How was it possible? I was sure it had to be my imagination. But it wasn't." Smith kissed her again. Brief, but with toe-curling intensity. "One taste was all it took. I will never forget, Zoe. Never."

"Come with me." Zoe ran her hand down Smith's arm, linking her fingers with his.

"Where are we going?"

"Your room."

"Okay."

Zoe laughed. "Since when did you become a man of few words?"

"When the moment is this important, actions speak louder."

Smith entered the code into the keypad, the elevator doors opened immediately.

"One question," Smith asked as the car began to move. "Why my room?"

"You're on a different floor than I. Or Ryder, Dalton, and Ashe. We probably wouldn't run into them, but..." Zoe shrugged. "This—the two of us— is none of their business."

"I agree. Are you sure you want to do this?"

"I'm sure." Zoe was ready. Without a doubt. "Unless you've changed your mind?"

"No. I haven't." Smith seemed to find the question highly amusing.

The ride was short, but it gave Zoe enough time to decide. One she had wrestled with since she stuck the condoms in her purse. When the elevator doors opened, she walked with Smith to his room, waiting while he slid the card into the slot. The familiar click had the light on near the handle turning green.

Zoe took a deep breath. "I've never done this before."

Chapter Twelve

SMITH SHOWED NO indication he heard what Zoe had said. When they were in the room—the door shut— and away from potential eavesdroppers, he casually dropped the key card on the desk, followed by his phone and wallet. Removing his jacket—which he carefully draped over a chair—Smith planted his feet, arms crossed over his chest.

"You've never done what before?" Smith raised an eyebrow. "Gone to a man's hotel room? Had dinner on the roof of a hotel?"

Zoe felt a wave of annoyance at Smith's attitude. He knew damn well what she meant, but he was going to make her say the words. A request for an explanation was bound to follow. Why couldn't he roll with the situation? For her sake, couldn't he pretend that he slept with twenty-five-year-old virgins all the time?

Zoe knew it was her own fault. She should have kept her mouth shut.

"I've never had sex," Zoe said, mimicking Smith's stance—though she added a touch of belligerence. "Is that a problem? Just say the word, and we can forget any of this happened. Or almost happened."

Smith ran a hand over his face, his head dropping forward. "I don't care how many men you have or haven't slept with, Zoe."

"I didn't have to tell you."

"Why did you?"

For some reason, the more calm and reasonable Smith sounded, the more Zoe felt the muscles in her shoulders tensing up.

"I don't know."

"Yes, you do." Smith skirted Zoe's body—and her dirty look—until he stood behind her. "Relax." He massaged the base of her neck. "You told me because this is the beginning of something and you don't want to start with a lie."

"Not telling you wouldn't be a lie." Zoe sighed. Smith had magic fingers.

"Yes, it would. By omission."

"That's a technicality."

"It's the truth." Smith kissed the curve between her neck and shoulder before tackling the knotted muscles. "I don't know where we're headed, Zoe. But wherever we end up, we need to keep the slate as clean as possible. If you didn't agree, you wouldn't have told me."

"I wasn't thinking about the future." Zoe wanted to have sex with Smith. That was a big enough step. She didn't want to think about anything beyond tonight.

"If you say so." Smith's lips moved from one sensitive area to another while his hands continued their quest to turn her into a limp noodle. A few more minutes and they might succeed. "I want you, Zoe. Is there anything I should know?"

"About sex? Don't tell me *you're* a virgin?"

"No," Smith chuckled. "I've done it once or twice."

Zoe snorted. "No need to downplay your experience. I won't blush or go screaming from the room."

"I like sex. End of discussion."

"Fair enough." Zoe pivoted, wanting to see Smith's face. "I wasn't traumatized if that's what you're worried about. There aren't any demons holding me back. I'm... picky." With her index finger, she traced the dent in his chin. "If you don't object, I pick you."

The flare of pleasure in Smith's green eyes was exactly what Zoe hoped to see.

"What sane, rational man would object to that?" Smith lifted her into his arms.

Zoe laughed. Secretly, she let herself enjoy the ride. "I can walk."

"Your legs are long. Mine are longer." In a few steps, Smith had them in the bedroom, shutting the door with one kick as they passed.

"Wait. I left my purse on the table."

"You won't need it." Smith set Zoe on the bed. Kneeling, he slowly unbuckled her shoe, kissing her ankle.

"I brought a box of condoms."

"How many?"

Fascinated by what Smith was doing, Zoe frowned. "How many what?"

"Condoms in the box?"

"Three."

"Honestly," Smith moved to the other shoe. "I should be insulted. But I will give you a pass—all things considered. Open the end table drawer."

Stretching to her right, Zoe did as Smith asked. Condoms. "Did you think I was a sure thing? Or do you always keep these next to the bed?"

"No, and yes."

It was a reasonable answer to Zoe. Arching her foot, she broke the seal on the box.

"Is that correct?"

"Probably." Smith's attention was on Zoe's legs as he ran his hand along her calf. "You will have to be more specific."

"The size of the condoms. Is that right?"

Smith looked up, his eyes twinkling. "What can I say? I'm a big boy."

Zoe studied the chart. *Big boy* was putting it mildly. If this were correct, the condoms she purchased wouldn't have done either of them any good.

"Might as well use them as water balloons," Zoe muttered.

Smith had moved to the back of her knee. His touch, more of a lingering caress made Zoe gasp. "Now I have your attention. Forget about the condoms. I'll take care of it when the time is right."

"As a mature woman, it is my responsibility to—Oh. My. God." Zoe collapsed onto the bed. Why hadn't she known that spot behind her knee was so sensitive? "What did you do?"

Smith, Zoe's leg resting on his shoulder, licked the area again. "Relax. Enjoy. Let me make you feel good."

If Smith kept that up, enjoying herself would not be a problem. Relaxing was another matter. Maybe she would, maybe she wouldn't. To be safe, Zoe decided to adopt a wait-and-see attitude.

"Lift your hips."

"You're going straight for my panties?" Zoe settled back, her weight resting on her elbows. "Shouldn't we do other stuff first?"

"Other stuff?"

Before Zoe could think of something they could be doing besides this, Smith had her underwear down her legs, tossing them over his shoulder. She liked him at her feet. But with her legs spread, and no panties, it was a bit awkward. At least from her perspective. Smith seemed completely at ease.

"Why don't you join me on the bed?"

"Shy?" Smith grazed the inside of her thigh, his touch as light as a whisper yet it ignited a million nerve endings. "Zoe Hart? Fearless guitar goddess?"

"I don't have my guitar at the moment. Or a bunch of stage lights between us." Zoe felt a vulnerability that had little to do with Smith's proximity.

"One on one. It's harder, isn't it?"

"I've never been very good at it." That was putting it mildly.

"You don't give yourself enough credit, Zoe." The timbre of Smith's voice dropped several octaves. Deep and filled with emotion, it resonated through her. "Let me show you just how good you are. How good we are."

That was where the talking stopped. Smith's mouth was busy doing spectacular things. After just a few kisses, nibbles, and swipes of his very talented tongue, Zoe couldn't remember her name let alone articulate it.

"So sweet. Are you with me, Zoe?"

Zoe's response was a moan. She reached for Smith, her fingers lacing through his hair, letting him know that she liked what he was doing. That she wanted him right where he was, doing exactly what he was doing. Smith seemed to understand. He touched her with increasing urgency. Over and over. Higher and higher. The flush of heat radiated throughout her body. Up. Down. Around. And back again.

Zoe knew the feeling—at least the way it started. An orgasm was not new to her. She had given herself more than she could count. This—what Smith had let loose—was not the same. It wasn't on the same planet or close to the same universe. Wild. Free. Uninhibited. It wasn't a release of tension. Or a mild pop of pleasure. Zoe had no frame of reference because she had no idea anything this intense was possible. She bit her lip, trying to keep her response to herself. Then gave up. Gave in. Gave herself—and her scream—to Smith.

Breathing hard, Zoe wondered how she could feel like a limp rag and strangely energized at the same time. She wasn't ready to run a marathon, but give her a few minutes, and one never knew.

"Thank you." Smith lay beside her, his chest pressing against her back, his arm around her waist, pulling her close.

"Why are you thanking me?"

"That gave me as much pleasure as it gave you."

Zoe laughed. "I find that impossible to believe."

"A different kind of pleasure," Smith conceded. "But it was just as intense."

"Does that mean you don't want me to return the favor?" Zoe slid her hand between their bodies, giving him a gentle squeeze. "I guess that's the end of tonight's entertainment. See you later."

Zoe barely moved an inch before Smith stopped her.

"You aren't going anywhere." Smith tugged on Zoe's arm. He had her flat on the mattress, leaning over her. "We aren't finished. Not by a long shot."

"Good." Zoe wound her arms around Smith's neck. "That was mostly bluff. I don't think my legs have regained enough strength to get me very far."

"Such gorgeous legs." Smith sighed, his green eyes fixed on his hand as it ran up Zoe's thigh. "Long and supple. Your skin is so soft."

To Zoe's amazement, she felt her blood begin to heat. What was this magic Smith possessed? She wasn't used to giving so much power to another person. Zoe preferred to be in control. Smith had his moment—and she had enjoyed every second. This round it was her turn to take control.

"Off with your clothes." Zoe used a maneuver she learned from her personal trainer to flip Smith onto his back. Straddling his hips, she loosened his tie. "Why are you still dressed?"

"I was busy." Smith didn't argue. Nor did he help. Relaxed, he lay back, happy to let Zoe do as she wanted.

"So you were," Zoe said with a happy sigh. She had never undressed anybody. It was more enjoyable than she expected. Of course, with Smith's naked body as her reward, she wasn't surprised. She moved to his shirt, making quick work of the buttons. *Oh, my.* Firm and strong without looking like a steroid-induced freak show, his chest was smooth to Zoe's touch.

"So damn sexy."

"You think so?" Smith's smile widened, his hands clasped behind his head. "Tell me more."

"Lift your arms." Zoe disposed of Smith's shirt. Had she said sexy? His upper body was the stuff of fantasies. And for tonight, all hers. "Instead of words, would you mind if I showed you instead?"

Smith smoothed back Zoe's hair, the heat in his gaze tempered with tenderness. "Be my guest."

Where to start? Zoe felt like a starving woman suddenly confronted with more food than she had ever seen. The options paralyzed her.

"Breathe," Smith whispered, kissing Zoe's palm.

Not realizing she had stopped, Zoe inhaled, filling her oxygen-deprived lungs. The overwhelming feeling of dizziness and panic quickly dissipated. She could do this. She *wanted* to do this. Bending, she kissed him. Tentatively at first, she found her confidence helped by Smith's groan of pleasure.

"You want me?" Zoe asked, biting into Smith's neck.

"God, yes."

Zoe reached back to unzip her dress. "Lose the pants," she commanded, moving off him.

Smith didn't hesitate. Before she could slip her dress over her head, he kicked off his shoes. Pants, underwear, and socks right behind.

"If you posed like this for your next album cover, you could retire a billionaire."

"I'll keep my clothes on—in public—and settle for dying rich. There's a reason the next level is called filthy."

"Because of the nasty things a person has to do to get there?" Zoe tossed her dress away.

Smith swallowed, raking her body with his gaze. "Naked isn't nasty. Not the way you do it. But yes. There are things I would never do. No matter how many zeros on the paycheck."

It was good to know that Smith had his line in the sand. A moral compass. Zoe was curious to find out what it was. Later. Much later.

"Condom." Smith caught the packet in midair. Zoe watched with interest and enjoyment as he rolled it on. Smith was bigger than she had imagined. Though hardly a freak of nature. Thoughtfully, she removed her bra. "What do you think? For the first time? Top or bottom?"

Smith smiled, his gaze riveted to her newly bared breasts. "You're steering this ship, sugar." His Southern drawl had thickened. "What makes you the most comfortable?"

Lying on her back, Zoe beckoned Smith with a crook of her finger. Now that the moment was at hand, she felt surprisingly calm—and playful. "How many virgins have you…?"

"Devirginized?

"I like that better than deflowered. Or popping my cherry. The Neanderthal who thought that one up must have been a real charmer."

"Call it what you want. Or call it nothing at all." Smith gave her a lingering kiss "I've been with one virgin. And she was my first."

"That's sweet."

"It was. Though I can't tell you for certain if she enjoyed herself." Taking her breast in his hand, Smith rubbed the tip with his thumb. Zoe hummed with approval. "All she said was that it was nice."

"It could have been worse. How was it for you?"

"I was sixteen. I didn't have anything to compare it to. Except for my own hand." When Zoe snorted, Smith grinned. "I came away thinking sex was the best thing ever. Nothing has happened since to change my mind. Though the degree of greatness varies—depending on the participants."

"Promise me one thing," Zoe said, drawing Smith between her legs. "If I'm a big disappointment? Don't tell me."

"You could never disappoint me, Zoe." Smith slowly entered her. His eyes darkened to the color of a forest on a moonless night. "Never."

There was no pain. Maybe a pinch. A slight discomfort. But it passed so quickly Zoe didn't give it a second thought. Smith filled her with long, slow strokes, concern in his gaze.

"Tell me if I should stop." Smith gritted the words through his teeth.

Zoe lifted her legs until they gripped his hips. "Stop?" she gasped with pleasure when Smith hit a particularly sensitive spot. Her legs tightened. "Don't. You. Dare."

If she was steering the ship, Smith was the wave carrying her along. It began as a gentle journey, but by the end, she was holding on for dear life and loving every second. Higher. Higher. Just when she thought the peak was in sight, Smith changed the rhythm, pushing her a little more.

"Now," Smith cried out, pushing Zoe over the edge, him right behind. Tumbling. Twisting. Finally, bursting into an all-encompassing light that illuminated everything with perfect clarity.

Gasping for breath, Zoe lay in Smith's arms, wondering what had happened. If that was sex, ninety-nine percent of the world must be doing it wrong. Otherwise, they would be walking around in a constant haze, never getting anything done because all they could think about was doing it again.

"Not a disappointment." Smith's chest rose and fell as if he had just completed the sexiest marathon ever. "As soon as my brain is working properly, I'll elaborate."

"That's okay." Zoe patted his hand. "The goofy smile on your face tells the tale."

"Goofy?" Smith nodded. "That sounds about right."

As the seconds ticked by, Zoe wondered what she was supposed to do. She felt wonderful. Loose limbed. Happily sated. But the thought of staying with Smith felt odd. Sex was one thing. Sleeping with him was another.

"I should go."

"What?" Smith frowned, grabbing Zoe's wrist when she tried to stand. "Stay with me."

Zoe tugged, but Smith wasn't letting go. "I don't like sharing a bed."

"How do you know?"

"I know." Zoe didn't want to elaborate.

"How?"

Smith was determined to have an answer. With a heartfelt sigh, she gave in. "The first foster home I was put in? There weren't enough beds to go around. It was big enough, but the other girl kicked out in her sleep. *And* had a very weak bladder."

"I don't kick." Smith cajoled, leading Zoe into the bathroom. "Nor do I wet the bed. Guaranteed. Shower or tub?"

"I was planning on taking a shower. *After* I got back to my room."

Smith adjusted the water temperature to his satisfaction. "This will save you the trip." Standing to one side, he motioned for Zoe to precede him.

Shaking her head, Zoe stepped into the spacious stall. Big enough for a basketball team's starting five, there was no need to share one showerhead when there were two perfectly good ones. Smith had other ideas.

"It conserves water," he reasoned.

"Share a shower, save the environment?"

Behind Zoe, Smith slid his arm around her waist, the other, slick with soap, covered her breast. "It's a side benefit. Not as good as this one. But every little bit helps."

Zoe lifted her face for Smith's kiss. "I'll stay. Though it's already late."

"We're both early risers." Smith nudged her backside with his erection.

"I suppose we could sleep in late." Zoe turned, her eyes sparkling. "Just this once."

Chapter Thirteen

SMITH HESITATED OUTSIDE the hotel room door. Ryder Hart had called him a few minutes ago, inviting him to stop by for a beer. There was nothing strange about it. Since the tour had begun, they usually found time to hang out in each city. Sometimes Ashe issued the invitation. Sometimes Dalton. Or Smith would invite them. It was casual. A way for them to unwind.

The difference between those times and this one was huge—even if he was the only one who knew it. It was hard to nonchalantly shoot the breeze with a man and drink his beer when he just spent the night having sex with his sister. His first instinct had been to make an excuse not to go. A trace of unexpected guilt had him worried that *not* to show up would look suspicious. It was irrational. Ryder had no reason to think that Smith's relationship with Zoe had gone beyond the mildly antagonistic stage. But crazy or not, he decided to play it safe.

Ryder answered the door a few seconds after Smith's hesitant knock. "Come on in."

"Hey, Smith," Ashe called out from his seat across the room.

"Beer?" Dalton asked.

Smith shook his head. "Water would be great." Smith felt a little drained—less sleep than usual plus a lot of physical activity will do that to a man. He knew that alcohol wouldn't help.

"Feeling under the weather?" Dalton tossed him the drink.

"Nothing major," Smith shrugged, breaking the seal on the bottle.

He noticed several guitars propped against the sofa. Sheet music was strewn across the table and various other instruments—a saxophone, some drumsticks, and a portable keyboard to name a few—littered the area. In other words, it looked like a musician's hotel room. Smith's wasn't that different. Music was their life. Work and play. Somebody was always picking out a song.

"Colleen surprised me last night."

"I don't want to hear about your sex life." Ashe tossed a wadded-up piece of paper at Dalton, smacking him in the temple. "Colleen is like a sister. And you know the rules about that."

Smith almost spit his mouthful of water across the room. Coughing, he wiped the liquid from his chin.

"You okay, man?" Ashe pounded Smith on the back—a little harder than seemed necessary.

"Swallowed wrong." Smith wheezed. He set the bottle on the table.

"I wasn't going to talk about sex," Dalton continued. "Though Colleen bought the most amazing nightie. Lace and satin."

Ashe snapped his fingers in front of his friend's eyes. "Earth to Dalton."

"Sorry. The image in my head was distracting. Where was I?"

"Colleen surprised you?" Taking a seat, a freshly opened beer in his hand, Ryder shook his head.

"Right." Dalton grinned. "Colleen is officially a full partner at *World Restorations.*"

"That's great news, Dalton." Ashe's smile was almost as big as Dalton's.

Colleen McNamara was an expert mechanic, but her specialty was car restoration. Having a place that allowed her to hone and show off her craft had always been her dream. Now, it was a reality.

"Next week when we're back in Los Angeles, we'll have a big celebration." Ryder raised his bottle, clicking it with Dalton's.

Smith and *The Ryder Hart Band* were taking a month-long break after their shows in New York. It gave everybody a chance to rest up and recharge. After that, they would spend the rest of the year in Europe. A week in London would begin the next leg of the tour.

Ryder turned toward Smith. "Any plans during the break?"

"I'll probably visit my family for a week. The rest I'll play by ear."

"Unplanned vacations are the best." Dalton picked up his drumsticks, absently tapping out a random rhythm. "Hey, Ryder. What was it you were saying before Smith arrived?"

"Nothing much," Ryder shrugged. "Alden received an interesting phone call this morning."

"Our manager's phone is practically attached to his ear," Ashe chuckled. "What made this call stand out?"

"It was a reporter from one of those entertainment news programs. And I use the word *news* very lightly."

Smith felt a frisson of unease. Perhaps it was the almost imperceptible change in Ryder's tone. Or the way Ashe and Dalton's attention seemed to have zeroed in on him. It was possible he was paranoid. Smith met Ryder's narrowed gaze. Or not.

"The reporter was asking for confirmation of the rumor that Zoe was involved with another musician."

"Who would that be?" Dalton asked with mock innocence.

"Why, none other than Smith Carson."

Smith felt like a deer in the headlights of three big, protective locomotives. He was surrounded, and they were between him and the hotel room door.

"Alden told the reporter that he had no comment." Ryder leaned forward as though ready to pounce if Smith gave the wrong answer. "I assume it's just an unfounded rumor?"

Smith had no worries that he could hold his own. Ryder was fit as hell, but so was Smith. Any damage would be mutual. However, he wasn't dealing with *one* overprotective brother. If he somehow managed to neutralize Ryder, Ashe, and Dalton would be waiting to happily get in their brotherly licks. Fighting would be counterproductive. Flight wasn't an option. Smith had a choice. Tell a bald-faced lie, or come clean and deal with the consequences.

"Zoe is an adult." Smith knew it was a lame start—and a foolish one. He had basically confessed without saying the words. On top of that, now, these men didn't give a rat's ass about Zoe's age.

"You're messing with my sister?" Ryder's tone was barely above a whisper, his expression blank. It was much more unsettling than crazed and over the top.

"It's none of your business."

Ryder exchanged looks with Dalton and Ashe. Some kind of message passed between the three. They had known each other for so long that words weren't necessary. Smith felt his temper start to rise. He hadn't done anything wrong. The hell if he was going to defend himself.

Smith rose to his feet. "I like Zoe. I'm happy to say that she likes me.

I understand that you feel protective. I have sisters, so I understand. So, I will say this, and then this conversation is over. I would never deliberately, or knowingly, hurt Zoe. If that's not enough for you, we can fight. But remember. I grew up in the country. There wasn't much to do for entertainment except beat the shit out of each other."

"I wouldn't mind knocking out a few of your pretty white teeth." Ryder stayed in his seat. He shrugged. "Unfortunately, Zoe has an independent streak a mile wide. I'm not scared of much, but my sister's wrath tops the short list."

"Then we're good?" Smith was relieved. A fight he could handle. He didn't want to risk losing Zoe as a result. If push came to shove, his chances of her siding with him against her brother were slim to none. Someday that might change. When they were closer, and she trusted him completely. But they weren't there yet. Not by a long shot.

"Treat her right, and we won't have a problem." Standing, Ryder held out his hand. His grip tightened as he leaned closer, his eyes chips of icy blue. "Hurt her? I won't worry about a fair fight. You will feel pain—and you won't see it coming. Understood?"

"That sounds fair." Smith had a similar conversation with his sister Charity's husband the day of their wedding. He understood right where Ryder was coming from.

"You know the same goes for us."

Smith exchanged nods with Ashe and Dalton. It wouldn't do any good to keep assuring them that he would never hurt Zoe. The only thing Smith could do was prove it. In this case, actions truly would speak louder than words.

"YOU'RE GETTING BETTER at that." Laughing, Zoe flopped onto her back.

"You know what they say about practice." Smith lay beside her, his hand automatically reaching for her.

It was a gesture Zoe was getting used to. Smith was naturally affectionate. Little gestures like the brush of his fingers across hers or touching her arm when they spoke. It was an intimacy she wouldn't have tolerated from another man. With Smith, it felt natural.

"You were pretty close to perfect before we started."

"We are learning each other's bodies. That's why the more we have sex, the better it gets."

Zoe couldn't argue with that. In the past four days, she and Smith had sex whenever—and wherever—they could find the time. Her dressing room between his show and hers had been interesting. Thank God she remembered to lock the door. When the stagehand knocked to remind her she was due on stage in five minutes, Zoe had been straddling a naked Smith and seconds away from an orgasm. While she called out breathlessly that she would be there, Smith laughed so hard he almost knocked her off. The only thing that saved her was strong thighs and a determination to get the pleasure that was so close at hand.

"I've learned that you have a spot right here that drives you crazy." Zoe kissed Smith below his ear.

Smith's response was somewhere between a moan and a groan. Pulling up the sheet to protect against the cold of the air conditioner, he tucked Zoe next to him. "Give me a minute. A man—even one in his prime—needs time to recover."

"I thought by the time a man reached twenty, his sexual prime was behind him. You're pushing thirty." Zoe gave an exaggerated sigh. "What am I going to do with you?"

"Come with me on vacation."

It wasn't the response Zoe had expected. She had been teasing. Smith sounded dead serious. Not that she hadn't thought about spending some of her vacation with Smith. She had. A lot. But they had played their last show. Their bags were packed, and in the morning, they were supposed to go their separate ways. Since Smith hadn't said anything, Zoe assumed he already had plans—that didn't include her.

"I'd like that."

Zoe tried to sound casual. Inside, she was a bundle of nerves. Smith wasn't just her first lover. Outside of Ryder, Ashe, and Dalton, he was the first man she had spent any real time getting to know. It was all so new. Figuring out how to handle each situation as it arose was challenging. To say the least.

"Have you ever been to—"

Whatever Smith had been about to say was interrupted by Zoe's phone. Not the usual ring. It sounded like a British police car on steroids.

"What the hell is that?" Smith demanded, almost jumping out of his skin.

"Sorry. I need to take this."

Zoe jumped out of bed, grabbed her phone, and rushed to the bathroom.

"Zoe—"

"Don't worry. I'll be right back."

Zoe leaned against the closed door, her heart racing. She had forgotten the special ringtone she had assigned Riesa Frost. Between Smith and the general madness of playing New York, the private investigator, and the reason Zoe had hired her, had been pushed to the back of her mind. It was after three in the morning. Midnight in Los Angeles. Riesa had instructions to call as soon as she had the information Zoe wanted—no matter the time.

"Hello?"

"Hi, Zoe." Riesa had a distinctively husky voice. "I know you said to call anytime, but I didn't expect the info to come in so late."

"No. I was awake." Zoe reminded herself to breathe. "What do you have?"

"I've found your mother."

"You're sure it's her?"

"One hundred percent. She's in Chicago."

Zoe's mouth went dry. Chicago? The place where it all began. Zoe hated that city. Ryder hated it more.

"How long has she been there?"

"She never left."

"What?" Zoe sank to the floor. "That can't be right."

"I checked, rechecked, and checked again. The information is correct."

All those years when Zoe and Ryder were living in hell, their mother had been in the same city? How was that possible? Leaving them with a monster was horrible enough. She ran. On a good day—when Zoe was feeling charitable—she used to give her mother a little leeway. The woman wanted to get away, and when she ran, it wasn't possible to bring along two small children. But to find out she hadn't run beyond the city limits? That was a revelation Zoe couldn't wrap her mind around.

"Zoe? Are you still there?"

"I'm here." Barely.

"The next step is up to you. I can contact her if you'd like."

"Do you have a phone number?"

"Yes. But I don't suggest that you call her directly, Zoe."

"Text me the number. And thank you, Riesa."

Zoe dropped the phone into her lap. There had always been a bit of doubt in her mind about what she would do if this moment came. Though she wanted answers, Zoe wondered if she would be able to follow through. Contacting her mother could open old wounds—and create new ones.

It was Ryder she worried about most. While Zoe's scars were psychological, his were mental *and* physical. Her suffering didn't begin to compare to her brother's. Deep down, Zoe knew it would have been better for all concerned if she forgot about the past.

With one phone call, that changed. Zoe was no longer worried about finding answers. She was angry. Bone deep and shaking with it. If she didn't confront her mother, she would never have another moment's peace. Excuses were off the table. Zoe wanted to burn the woman down.

"Zoe?" Smith knocked on the door. "Are you all right?"

"I'm fine," Zoe called out.

It was a lie. A big fat one. Zoe couldn't tell Smith the truth. He would try to interfere. Or worse. He would tell Ryder. Maybe when it was over. When the rage boiling in her blood had cooled to merely majorly pissed off.

No, Zoe wasn't fine. But she would be. As soon as she took care of some long overdue unfinished business.

Standing, Zoe checked her image. She had forgotten she was naked. It didn't matter, but it *was* vaguely interesting. Her cheeks were flushed and her eyes unnaturally bright. All things she could explain if necessary. But she didn't feel like talking.

Reaching into the shower stall, Zoe turned on the water, then stepped in.

"I need somebody to wash my back," she called out, raising her face to the spray.

"Will I do?"

Zoe knew Smith wouldn't let her down. Leaning back, she sighed when her back met his solid frame.

"You're exactly who I had in mind."

Chapter Fourteen

THE PLANE SAT on the tarmac fueled and ready for takeoff. There were definite advantages to having part ownership in a private jet. Using it to visit your scumbag of a deserting mother was one of them.

Zoe stepped from the taxi. As she waited for the driver to take her bags from the trunk, she checked her purse one last time. Wallet. Comb. Sugarless gum—cinnamon flavored. No handgun. Zoe hadn't seriously considered taking one with her. She didn't own a gun and didn't want to. But there was a fleeting moment when the thought had crossed her mind. The look of horror she imagined in her mother's eyes made it tempting.

However, this trip was not about causing bodily harm to the woman who gave birth to her then cavalierly walked away. Zoe's initial blood vessel-bursting reaction to discovering her mother's whereabouts had cooled considerably. It was impossible to maintain that level of anger. It was too exhausting.

Shower sex with Smith had helped. Any sex with Smith helped. He had the touch—one she had missed since leaving him in New York.

"We are approximately thirty minutes from takeoff, Ms. Hart." Cary Staul, the pilot that regularly flew the jet, joined Zoe as she walked to the plane.

"Thank you, Cary."

"Any change in your itinerary?"

"No. This is a short trip. We'll be returning to Los Angeles this evening."

Zoe had left her house dressed for comfort. Loose-fitting linen pants and a silk t-shirt in contrasting colors of teal and orange. Strangely, it was a copasetic combination. Her hair was twisted into a messy bun held with a simple antique silver clip. Before landing in Chicago, she would deck herself out to the nines. But during the trip, she wanted to relax as much as possible.

"Good morning, Ms. Hart." A perky young woman dressed with her dark hair pulled into a ponytail and wearing a dark blue blazer and matching skirt greeted Zoe. They didn't employ a full-time flight attendant. Each trip was different. Sometimes they had somebody to serve drinks and meals. Sometimes they didn't. The length of the trip tended to be the deciding factor. But they did have a service on call that kept it cleaned and stocked.

"The bar and refrigerator are filled with your favorites. Drinks and snacks—including fresh fruit and an assortment of sandwiches."

"Great. Thank you."

"And your guest has arrived."

"My guest?"

The woman giggled. Not terribly professional, but Zoe was too busy racking her brain to notice.

"I showed him where to find everything. Have a safe trip."

Zoe paused outside the main cabin's privacy curtain. *Him*? Ryder, Dalton, or Ashe. One of them might be calling himself her guest, but *she* was not a happy hostess. Determined to kick their ass off the plane, Zoe plowed forward.

"I thought we agreed that I would handle this by myself."

"I didn't agree to anything. And it's nice to see you too."

"Smith?"

"Hello, Zoe."

They had said goodbye in New York. Zoe had made up an excuse about needing work waiting for her in Los Angeles. Smith looked skeptical, but he hadn't called her on it. Instead, he gave her a mind-melting kiss and left to visit his family, leaving any discussion of her joining him later in the month up in the air.

"I thought you were in Alabama."

"I was."

It hadn't been a full week, but Zoe had missed him more than she would have thought possible. She had quickly discovered that leaving her lover was different than saying goodbye to a man she merely desired. Her gaze took in every detail of Smith's appearance. He never had gotten that haircut. A little shaggy, the disheveled look worked for him. His jeans were faded, but his white cotton shirt looked new.

When Zoe's eyes met Smith's, it felt as if her heart did a barrel roll. Without another word, she walked into his open arms.

Smith breathed deeply. "You always smell so damn good."

"So do you."

Zoe whispered the words, her lips brushing his. Smith let out a growl.

"Not enough."

Zoe agreed. She wasn't satisfied to let Smith kiss her, insisting on full participation.

"I needed that," she said.

"Me too." Smith kissed her again, his fingers loosening the clip that held her hair in place until it cascaded down her back.

"Now leave."

"Not going to happen." Smith took his seat. "Better buckle up. I hear we'll be taking off in a few minutes."

"I could have you thrown off."

Smith crossed his arms. "You could try."

"Fine." Zoe sat opposite him. "If you feel like a plane flight to Chicago, be my guest. But when we get there, you're on your own."

"Chicago? Is that where we're going. Ryder didn't say."

"Because he didn't know." Zoe's eyes narrowed. "Why are you conspiring with my brother?"

"Hardly a conspiracy. Water? Juice?" Smith had his head in the mini-fridge.

"Hot tea. But I'll get it after takeoff. Why are you here, Smith?"

"I was worried about you."

"You didn't say anything in New York."

"You weren't ready to talk," Smith said. He set his bottle of orange juice on the table before fastening his seatbelt. "I was going to wait until you called me. After a few days, I decided the move would have to be mine."

"So, you went to see Ryder?"

Briefly, Smith told her what had transpired in New York between him and Ryder. Not to mention Ashe and Dalton. Zoe hadn't realized her brother knew about her and Smith. It seemed she was wrong.

"You should have told me sooner."

"It was between us men. And before you blow your top, I know how that sounds." Smith gave a philosophical shrug. "We weren't deciding your life, Zoe. Just coming to an understanding."

"Men," Zoe scoffed.

Zoe wasn't angry. She wasn't even surprised. Ryder had always looked out for her, and though she didn't need him as much as she once did, he would always be her big brother. She wouldn't have it any other way.

The plane taxied to the runway and a few minutes later, they were in the air. Zoe didn't speak or look at Smith as she left her seat, but her mind was working overtime. Methodically, she fixed her tea. Little tasks that she could do in her sleep helped her think.

"What did Ryder tell you?"

"That you had hired a private investigator to find your mother and that you were on your way to meet with her."

The heat from the tea felt good against Zoe's cold hands. She stared at the liquid, a frown forming between her brows.

"From the moment I took my first breath, Ryder has always looked after me. Protected me. Chicago holds such horrible memories. He used to insist on including it on our tour schedule as some kind of test that he was stronger than his past."

"But you skipped Chicago this time."

"Because—for the first time—Ryder truly has left it behind him."

Smith nodded. "Not telling him where you were going was your way of protecting your brother?"

"Ryder wouldn't thank me, but yes, I want to spare him as much of this as possible."

"I know a little about your childhood—the abuse." Smith hesitated. "I want to say the right thing, but…"

"There is no right thing, Smith."

"I want to understand."

"No!" Zoe's tone was sharper than she intended. Slowly, she exhaled. "You can't understand, and that's the way it should be. You had loving, supportive parents. Ryder and I had a monster for a father."

"And your mother?"

Zoe had been filled with so many emotions over the past week—all directed at the woman who gave her life. From anger to sadness to disbelief and every emotion in between. If she were honest with herself, it had been going on a lot longer than a week. For most of Zoe's life, she tamped down the pain, channeling it into her music and an *I don't give a shit* attitude. Well, Zoe *did* care. More than she wanted to admit.

"Are you sure you want to hear this? Once the ugly is out there, you can't push it back in."

Smith moved to the seat next to Zoe. He didn't take her hand. Instead, he held his out, leaving the choice up to her. "Will it help you to talk?"

"Hell if I know." Linking their fingers, Zoe gazed into Smith's deep green eyes. "But if you're willing, so am I. Ready?"

As if sensing the question was directed more at herself than him, Smith squeezed Zoe's hand.

"I don't remember my mother." Zoe scoffed. "Let me rewind. My mother didn't stick around long enough to leave me any memories. She left when I was about three months old. Ryder vaguely recalls her, but it's more shadows than reality."

When she was a little girl, Zoe would ask Ryder why they didn't have a mommy. He would say he didn't know, but they had each other. Zoe wasn't sure when she stopped asking. She just did. Nor was she certain when their father started beating Ryder.

"Ryder always had bruises. Big splotches. He hid them from prying eyes with oversized shirts and his wits. The Monster. That's what we called him when we were alone. To his face, it was always sir."

Zoe knew early not to ask questions. She spoke as little as possible. Invisible. Ryder taught her that. Hide under the bed. Hide period. Ryder drew the attention toward himself. Ten years. That was how long she lived under the same roof with the Monster. In that time, she didn't think he had spoken more than a handful of words to her. Years later, when she was in foster care, Zoe had a revelation. It hadn't been necessary for her to hide. To the Monster, she didn't exist. Ryder wasn't as lucky.

"Nobody knew what was happening to Ryder?" Smith seemed to find the idea incomprehensible. In the world he grew up in, it probably was.

"I don't know." Zoe hadn't thought much about it. "It was a poor, working-class neighborhood. They had their own problems without getting involved in ours." Seeing the anguish on Smith's face, Zoe smiled. She couldn't quite make it reach her eyes. "I guess it's a perfect argument for nature over nurture. That bastard tried his hardest to break Ryder, but he couldn't. My brother is a strong, caring, compassionate person. Always was. Always will be."

"You shouldn't feel guilty, Zoe."

"Ryder was beaten, Smith." Tears clogged Zoe's throat. A drink of tea helped a little. "Not a swat on his butt or even a slap across his face. I'm talking about a grown man wielding a leather belt. Or his fists."

"Son of a bitch."

"Ryder still suffers from the time he took a baseball bat to the knee. How can I not feel guilty?" Smith wiped the tears from Zoe's cheeks—tears she didn't realize were there. "The best day of my childhood was the day my father blew his brains out. How messed up is that?"

"That makes complete sense to me. You were free. You *and* Ryder." Smith brushed his lips across her forehead. "Let me get you some fresh tea."

Zoe didn't want more tea, but she let Smith fuss. It made them both feel a little better.

"I wish that was where the story ended. Ryder and his friends started a band. Three years later, they made room for me. And the rest is history."

Smith set down the cup, taking his seat. "You won."

"We did, didn't we? I like that." Zoe took the manila envelope from the bag. "Naturally, I couldn't be happy with winning. I wanted a clean ending. No loose ends allowed. So, I went looking for our mother. What the hell happened to April Hart?" She tossed the envelope onto Smith's lap. "Ryder was right—as usual. I should have let that sleeping bitch lie."

Zoe got to her feet, leaving Smith with the private investigator's report. The first time she read it, Zoe was certain it couldn't be right. It had taken three times before the truth sank in fully.

"Is this a joke?" Smith asked, a look of disbelief on his face.

"Wouldn't that be nice? Sick," Zoe conceded. "But it would mean that none of it was true."

Smith tossed the envelope aside. "You know what this means?"

Nodding, the expression in Zoe's eyes turned to ice. "My father was an alcoholic bastard who took his anger out on a helpless child. But my mother? *She* was the Monster."

Chapter Fifteen

THE TRAFFIC WAS a mess. It took twice as long to get from the airport to mid-town Chicago as it should have. Zoe had arranged for a car to pick her up, thinking it would be easier than trying to maneuver a rental car through unfamiliar streets. The driver seemed to know what she was doing, zipping from lane to lane whenever she saw a chance at an open space. It made for an interesting ride.

Smith frowned, adjusting his tie for the fifth time. His nerves surprised Zoe. He always came off as the most laidback guy in the room.

"I hate traffic," Smith muttered.

"Name somebody who doesn't."

"All these cars jockeying for position. It isn't natural."

Zoe smiled. "Are you trying to distract me, or does traffic really make you jumpy?"

"A little of both. How am I doing?"

Nothing was going to take Zoe's mind off the meeting with her mother, but she appreciated Smith's efforts.

"Great. Remind me to thank you properly on the flight back to Los Angeles."

"Oh, I will." Smith waggled his eyebrows.

Chuckling, Zoe stared out the tinted windows without really seeing anything. To the uninformed, she and Smith looked like any other upscale couple. She had been surprised to find out that he packed a suit and tie.

"I didn't know where you were taking me," Smith explained as he buttoned his shirt. He had pulled the suit from his bag when he observed Zoe's outfit hanging near the bathroom.

Still dealing with the idea of an unexpected passenger, Zoe had planned to leave Smith to his own devices after they landed. She had a clear vision of how she wanted to approach the meeting with her mother, and he wasn't part of it.

"Your face is too well known for you to casually walk around. Why don't you stay here? I shouldn't be gone more than a few hours."

"*My* face is too well known? How many magazine covers did you grace last month alone?"

"Two." Zoe had agreed because the periodicals didn't push for an in-depth interview. They were happy to let her talk about fashion and the charities she supported. Plus, she had received final approval on the stories.

"*Vogue* and *Rolling Stone*," Smith said. "Those are the big boys. Don't shrug it off."

"I'm not."

The truth was, the Rolling Stone offer had flattered Zoe. But *Vogue*? When she was in high school, the magazine had been her Bible. She had haunted the local library so that she could be the first person to read each month's issue. The idea of her face on the cover wasn't a dream come true. Back then, when she was an invisible high school student just trying to make it from day to day, Zoe hadn't considered it a possibility.

The car braked at a stoplight, two blocks from their destination. Zoe took Smith's hand, glancing at the watch on his wrist. She had a thing about being on time. As a result, she always gave herself a hefty cushion. Even with the traffic, they were twenty minutes early.

"Nervous?" Smith kept hold of her hand.

"Is anxious different than nervous?"

"They probably live in the same vicinity."

"I need to do this, but I wish it was over and done with." Zoe realized she was gripping her purse for dear life. Consciously, she focused on relaxing each finger. "I spent eighteen years in Chicago, but I didn't see this part of the city until we stayed here during the band's first big tour."

"Ms. Hart?" The driver's voice came over the intercom. "It says in my instructions that I'm supposed to pull into the alley behind the hotel. I just want to confirm."

"That's correct."

"Got it. Thank you."

"Meeting in a hotel instead of her home? Is this supposed to be a slap in your face?" Smith asked.

Zoe had wondered the same thing. In the end, she had left it up to Riesa Frost to arrange the meeting. The private investigator had been surprised when April Hart—now April Danvers—had dealt with everything herself instead of going through a lawyer.

"She doesn't want anybody to know about her connection to me." That was Zoe's interpretation. "For over twenty-five years, she's lived a lie. The last thing she wants is for me to come to her home."

"She's afraid that you'll bring it tumbling down around her ears."

Smith summed it up perfectly. Zoe held all the cards. She could have used her muscle to insist on a different venue for their meeting. But she liked the idea of her mother thinking that Zoe was a pushover. When the truth hit, it would be too late to do anything about it.

The car pulled to a stop. Near the back entrance, a man in a conservative dark blue suit waited.

"You can still change your mind," Zoe told Smith.

Smith raised his arm, flexing the muscle. "If your mother asks, I'm your bodyguard."

Smith had the bulk, but his face was too pretty. Zoe had never met a bodyguard who hadn't had his nose broken at least once. He wasn't going to fool anybody. However, now that she was here, she was glad he had insisted on coming along.

"I don't need protection." Zoe met his gaze. "But I could use a friend."

"Then that's what you'll have." Smith touched her cheek. "Always."

Smith's words were exactly what Zoe needed to bolster her confidence. Sitting up straight, Zoe nodded. She could do this. It was past time to put the period on the final chapter of her childhood. Whatever happened, she was determined that this was the end.

"Hello, Ms. Hart." The man in the dark suit held out his hand. "It's nice to see you again. And Mr. Carson. What a nice surprise."

"Thank you, Thomas." Zoe remembered the manager from the last time she stayed at the hotel. "I hope we haven't caused you too much bother."

"Not at all." Thomas held the door for them, taking the lead to the service elevator. "It's my pleasure to be of service. The party that you're meeting has already checked into room seven fifteen. Would you like me to accompany you or shall I leave you here?"

"Thank you, but we'll be fine on our own."

"When you're ready to leave, send me a text. I will make certain your car is waiting to pick you up."

"I was wondering if she would make me wait." Zoe hit the button for the seventh floor.

"Her attempt at a power play?"

"Maybe. You read the file. April Danvers has money and influence."

"Through her husband."

"Initially. But over the years, April had maneuvered herself toward the top of Chicago society. I imagine she's used to getting her own way." Zoe straightened her jacket. "How do I look? Too much?"

After much internal debate, Zoe had chosen a two-piece suit. The skirt and jacket were tailored perfectly to her body. The color of rich cream, it was deceptively simple in design, accented only by a row of brushed gold buttons. It didn't scream money, but it was obvious to anybody with an eye for such things that the suit hadn't come off the rack.

Zoe wore her blond hair pulled back into a severe bun at the base of her neck. She had wanted a look that said cool and composed. Elegant. However, she wanted to be true to herself. Her red leather pumps added four inches to her height, and while they didn't scream rock and roll, they sent a message. Zoe Hart was an individual. Don't mess with her or you might get one of her spiked heels up your ass.

"You're gorgeous. And a little scary. Like a white-clad dominatrix."

"That sounds like a compliment."

"It was," Smith assured her.

Stepping from the elevator, Zoe shot Smith a speculative look. "How many dominatrices have you met?"

"In person? One. And before you ask, the answer is no. I did not partake of her services. A friend introduced us."

"You have some interesting friends."

Smith held out his arm, smiling when Zoe complied by placing her hand above his elbow. "I'll introduce you sometime. Barney and I went to high school together."

"What did he grow up to be? Besides, a man who walks on the kinky side of life?"

"An Alabama Supreme Court Justice."

"Are you serious?"

"As a judge."

"I think the phase is *sober as a judge*, but you get points for the attempt."

Their nonsensical conversation had gotten them to the room at the end of the hall.

"Not the penthouse suite, but this is one of the hotel's better rooms," Smith said. "Maybe dear old Mom wants your reunion to be a special one."

"If that was your attempt at a joke, it's too soon."

"When should I try again?"

"Just this side of never." Zoe gave the door a brisk wrap.

"*Just This Side of Never*," Smith mused. "Good song title."

The man was unbelievable, Zoe thought. Unbelievably wonderful. Smith knew how difficult this was for her. It wasn't possible to completely push away the dark cloud that hovered over her head, but he had lightened it considerably.

The door slowly opened. *Here we go.* Zoe's spine stiffened, and her chin rose a good inch. The woman—her mother—had a similar stance. Dark brown eyes, so like her own, looked back. Cool. Not a flicker of emotion. Zoe knew that look. She had used it often enough. The revelation was not a happy one.

"Won't you come in?" April Danvers asked with a voice as cool as her gaze.

Zoe entered with Smith right behind. The air smelled of expensive perfume. Next to the chintz-covered sofa sat a cart filled with a silver coffee service, a tray of tiny crustless sandwiches, and iced cakes in a variety of pastel colors.

"Have a seat. Would you like a cup of tea?"

If the décor had been different, Zoe would have sworn she was dealing with the Mad Hatter. At least *his* party had some flare.

"My name is Zoe Hart." Zoe remained standing. Smith was a few paces behind. Without saying a thing, he was telling Zoe that he had her back.

"I know who you are, young lady. We are here because that private investigator made it clear that I had no choice in the matter."

Besides the eyes, Zoe could see some other similarities. The cheekbones. The color of their hair—though a good beautician could be responsible for that. However, one thing they did not share was their stature. April Danvers—even in heels—hit Zoe just below her shoulders. Towering over the woman was another reason that Zoe remained on her feet.

"You always have a choice, Mrs. Danvers."

"That's where you're wrong." Gracefully, April Danvers took a seat, legs together, ankles crossed. "I had no choice today or when I left your father."

"He threw you out? Refused to let you come back—even to visit your children?"

"No. He wanted me. In fact, I was his world." April added a drop of cream to her cup of tea. "It became unbearable. I had to account for every second of every day. If I wanted to leave the apartment, he had to go with me. One time when I tried to rebel, he had the audacity to hit me."

"How many times?"

April frowned. "Pardon?"

"How many times did he hit you?"

"Just the once. He apologized, and I pretended that I accepted. But once was enough."

"So as soon as I was born, you left."

"Yes."

"What about Ryder and me?"

"What about you?" April seemed genuinely surprised by the question. "I had no money. No way of taking care of a toddler and a newborn. You were better off with your father."

"Better off with—"

"I had to travel light."

Zoe felt as if she were floating above herself, witnessing the exchange. What other explanation could there be? Either the woman was crazy, or none of this was happening.

"You didn't travel very far. About ten miles by my estimation."

"I was lucky. I met my husband while—"

"I don't care about your amazing rags-to-riches story." Zoe's head began to pound.

"So, we are finally getting to the real reason we're here. Here it is." Taking a piece of paper from the table, April held it out with a look of disdain.

"What is that?" Zoe didn't move.

"A check. It's a lot of money. You would be smart to take it. This is the only offer I am going to make. Naturally, you will need to sign a nondisclosure agreement. "I won't have you coming back every few months asking for more."

"Do you think I'm here to blackmail you?" Zoe looked at Smith. Amazed, he simply shrugged.

"Why else?" April set the check within Zoe's reach. "I understand you've had a bit of success with your music."

138

"A bit," Smith muttered. The sarcasm in his tone was lost on April.

"However, you won't be young and pretty forever. When your looks begin to fade, you'll be glad to have a nice nest egg. My advice it to invest it wisely. Don't blow it on whatever."

Zoe had promised herself to remain calm and classy. She wanted answers to a few questions. Anger and accusations might be momentarily satisfying, but in the long run, there wasn't any point. Ten minutes with April and her smug, condescending attitude, and Zoe was ready to throw a little dirt.

"Is your marriage legal?" Zoe smiled when April's hand jerked, sending a splash of tea into the saucer. "You didn't divorce my father. Which, if I'm not mistaken, would make your son a bastard."

"There is no need for that kind of language." April set aside her cup and saucer. "My husband and I renewed our vows fifteen years ago."

"Shortly after your first husband committed suicide." At her sides, Zoe's hands clenched. "That means you kept track of us. You said that my father slapped you once. What about Ryder?"

April swallowed, her gaze darting around the room before settling on her clasped hands. "I don't know what you mean."

"You evil bitch." Smith ground out the words. Knowing he was as outraged as she was helped Zoe stay relatively calm.

"You knew."

"I—"

April flinched when Zoe stepped forward. "That man beat Ryder. Not slapped, April. Beat. And not just with his hands. Do you have any idea how much damage a baseball bat can do to a child's knee?"

"He promised to stop." April raised her chin defiantly. "And he swore he would never raise a hand to you."

Zoe didn't tell her that he had kept that promise. April probably didn't care one way or the other. But Zoe wanted no part in easing what little conscience the woman might possess.

Without giving April another glance, Zoe turned to Smith.

"I'm finished."

With a nod, Smith walked with Zoe to the door.

"Wait," April called out. "Are you going to tell my husband and son? What about the press?"

The click of heels running after them filled the room.

"Go home, Mrs. Danvers." Smith put himself in front of Zoe.

"Take the check." April tried to shove it at Zoe. "Sign the agreement."

"Shove it up your ass."

April's shocked expression was the last memory Zoe would have of her mother. Their eyes met one last time before Zoe slammed the door.

After that, everything became a blur. Thank God for Smith or Zoe might have ended up wandering the streets of Chicago. He took care of texting the hotel manager and getting her to the car.

"Is she okay?" the driver asked when she caught sight of Zoe.

"She'll be fine." Smith bundled Zoe into the backseat. "Just get us to the airport as quickly as you can."

Smith buckled Zoe's seatbelt then took her into his arms. "I'm tired," she whispered. Between the hotel room and the car, Zoe had lost all her fight.

"Then rest. I've got you. Cry if you want."

"No."

"It might do you good."

"I've shed my last tear over that woman." If Zoe cried, it would be for Ryder, not herself. But not now. She didn't have the energy.

"Your skin is like ice."

Smith adjusted the vents, turning the blast away from Zoe. Closing her eyes, the second her head met his shoulder, every muscle in Zoe's body seemed to dissolve. She knew they were still there—hiding somewhere—but at the moment, she couldn't have raised so much as a finger if she wanted to.

Unlike the ride from the airport, the return trip flew by. It seemed as if they hit every green light and traffic magically moved out of their way. Or perhaps it took hours. Zoe didn't know or care. She felt safe. She knew she could count on Smith to take care of everything.

Zoe trusted Smith. Without reservation. She knew that was an important piece of information, but why? Later, she thought. Right now, her brain wasn't up to worrying about anything beyond how good Smith smelled and how right it felt to be in his arms.

"Stay where you are."

Frowning, Zoe opened her eyes. Before she could wonder where Smith had gone, he was lifting her from the car.

"You're strong," Zoe sighed.

"So are you. The strongest woman I've ever known." Smith brushed his lips across Zoe's temple. "But right now, let me take care of you. Can you do that? Just for a little while?"

Nodding, Zoe shut her eyes. That sounded good. *Just for a little while.*

Chapter Sixteen

"WHERE ARE WE?" Zoe rubbed her eyes, looked out the window, then rubbed her eyes again. "And how did we get here?"

"That big thing they call an airplane took us to Birmingham. The vehicle that I'm driving is called an SUV." Smith patted the dashboard. "A Cadillac is kind of flashy for this neck of the woods, but it was this or an Escort."

"Birmingham?" Zoe came fully awake. "As in Alabama?"

"You know your geography," Smith said. "Of course, Birmingham was almost two hours ago. We just passed through South Ridge."

"How did I sleep through a plane flight *and* a two-hour drive?" Zoe looked at her lap, her head whipping around. "This isn't what I had on in Chicago."

"I thought you would be more comfortable in jeans and a t-shirt."

Zoe was flabbergasted. Smith had managed to get her onto a plane. Change her clothes. Remove her from the same plane and get her into a rental car. Then he drove to South Ridge, Alabama? Zoe didn't know which of those facts she found the most disturbing.

Yes, she did. Alabama? Where Smith's family lived? Hell no.

"Smith." Zoe tried to keep the rising feeling of panic from her voice. "I'm not in any condition to meet the parents.'"

"I called ahead. I didn't give Mom and Dad the details. I simply told them that you were worn out from the tour and needed a few days to rest. They agreed that there isn't a better place than the country."

For some reason, all Zoe could think of to say was, "I'm not wearing a bra."

"Those things are a lot easier to take off than put on."

"What about the one I was already wearing?"

"It was one of those all in one thingamajigs. You know." Smith made a sweeping motion. "A slip *and* a bra?"

Zoe had a faint memory of Smith removing her clothes. It seemed the beginning of a nice dream. For some reason, she couldn't recall the rest of it, but she would have loved to be a fly on the wall when he tried to figure out her bra. It was so absurd Zoe had to laugh. Once she started, she couldn't seem to stop. She didn't like finding herself on this rollercoaster of emotions. It wasn't like her. She wanted the old Zoe back. Keeping her feelings pent up was much less exhausting.

When Zoe had control, she took a deep breath, sending Smith a sheepish look. "This has been quite a day. Are you sorry you came along?"

"Why would you think that?"

"Mother from hell? Then you had to deal with me when I fell apart."

Smith shook his head. From his quick glance, Zoe got the impression he wasn't happy with her assessment.

"How much sleep have you gotten in the last week?"

"Enough," Zoe muttered—if you could call a few hours of fitful tossing and turning sleep.

It didn't take a mind reader to know that Smith didn't believe her.

"You twisted yourself into a knot. You were anxious about meeting your mother, but it was worrying about Ryder that did you in."

"Can you blame me?"

"After hearing what that woman had to say? No." Smith's fingers tightened on the steering wheel. "You were fierce, Zoe. I don't know if it means anything, but I was proud of how you handled the situation."

"It means a lot." Zoe reached for Smith's hand, never doubting he would meet her halfway.

"When you finished with her—for good—your mind and body needed a major rest. You didn't *break* down. You *shut* down. It was self-preservation."

"I don't know what I would have done if you hadn't been there."

"You would have stayed strong and gotten yourself back to the plane,"

Smith said with complete conviction. "I'm glad I was there, so you didn't have to."

So was Zoe. What amazed her was that he hadn't dumped her and run—as far and as fast as possible. Smith knew it all. The ugliest of the ugly. He learned about her father and had witnessed her mother first hand. Yet he was still here. Not just here, but taking her home to his family.

"Are you sure this is a good idea?"

Smith understood without her spelling it out. "My parents can't wait to meet you."

"But—"

"You aren't your mother or your father, Zoe. Because you're still a little wobbly, I won't get angry at you for suggesting otherwise."

"Gee, thanks."

With a wink, Smith kissed the back of Zoe's hand. "You're welcome."

Zoe wasn't completely convinced, but she didn't doubt that Smith meant what he said.

"What time is it?" For the first time, Zoe noticed the position of the sun in the sky.

"Quarter to seven."

"It's been four hours?" Zoe couldn't remember the last time she slept that long for one stretch.

"More like four and a half." Smith hit the turn indicator, slowing the SUV. "You were out so hard, I whipped out a mirror to make certain you were still breathing. Then you started to snore, so I relaxed."

"I don't snore," Zoe said with smug certainty.

"How would you know?"

"Three ways. Ryder, Dalton, and Ashe." Zoe counted her bandmates off on her fingers. "We used to sleep on the bus to save money. If I snored, they wouldn't hesitate to tell me."

"Fine. It was more of a cute snuffle than a full-blown snore." Smith expertly maneuvered the long, winding road. "I was jealous of Dalton and Ashe. Before you let me into your life."

"They're my brothers."

"I know that. Now."

"You believed the gossip." The news didn't bother Zoe as much as it surprised her. "Shame."

Smith smiled, recognizing teasing when he heard it. "I was crushing pretty hard on you, gorgeous. And you barely acknowledged my existence."

"I sent a sneer or two." Zoe's gaze moved from the scenery to Smith's profile. "Do you want the truth?"

"Does a cow love clover?"

"I have no idea. But I'll take that as a yes, farm boy."

"Take it as a hell yes. If at all possible, I always want you to tell me the truth."

Zoe appreciated the qualifier Smith added. Sometimes—for more reasons than she had time to catalog—the truth was out of reach. But she could promise him *if at all possible.*

"You made me nervous."

"Me?" Smith grinned, his green eyes twinkling. "Now isn't that a nice thing to hear. You made me—"

"Horny?"

"That's a given." It was Zoe's turn to grin. "I was going to say that you made me want something I couldn't put a name to. You, Zoe Hart, can be damned frustrating. A real pain in my ass."

"Flatterer."

Smith's eyes left the road for a second, gauging Zoe's expression. Shaking his head, he laughed. "Leave it to you to take that as a compliment."

"Of the highest order." Through the long row of pine trees, Zoe caught sight of a house. "Are we on your family's property?"

"Technically, we have been for the last ten miles."

"What does technically mean?"

"As soon as I had some money, I wanted to share it with my family. Updating the house. A new truck. It was like pulling teeth, but Mom and Dad finally agreed. When I offered to buy some surrounding farmland, they jumped at the idea."

"So, you own all of this?" It was beautiful. There were open fields as far as the eye could see. "It must be a lot of work."

"It is. But not for my parents. They had a plan. I would buy the land from any farmer willing to sell, then lease it back. If there comes a time when a member of the family wants to buy it, half the money that has been paid in rent will count as a down payment."

Zoe was impressed. Smith's parents were good people. And they had raised a good son.

"Has it worked out?"

Smith nodded. "Ten families wanted to sell. That was five years ago.

The farms are thriving, and a few have made overtures about buying their land back."

They rounded the last turn. On a small hill sat Smith's childhood home, illuminated by the early evening sunlight. It wasn't what Zoe had expected. More homey than grand, it looked like the kind of place a regular family lived—not the parents of a rock music superstar.

The wraparound porch was decorated with hanging fuchsias in a riot of purples and pinks. On one end hung a wooden swing flanked by two rocking chairs. The long, built-in bench had cushions designed for comfort, though it was obvious the teal blue color was chosen to match the shutters that framed the windows.

"It's wonderful, Smith."

"Spruced up considerably from when I was a kid. But even when the steps sagged and the paint was faded and peeling, it was always a home."

Zoe knew what Smith meant. It wasn't the house, it was the people inside. The affection and unconditional love. Ryder had given that to her. Though they had nightmare parents, they had each other. Zoe had never taken it for granted, but after today, she knew exactly how lucky she was.

The front door opened. First out loped a long-eared brown dog with big feet and a goofy smile. Right behind ran a curvy woman with short dark hair. Until she spoke, Zoe thought it was one of Smith's sisters.

"There's my baby boy."

"Hello, Mama." Smith picked her up, swinging her in a circle.

Nellie Carson kissed both of Smith's cheeks, hugging him close. "I swear you get more handsome every time I see you." Nellie smiled at Zoe. "He takes after his father. Put me down, Smith, and introduce me to your friend."

Smith kept his arm around his mother's shoulders. "Mama, I would like you to meet Zoe Hart. Zoe, this is my mother, Nellie Carson. And this," Smith knelt by the dog, giving him a scratch behind the ear, "is Almond Rocca. Named after Mom's favorite candy. We just call him Al."

"Welcome."

When Nellie moved in for a hug, Zoe's first instinct was to step back. But Smith's mother didn't give her the chance. Her embrace was filled with so much warmth and affection, Zoe found she didn't mind.

"It's nice to meet you, Mrs. Carson."

"Such lovely manners." Nellie smiled, the twinkle in her blue eyes reminding Zoe of Smith. "But it's Nellie. And this is Smith's father. Ben, come and meet Zoe."

Zoe didn't know if Ben Carson noticed her wariness, or if he was naturally more reticent than his wife, but instead of a hug, he held out his hand. It was big and callused. The hand of a man who had worked the land his entire life.

"Even prettier in person." Smiling, Ben held onto Zoe's hand a second longer. "We're big fans around here. How many times have you played *The Ryder Hart Band's* last album?"

"Whenever I'm working around the house."

With a strong and true voice, Nellie sang a few bars of *Understanding Goodbye*. Zoe was impressed. It wasn't an easy song to navigate. She should know, she wrote it that way as a challenge for Ryder. Even he had nights when he decided it was too much and opted to leave it off the playlist.

"Did you ever think of singing professionally? You have the voice for it."

Nellie waved off Zoe's compliment, but the flush on her cheeks made it obvious she was pleased.

"I don't have the temperament. Or the ambition. I wanted to raise a family and help Ben farm our land. But I don't mind admitting that I've gotten a kick out of watching Smith's success."

"What's wrong with us?" Ben said, shaking his head. "You came here for a rest, and we're keeping you standing around."

"Ben's right. Come with me. Dinner will be ready in a few minutes. You can have something to drink while I finish. Smith, you and your father bring in the luggage."

"I'm fine. Honestly." Zoe looked to Smith for help, but he simply grinned.

"Don't argue with Nellie. She looks like a strong wind would blow her over, but she rules this place with an iron fist."

"He's right," Nellie said as she and Zoe walked up the front steps. "I grew up in a big family where I was the only girl. I learned early on to stand up for myself, or I would have been buried under all that testosterone. Sit here at the counter and keep me company."

Zoe breathed in the smell of fresh baked bread. Her mouth watered, reminding her that she hadn't eaten anything since yesterday. Her stomach wasn't in the mood that morning. Or that afternoon.

"Would you mind if I made a phone call?"

"Not at all." Smiling, Nellie tied an apron around her waist. "There's a lovely view from the back porch and plenty of privacy. Take a glass of lemonade with you."

It wasn't a suggestion. Thanking Nellie, Zoe made her way through the sliding doors, glass in hand. She took a sip. Perfection. Just the right amount of tart and sweet. Nellie knew her stuff. About lemonade and views. From the back porch, Zoe could see a small pond backed up by a tree-covered hill. It was like something out of an issue of *Better Homes and Gardens.* Even the sun was doing its part, producing shadows and light that danced across the stone-paved path and the cheery flowers that ran its length.

Taking a seat, Zoe checked her phone. *Oh, boy.* There were more missed calls and texts than she could count. No point in wading through them all. She knew who they were from. Not sure what she would say, Zoe hit the first name on her contact list.

"Where the hell have you been?"

"Hello to you too, brother dear."

"Do you know how worried I've been? How worried we've all been?" Zoe could picture Ryder pacing the room. "If Smith hadn't called, I don't know what I would have done."

"Smith called you?" Why hadn't he mentioned it to her? "What did he say?"

"Just that you were fine and not to worry. It wasn't a terribly satisfactory conversation," Ryder said. "He also mentioned that he was taking you to Alabama."

"That's where we are. Out in farm country."

"Are you okay?"

Even before she met with their mother, Zoe had debated with herself how much to tell Ryder. She wouldn't lie. But unless he asked something specific, she had decided the less he found out, the better. He lived with too many bad memories. She wasn't going add to them.

"I'm fine." Now that the initial shock and anger had worn off. "It was pretty much what I expected."

"I don't care about the details, Zoe. Just answer one question. Did you get what you needed?"

Zoe didn't answer right away. She gave herself a moment. When she started the search for their mother, it was for closure—or that was what she told herself. For so long, she had been angry with a phantom. An idea more than a person. Zoe realized she had been looking for a face to accompany her hate. Closing her eyes, she tried to conjure up the face of April Danvers. It had been a few short hours, but already it was fading. Along with it, Zoe's anger.

Breathing in the clean, country air, Zoe smiled.

"It's over, Ryder. I'm sorry that I dredged it up. It wasn't fair to you."

"Fuck that, little sister."

Zoe laughed. Ryder wasn't averse to swearing, but he seldom directed it toward her. When he did, she knew his emotions bubbled close to the surface.

"We aren't the same people, Zoe. Finding our mother was important to you. Never apologize for that."

"Well, she won't be joining us for Thanksgiving dinner."

"Holy shit." Ryder exploded, causing Zoe to hold the phone away from her ear. "Was that ever a possibility?"

"God, no," she rushed to assure him. "That was my attempt at a joke. Pretty lame, wasn't it?"

"Lame? My heart almost stopped." Ryder let out a heavy sigh. "That kind of humor should be reserved for when I've had a few drinks."

"Or never?"

"There you go."

"I don't know how long I'll be in Alabama. If it's more than a day or two, I'll let you know."

"Take your time. Quinn and I are going up to the mountain cabin. Dalton and Ashe are planning some kind of getaway with their ladies."

"You were waiting to hear from me." Zoe loved her family. And they loved her. "I'm lucky to have you, Ryder. All of you."

"Never forget it goes both ways."

"I won't. Take care. I love you. And Ryder?"

"What is it, kid?"

"Give Quinn my love."

There was a pause. Under his breath, Ryder muttered, "Well, I'll be damned."

"You shouldn't be surprised. You love her, how could I not?"

"I have the best sister in the world."

"Yes, you do."

Ryder laughed. "Have a good time. I love you, kid."

Feeling better than she had in days, Zoe set the phone aside.

"Was that Ryder?" Smith walked from the house.

"Yes. Thank you for calling him. I forgot until now."

Taking a seat, Smith stretched out his long legs, crossing them at the ankles.

"Your brother was not a happy camper. Especially when I was skimpy on the details."

"Ryder appreciated hearing from you."

"Really?" Smith didn't sound convinced. His voice morphed into a pretty good imitation of Ryder. "*Where's my sister? What the hell is going on? If you let anything happen to her, I will track you down like the dirty dog you are.*"

"I'm pretty certain that Ryder has never used the term *dirty dog* in his entire life."

"I may have embellished—slightly," Smith admitted, his smile matching Zoe's. "There was some mention of messing up my pretty face, but because I understood Ryder's concern for you, I chose to ignore it."

"That's big of you." Zoe lifted her face, enjoying the gentle breeze. It smelled of roses and… "What is that scent? It's wonderful."

"Jasmine." Smith shot her a sideways look. "I thought you didn't like flowers."

"I don't like men who pay for outrageously expensive arrangements of flowers with the idea it will impress me into bed."

"So, it's the men—not the flowers—that pisses you off."

"It's never taken much to piss me off," Zoe laughed. "Though recently—"

"Yes?"

"I don't have the energy. Maybe I'm getting old."

Zoe could have said that she felt more at ease with herself and the world in general. If she removed the past week from the equation, her outlook had mellowed considerably. She wasn't ready to examine the reason. Though she suspected a big part of it had to do with the man sitting next to her.

"If you're old, what does that make me?"

"Ancient?"

"Hey!" Smith frowned with mock outrage. "I still have enough gas in the tank for you, gorgeous.

"You'll have to wait until later to prove it," Ben Carson called out from the doorway. "Your mother says to stop hogging Zoe and bring her in for dinner."

"That wasn't the least bit embarrassing." Zoe took Smith's hand, letting him help her to her feet.

"*That* was Dad's idea of a joke. If he didn't like you, he would have politely invited you in to eat. Nothing more."

"How can he like me? We just met."

"Dad prides himself on his ability to quickly take the measure of a person. And," Smith shrugged. "I may have mentioned you a few times." Just before they entered the house, Smith gave Zoe a sizzling kiss. "Maybe more than a few."

"Is that something you do on a regular basis?" Zoe kept hold of Smith's arm until her equilibrium returned. Something about his kisses temporarily threw her balance out of whack.

"What? Talk to my father about you?"

"Me. Or any of your many, many lady friends."

Smith tipped Zoe's chin until her gaze met his, his green eyes caressing her face. "You're the first. The first I've spoken about. The first I've brought to meet them. Interpret that however you wish."

"I—" It wasn't often that Zoe found herself at a loss for words. If nothing else, she could fall back on some variation of *screw you*. Not this time. Her mind was a blank.

"Relax. Close your mouth." He tapped her bottom lip. "It's time to eat, and my mother hates it if we let her food get cold."

Zoe didn't have time to reflect on Smith's words. The moment they stepped into the house, she was too busy enjoying herself. The unrestrained laughter and familial affection gave a glow to the Carson home. It had little to do with gleaming hardwood floors or the comfortable-looking overstuffed furniture. As with anything truly special, it was the people who made it that way.

"Sit down, everybody," Nellie said as she carried a blue-and-white tureen from the kitchen. Before she had taken two steps into the dining room, Smith had plucked the covered bowl from her hands. "Thank you, sweetheart. It's nothing fancy, but it will stick to your ribs."

"Nothing fancy, she says." Smith lifted the lid. Breathing deeply, his eyes closing with pleasure. "Chowder?"

"My little patch has produced more corn this year than I can remember. I hope you like it, Zoe. When Smith called to let us know you were coming, I was so excited that I went on a baking frenzy."

"All of this is homemade?" Zoe took a roll from the heaping basket to her left. "Until recently, I had never met anybody who cooked for themselves."

"Would you like to know the secret of a good cook?" Ladle in hand,

Nellie filled a bowl. "Passion. I love to chop and dice and knead and mix. For my birthday a few years ago, Smith bought me lessons. In Paris! Can you imagine?"

"Two weeks in our own little apartment." Ben exchanged smiles with his wife. "Nellie spent the day in the kitchen, and I toured some local farms. We spent the nights together. If you know what I mean."

"Benjamin Carson!" Color bloomed on Nellie's cheeks. "He means we went to a lot of amazing restaurants. And walked for hours."

"The food was good. But not as good as yours."

If Zoe's mouth hadn't been full of creamy, corny goodness, she would have agreed with Ben. She had eaten at some of the best restaurants in the world. If anything had tasted better than Nellie's chowder, Zoe couldn't think what it was. And the bread. Warm and soft, it melted in her mouth.

"Do you mind if I ask you a question?" The meal served, Nellie took her seat. "You won't hurt my feelings if you say no."

"You can ask," Zoe said cautiously.

"But she might not answer."

"I didn't say that." Under the table, Zoe kicked Smith. She wished he had put her in something with more heft than a pair of electric-blue high tops. Or that he wasn't wearing a pair of leather boots.

"It's what you meant."

Zoe's eyes narrowed, warning Smith that she would make him pay. "What Smith means is that when my brother and his friends formed *The Ryder Hart Band,* they agreed to let their music do the talking. When I joined, it was already an unwritten rule. Our personal lives are nobody's business. However, that applies to the media. Not you, Nellie."

"If you're sure." When Zoe nodded, Nellie's eyes lit with interest. "What is it like to be the only woman in a rock band?"

"A pain in the butt."

Nellie and Ben burst out laughing. That broke the ice. Zoe went on to recount several stories about her early days on the road.

"On a good day, we had enough money for a hotel room. One room."

"That must have been awkward." Ben was so focused on Zoe he buttered his thumb instead of his bread.

"It was at first. But mostly for Ashe and Dalton. In those days, they were two of the biggest lady's men on the planet. But around me, they were jumpy as all get out. They were scared to death of walking in on me naked, so most of the time, they would sleep on the bus. As my brother,

Ryder appreciated their attitude. But that didn't stop him from teasing them unmercifully."

"I think it was sweet," Nellie said.

"I agree—in retrospect. At the time, it was annoying. I desperately wanted to fit in. Joining the band was a dream come true. All I wanted was to be one of the guys."

"Oh, darlin'," Ben patted her hand. "That was never going to happen."

"You're right." Zoe could smile about it now. "Luckily, we found our way. Our mutual love of music helped. And long hours traveling in cramped quarters from crappy gig to crappy gig. An experience like that either tears a band apart or makes them solid as a rock."

"You became a family."

"That's right," Zoe nodded, pleased that Nellie understood. "I hate to roll out the well-worn trope, but it fits. Us against the world. Nobody handed us success. Talent helps. So does luck. Sometimes I think we made it because we wanted it so much. I'm sure Smith has shared a few stories of his own on that subject."

"To hear Smith tell it, the music business is all rainbows and lollypops." Nellie patted her son's hand. "I know better. However, as a mother, I appreciate that he didn't want me to worry."

"You were going to worry no matter what I said."

"That's what mothers do."

Zoe waited, expecting a shot of pain in the region of her gut. When it didn't come, she met Smith's worried gaze. She shook her head, mouthing the words, *I'm fine.* And she was. If this were the final test, Zoe had passed with flying colors. The big bad witch was well and truly dead.

"I hope you saved room for dessert." Unaware of what had passed between Zoe and Smith, Nellie pushed her chair back from the table. "It's chocolate cake."

"Sounds great."

"A sliver is not considered a serving in the Carson household," Nellie warned Zoe. "We serve cake by the slab."

"Is that your mother's way of saying I need fattening up?" Zoe whispered when Ben and Nellie had taken the dishes away.

Smith kissed Zoe's temple. "It's her way of saying that she considers you family."

"Oh." Zoe blinked in surprise. "Okay."

Chapter Seventeen

ZOE SNUGGLED UNDER the soft cotton sheets that smelled as fresh as a summer rain. The curtain fluttered, the open window allowing a cool breeze to swirl about the room.

Back in Los Angeles, Zoe slept on the best mattress known to man—at least that's how it was hyped. She didn't have any complaints. Not a great sleeper to start with, when it was quickly delivered and efficiently set up, she hadn't expected miracles. In her experience, a mattress was a mattress. However, after five minutes on the Carsons' guest room bed, Zoe knew with certainty that she had wasted her money. The expression was out like a light. Until now, she hadn't understood the true meaning of that phrase.

Peeking over the patchwork quilt, Zoe noticed the slightest sliver of light on the eastern horizon. For an early riser or a farmer—in this example, she supposed they were the same thing—this room was perfect. The large window was located directly across from the bed, making it impossible to miss the break of dawn. On a normal day, Zoe would have rolled out of bed, wide awake, and pulling on her workout clothes.

Not this morning. Zoe was too relaxed. Her mind and body felt too loose to want to do anything but stay where she was—at least for a few more minutes.

There was a lot to be said for the peace and quiet of non-city life. Just as the thought crossed Zoe's mind, a rooster decided to do his job, announcing dawn's arrival with a full-out cock-a-doodle-doo. The sound didn't shatter the mood. Just the opposite. She would have been disappointed if it hadn't happened. Zoe had zero personal knowledge of a working farm. But in her mind, a rooster was supposed to be part of the experience.

"Psst." Smith slipped through the bedroom door, his long legs making short work of the distance to the bed

"Are you trying to get my attention or are you suffering from a medical condition that makes you sound like a punctured tire?" Zoe smiled as Smith lay next to her on the bed. "If it's the latter, we need to get you immediate medical attention."

"I have a medical condition, all right."

Staying outside the covers, Smith spooned Zoe. Even through a sheet and quilted cover, she had no problem feeling his *condition*. The bulge hit her smack below the curve of her butt. She sighed with pleasure when his lips found the back of her neck. It wasn't the worst way to begin her day.

"You're a guy. Isn't that pretty common in the morning?"

"Yes. But it's exacerbated by the fact that you refused to let me share your bed. I tossed and turned most of the night."

"Really? I slept like a baby."

"If I'd had my way, you would have slept like a satisfied, multi-or-gasmic woman."

"Now that's just mean," Zoe moaned, her body responding to Smith's words—as well as his obvious need for her.

"You're sorry. I'm sorry. There was no need for either of us to suffer. My parents wouldn't have minded if I slept in here."

"Really?" Zoe wasn't convinced. "Even knowing that neither of us would have done much sleeping."

"Let's not go there. I refuse to think about what my parents do behind closed doors, and I'm pretty sure they return the favor." Smith gave a small shudder before pulling Zoe closer. "If you had agreed to let me sneak in here, nobody would have been the wiser."

Zoe had been tempted. Especially when Smith couched the suggestion with a round of bone-melting kisses. He had no idea how close she came to caving in.

"Nellie and Ben graciously invited me into their home. I'm not going behind their backs just to appease your baser instincts."

"Me? Base?" Smith nuzzled Zoe's ear, his hand slipping beneath the covers to cover her breast. "I don't know what you're talking about."

"This is a bad idea."

"Best idea ever. But not here." With one last kiss to her bare shoulder, Smith left the bed. "Meet me downstairs in five minutes. My brothers are taking care of the chores this morning, so Mom and Dad are still in bed for a change."

"Do you think they're sleeping? Or…"

"Hey. Do not put that image in my head. Ever." Smith lightly swatted Zoe on the butt. "Five minutes, lazy bones."

"Ten. I haven't been to the bathroom. And I need to make the bed."

"The bed will wait until we get back."

Zoe never left a messy bed. Even in a hotel, she straightened the covers. It was a habit she acquired as a little girl and had never attempted to break. She didn't think her need for a neat and tidy bedroom was odd. It simply was. End of discussion.

Sliding from under the covers, Zoe shook her head. Fast and efficient, before Smith could blink, she had the bed looking neat as a pin. Smith stared, his eyes filled with admiration. Though whether it was for her bed-making skills or that she was naked, Zoe couldn't say. However, when he reached for her, admiration turning to hunger, she had her answer.

"Watch it." Zoe swatted away Smith's hands. "This is a no groping zone."

"Then put something on, woman. I'm only human."

Grabbing Smith, Zoe gave him a kiss that left them both wanting more.

"Five minutes." Slightly breathless, Zoe pushed a reluctant Smith from the room.

"Don't keep me waiting."

Leaning against the closed door, Zoe took a moment to let herself enjoy what could only be described as happiness. She knew the feeling, but it rarely happened when she didn't have a guitar in her hands. Until Smith.

Whatever this thing was between them. Wherever it led. Zoe knew one thing for certain. Smith had given her a gift. Not just sex—though she couldn't discount how much that meant. He gave her laughter. Friendship. One more person in her small precious circle that she could believe in and count on.

No matter what, they were gifts that Zoe would always treasure and never forget.

SMITH DIDN'T WATCH the sunrise. He had seen it from this vantage point hundreds of times. Instead, his eyes were on Zoe. It was as if that morning, the light was just for her. The blond hair that flowed freely down her back glowed, but not as brightly as her eyes. Zoe seemed transfixed as she sat beneath the old cedar tree. If humans were made in God's image, then Smith had no doubt that God was a gorgeous blonde with legs that went on forever and skin the color of rich cream.

Smith's guitar goddess had turned golden.

Zoe sat with her knees pulled up to her chest, her arms wrapped around her legs, providing the perfect resting place for her chin. Turning her head ever so slightly, she sent him a smile. Beautiful. Joyful. And utterly breathtaking.

There were few true revelations in life. It wasn't about sudden flashes of insight. Smith knew that feelings and ideas tended to sneak up on him. Instead of blooming overnight, it often took months—sometimes years—before it happened.

Zoe was the perfect example.

When they first met, she was a pretty teenager with a chip on her shoulder. In the same business, they weaved in and out of each other's lives. Their relationship—if they could call it that—was strictly professional. Until a year ago, he didn't think they had exchanged more than half a dozen words—Zoe usually growling her end of the brief conversation.

Smith couldn't pinpoint the moment he noticed that Zoe had grown from a girl to a woman. It was gradual. One second, she was somebody's kid sister; the next, she was all grown up. Somewhere along the way, she had left pretty behind, skipped beautiful, and hit full-on gorgeous. All the while, she maintained the screw-you attitude. Smith had to admit, her sharp tongue had been a major part of her appeal.

Wanting Zoe had seemed simple enough. But from the start, it was more than simple desire.

Making music was a dream come true. Making a living at it was the dream with a big, fat cherry on top. His professional life was exciting. Hectic. Often stressful. That was why he did his best to avoid drama when the lights went down. He had dropped more than one woman for the simple reason that they created more trouble than they were worth.

Then there was Zoe. On paper, everything about her should have had him running for the hills. No looking back. Not that she was high maintenance. Just the opposite. Zoe was the most independent, self-sufficient woman he had ever known. It never occurred to her to ask for help because she was certain she could handle any situation on her own. And she could. Zoe hadn't needed him to accompany her to Chicago. Luckily, Smith was the kind of man who had no compunction over inserting himself where

Zoe didn't think she wanted him. If he had sat back and waited, they wouldn't be lovers. And she wouldn't be sitting with him, watching the sunrise on a hill in Alabama.

"You're officially forgiven for making me leave my warm bed." Zoe raised her face to the light. "Is this your favorite spot?"

"Yes. I'm glad I could share it with you."

"Thank you." Zoe's dark brown eyes met his. "For this. For everything."

Smith could have sworn his heart stopped for just a second then started to race, pounding wildly in his chest. He knew what love looked like. What his parents shared was a healthy, beaming example. They made it seem so easy. Two people with the same interests, working toward the same goals. A simple life filled with work, family, and a healthy dose of play. That was how he thought it would be for him. True, his life was slightly more complicated, but he saw no reason why falling in love shouldn't be smooth. Like gliding on glass. No bumps allowed.

Leave it to Smith to fall for Zoe Hart. The only thing smooth about her was her skin. And bumps? It was like maneuvering a dirt road after a hard winter. The potholes weren't just deep. They were cavernous. If he lost focus for one second, every hard-fought inch of progress he had made with Zoe would be lost.

As Smith gazed at Zoe's profile, he mentally stepped back. The situation wasn't simple, but the question was. If given a chance, would he do things differently? Loving Zoe would never be easy. But who the hell cared? She was a vibrant, passionate woman with a surprisingly wicked sense of humor. The sharp edges were part of her charm.

The question was simple, and so was the answer. Smith loved Zoe. He wouldn't change a thing. Not about the past or her. She was perfect. Perfect for him.

That settled, Smith was left with one problem. And it was a big one. He knew how he felt. He was in love. All in. All the way. He was almost positive Zoe felt the same about him. Almost being the operative word.

All Smith had to do was convince Zoe. There was no harm in keeping it to himself a little longer. If he blurted it out, she might pull away. Love was a scary word. Nobody knew that better than he did. He wasn't going to take the chance on blurting out his feelings until he was certain that if she ran, it was straight into his arms.

Slowly—how appropriate—Smith ran his hand up Zoe's arm, his fingers playing with the flutter of lace that covered her shoulder. White and looking like it weighed less than a feather in flight, the dress hung loosely on Zoe's slender frame, the material flowing gracefully around her legs when she walked. With her blond hair, it made her look like an angel. The image was more sweet than sexy until Smith caught a hint of the devil in her dark eyes.

"Nice dress."

Zoe fanned out the full skirt, giving Smith a flash of her bare feet and their red-tipped nails.

"Since I didn't think we would be helping your brothers with the chores, I took a chance. Is it too much for a day on the farm?"

"For slopping hogs?" Zoe laughed. Just as Smith meant her to. His hand touched her leg just above the knee "For kissing me as the sun rises? It couldn't be better."

Together, they fell onto the blanket that Smith had laid out after they arrived. Rolling to his back, he took Zoe with him until a curtain of her lemon-scented hair hung around them. Nobody was around to see them besides a few disinterested cows and the birds that sailed gracefully over their heads.

"Was this your plan all along?" Zoe asked as she tugged Smith's shirt over his head.

Smith took a foil square from his pocket. "I wasn't a Boy Scout, but…"

"Always prepared?"

Shifting positions, Smith smoothed back Zoe's hair, his green eyes locking with hers. *Always.* The word had more meaning than she realized. Zoe was in his head. She owned his soul. He kissed her once with sweetness. Twice with a growing intensity. He was going down for the third time. Drowning and happy with it. Brushing his lips against Zoe's ear, Smith whispered what was in his heart.

"Always."

THERE WERE FOUR vehicles parked by the house that hadn't been there when Smith and Zoe left. It was still early by city standards. But on the Carson farm, there was no such thing. Smith could almost smell bacon sizzling in a cast-iron skillet while his mother cranked out an endless supply of fluffy pancakes. From the looks of things, his siblings had dropped by for a big breakfast. They would have a warm greeting for him, but it was Zoe they were here to see.

"*Cowboys Do It with Their Spurs On?*" Zoe read the bumper sticker on the back of the black Ford pickup truck. "I may not know the difference between a pig and a hog, but I know a cowboy works on a ranch. Who does that belong to?"

"A hog is simply a pig that weighs more than a hundred and twenty pounds. Just for future reference."

Zoe laughed as Smith helped her from the SUV. Choosing not to put her shoes back on, she had the straps of her sandals looped over one finger. "That's more information than I wanted. And the cowboy?"

"Margot's fiancé. Craig did the rodeo circuit until last year. My sister loves him, so we tolerate him."

Near the Ford sat another truck, a mini-van and a beat-up hatchback that had seen better days. Smith planned to buy Petula a new car when she finished graduate school next spring. His way of telling her how proud he was of the future teacher. However, from the looks of the twenty-year-old Civic, he wasn't going to wait. Her birthday was coming up in about a month. As soon as he was back in Los Angeles, he would make the arrangements.

"Come on," Smith took Zoe's hand. "Are you ready to meet the rest of my family?"

"All of them?" Zoe looked a little leery at the prospect.

"As a group, the Carsons are only slightly less intimidating than a rampaging hoard of Mongol warriors." When Zoe stopped in her tracks just outside the house, Smith laughed. "I was joking."

"I need to change my clothes." Zoe raised a hand to her head. "And comb my hair."

Touching her cheek, Smith marveled at the glow of her skin. He liked to think he had something to do with the rosy glow.

"You look fine. Better than fine."

"Give me a minute? Please?"

Smith took Zoe into his arms. She was nervous. His badass woman was jumpy at the thought of a room full of Carsons. Who would have guessed? Teasingly, he whispered, "You were supposed to be gone for less than a day. Why did you bring four suitcases?"

"Because you never know when a big old farm boy is going to kidnap you. *And* because I can." Zoe tapped his chest, the smile he had been looking for curved her lips. With a quick kiss, she hurried into the house and up to her room.

Chuckling, Smith watched Zoe's long legs eat up the stairs three at a time.

"Was that streak of white the famous Zoe Hart?"

"The one and only." Smith greeted his oldest sister with a warm hug. "She wanted to freshen up before taking on the Carson kids."

"This mass get-together at the homestead wasn't planned," Charity informed him, holding him close. "A little FYI in case you thought we were ganging up on your girlfriend."

"It hadn't occurred to me until you mentioned it. I assumed you were here to bum a free meal off our parents."

"*That* is always a possibility."

Laughing, the siblings walked to the kitchen. Smith kept his arm around Charity's shoulders. She was the spitting image of their mother with the same kind heart and cheerful disposition. It couldn't have been easy as the oldest of six. Charity had the most responsibilities simply because she had been here the longest. That said, Smith couldn't remember his sister rebelling against her role. Not that she was a saint—heaven forbid. Charity had a bit of the imp in her. She seemed to know when to hold her siblings in check and when to let them loose—usually with her leading the charge. In Smith's opinion, Charity was the best oldest sister ever.

"Would you listen to that?" Charity asked as they drew near the kitchen, shaking her head, not with dismay but affection.

It was loud. Shouting. Laughter. Good-natured arguing. In other words, a typical Carson family get-together. All Smith could think was that it felt good to be home. Los Angeles was his base of operations. He was comfortable there. More than comfortable. He had a house in Colorado. An apartment in London. But no matter how long he was away or how many years passed, this would always be the place he felt safe and loved.

"Smith!"

When his brother Ethan shouted his name, the group turned almost as one, erupting into a chorus of shouted hellos. It was a sea of familiar faces all smiling, all happy he was there. Going home again was never a problem for Smith. In his heart, he had never left.

ZOE SAT ON the bed looking at her open suitcases. It wasn't like her to leave them unpacked, but it had been a crazy twenty-four hours. One day. It was hard to believe that yesterday at this time she was in Los Angeles. She hadn't boarded the plane. Hadn't been surprised by Smith. And she hadn't met with her mother.

It felt like a dream. Rationally, Zoe knew it had happened. April Danvers had been real—disturbingly so. She had a couple of new mental wounds to prove it. However, they weren't as deep as she initially thought. The bleeding had been minimal and was already healing nicely. Zoe doubted there would be much scarring—if any.

After years of wondering why her mother had abandoned her children, Zoe had the answer. The woman had walked away without a backward glance. There was no regret. No guilt. April had latched onto a big fat fish who had elevated her to a life of comfort and privilege. Zoe could have demanded every minute detail. Zoe wasn't a reporter looking for the who, what, where, or when. She found out the only thing that mattered. The why. April Danvers was a self-serving, egocentric, cold-hearted bitch with about as much motherly instinct as an alley cat.

It wasn't pretty. Zoe hadn't expected it to be. The story hadn't been tied up with a pretty bow. She could live with that. The important thing was that it was over. Well and truly finished.

Zoe pulled herself back to the task at hand. What to wear to meet Smith's brothers and sisters. Yesterday, there hadn't been time to worry about what she looked like. Smith had plopped her down in Alabama without warning. Her head had been fuzzy from sleep and mama drama. Nellie and Ben had been so warm—so welcoming—that there wasn't time to think about her messy hair, wrinkled clothes, or smudged makeup.

Running a comb through her hair, Zoe mentally went through her clothing options. She hadn't packed with farm life in mind. Designer outfits. High-heeled leather boots. Jackets that were more for show than practicality. That left her with jeans—always a good bet—and an assortment of shirts.

Just get dressed. Grabbing what she needed, Zoe laughed at herself as she shimmied into her jeans. She had taken less time deciding want to wear when she met the Queen of England. It had been an honor, but she hadn't been out to impress Elizabeth II. Smith's family was another matter.

As she approached the bottom of the stairs, Zoe could hear the conversation and laughter spilling throughout the house from the kitchen and dining room. Somebody had put on some music. *Bluegrass*? She recognized the style immediately. A truly American art form. Musically, there wasn't anything Zoe didn't like. If she could play along, she was a fan.

"I was about to come and get you." Smith walked toward her, a cup in each hand. "I wouldn't have blamed you for running."

Zoe gratefully accepted the coffee, sipping the steaming liquid. Black as ink. Smith remembered.

"I never run from anything."

There was a glint in Smith's green eyes that matched his smile. "Tough as nails. With a sweet, soft center."

"Shh," Zoe warned. "I have a reputation to uphold. Sweet and soft are not part of the Zoe Hart brand."

"I don't care what you show the rest of the world." Smith kissed her lightly. "I know the truth."

"Do you now?"

"Without a doubt. But don't worry. Your secret is safe with me."

"I'm pretty much all out of secrets." It was hard to believe but true. "Consider me an open book."

"You don't look very happy about it."

"More bemused than unhappy."

"That seems fair," Smith said after some consideration. "What do you say? Are you ready to meet the rest of the family?"

Zoe fell in step with Smith. However, when a burst of laughter hit her ears, she couldn't resist one last question. "How many people are in there?"

"Counting spouses, a cowboy, and grandkids?" Smith did a quick calculation in his head. "Nineteen."

"What?" Not exactly a mob, but more than Zoe had anticipated.

When Zoe would have stopped, Smith put a hand in the middle of her back, helping to propel her forward. "Think of it this way. You meet them all at once instead of in dibs and dabs. Like pulling off a Band-Aid."

"Slow or fast, there is always pain involved."

"Not in this case," Smith promised.

Zoe nodded. Smith was probably right. But just in case, she plastered her best fake smile on her lips. What was the saying? Hope for the best, prepare for the worst. Taking a bracing sip of coffee, Zoe pulled back her shoulders. She wasn't certain, but she would have sworn she heard Smith chuckle.

"Ready?" Smith asked, his lips twitching suspiciously.

"Ready." Zoe would kick his ass—later.

Chapter Eighteen

ZOE HAD PLAYED three-hour shows in sweltering heat that hadn't exhausted her as much as meeting Smith's family. Breakfast had run into lunch which was threatening to trickle into dinner. Needing a moment alone, Zoe snuck off the patio, destination unknown. Just a little peace and quiet.

Not that there was anything wrong with the Carson family. Just the opposite. They were a big, boisterous, warmly welcoming bunch. And good looking. One look around and Zoe discovered that Nellie and Ben had produced an enviable array of good-looking individuals. From Charity to the twins, Ethan and Timothy—if they hadn't been wearing different-colored shirts she never would have figured out which was which. Margot's boyfriend fit right in. With their equally bright smiles, the couple looked like they had stepped out of a milk commercial. Finally, there was Petula. Except for the blue eyes, there was no doubt that she was Smith's sister.

Zoe wedged her way through a hedge, finding herself face to face with the side of a barn. Blue, not red. A city girl through and through, the closest she had been to one of these buildings was at a Tuscan villa. The one in Italy had been converted into a wine tasting room with leather bar stools and a million dollars' worth of art hanging on the walls. In other words, there was no comparison.

It didn't take much muscle to push open the tall wooden door. Not even a peep from the well-oiled hinges. The inside of the barn smelled like… Fresh hay and…

"It's Eau de cow manure."

With a gasp, Zoe spun around to find Ben Carson rubbing the muzzle of a contented-looking horse.

"I didn't realize anybody was in here."

"Surprised?" Smith's father chuckled. "Occasionally, even the architect of that brood needs a breather from them."

"They are very… vocal."

"Well put. Any experience as a diplomat? No?" Ben picked up a brush, offering it to Zoe. "Go on. Tammy Sue loves when you give her attention. It's relaxing for the horse and the human."

"Maybe not." Zoe liked the idea of large animals better than the reality. "Tammy Sue looks pretty Zen without any help from me."

Ben wouldn't take no for an answer. She now knew where Smith inherited the trait. Tentatively, Zoe ran the bristles over Tammy Sue's coat. Despite Ben's reassuring words, she was prepared for a full-out horse revolt.

"See? Nothing to it."

Zoe had to admit it wasn't the worst thing she had ever tried. She found a rhythm and it was kind of relaxing. However, Zoe was not one to push her luck. She never bet more than a hundred bucks at the blackjack table and five minutes was her limit grooming an animal that, if she made up her mind, could stomp Zoe to a pulp.

"Thank you." Zoe directed her words to Ben as well as Tammy Sue. "If I had a bucket list, brushing a horse would officially be crossed off."

"No bucket list? Does that mean you've done everything you want to do with your life?"

"I've done a lot." More than she had once thought possible. "But everything? No."

Ben walked with her out of the barn. His hair was thick and dark, but in the sunlight, Zoe could see a few strands of silver creeping in. If Zoe hadn't known better, she wouldn't guess that he was the father of six or that he was halfway into his fifties. Ben had a spring in his step that men decades younger would envy.

"When I was a boy, I dreamed of seeing the world. I even flirted with the idea of joining the Navy." Shutting the barn door, Ben checked to make certain the latch was secure.

"What about the farm? Smith told me it has been in your family for generations."

"The Navy was a momentary pipe dream. And I'm glad. It's hard to imagine a life without my Nellie. From the day we met, she was all that mattered."

"No regrets?" Zoe asked.

"I have the woman I love. A healthy family. And all of this." Ben stood on the porch, looking at his land with pride. "And thanks to a very generous son, I've seen some of the world. Can you keep a secret?"

Smiling at the conspiratorial tone of Ben's voice, Zoe nodded. "My lips are sealed."

"I enjoyed Paris. Mainly because Nellie was having a blast. But I was glad to get home. I guess when it comes down to it, I like the idea of traveling better than actually doing it. How about you?"

"Do I like to travel?" When Ben motioned for her to sit, Zoe settled in one of the rocking chairs. "Yes. I guess I do. When I first joined the band, we were dirt poor and traveled in a tiny bus that was always breaking down in the middle of nowhere. But even then, I loved it. Ryder, Dalton, and Ashe would complain about the crappy accommodations and crappier gigs."

"And you?"

"I was with my friends playing my guitar. And somebody paid me to do it. Not much, but it was never about the money."

"A few bucks in the bank doesn't hurt."

"True," Zoe laughed. "Believe me, I wouldn't want to go back. It was fun when I was eighteen. You wouldn't believe the musicians I met. Some were on the way up, some on the way down. And some were stuck in the middle. All of them taught me more than I could have ever learned in a fancy music academy."

"You worked hard." Ben knew what that was like. "You still do."

"With a lot more perks. You might say that luxury has become my welcome companion."

"Nice turn of phrase."

The compliment pleased Zoe. "It's kind of what I do."

"Kind of?" Ben threw his head back, his unrestrained laughter catching the attention of several barnyard animals.

"I missed the joke."

Wiping his eyes, Ben sighed. "I wasn't laughing at you."

"Okay." Because she liked him—and he was Smith's father—Zoe was willing to give him the benefit of the doubt.

"Honestly. I've heard the songs you've written. They touch me. In here." Ben placed a hand over his heart. "When you said '*it's kind of what I do,*' the words struck me as a huge understatement. It would be like saying you '*kind of*' play the guitar."

Understanding, Zoe grinned. "I would never say that. The guitar is… Hell, why beat around the bush? I kill the guitar."

"No argument here," Ben nodded. "And I come from a family of musicians."

"Really? Tell me about them." Zoe sat forward. She loved this kind of story.

"Just a second. Do you drink beer?"

"I would prefer some of Nellie's lemonade."

Ben disappeared into the house, returning with an open bottle and a filled glass. He handed Zoe hers before taking his seat on the padded swing. Thoughtfully, he took a sip of his drink.

"I was lucky enough to know my great-grandfather. He lived to be a hundred years old. Long enough to hold his first great-great-great-grandbaby in his arms." When Zoe let out a low whistle, Ben shrugged, a grin on his lips. "We Carsons start reproducing young."

It wasn't the ages that impressed Zoe as much as the rooted family tree. In her world, there was Ryder. Period. She had never met one grandparent, let alone a whole string of them. It must have been nice, she thought. Ben knew where he came from. Then again, for most of Zoe's life, she had known exactly where she was going. Or at least where she wanted to end up. There was something to be said for that.

"Did your great-great grandfather play an instrument?"

"He did. Smith learned to play on that very guitar." Ben rocked his feet back and forth, the swing moving with him. "On Saturday night—without fail—my folks would turn on the radio. *The Grand Ole Opry.* The family would gather. Listening to every word—every song. After, we would spend the rest of the evening playing and singing."

"You play?"

"I sing," Ben corrected. "Enthusiastically. That's my way of saying that my voice leaves much to be desired. However, Smith comes by his talent honestly. His grandmother has the voice of an angel. She and my father are cruising the Greek Islands, or they would be here. I think the two of you would hit it off."

More family. Ben's mother was probably a lovely woman, but she had enough Carsons on her hands without anymore. Silently, she said a thank you for Greek Island cruises.

"Your son grew up on country music?" Hard-rocking Smith Carson? "Were you surprised that he didn't end up in Nashville?"

"Blame his mama for that one. Nellie loves all music, but her first love is rock and roll. The classic stuff. She turned me on to groups you're way too young to know about."

"You think so?" It sounded like a challenge to Zoe. "Try me."

"*The Scorpions?*"

"That one is too easy. *Rock You Like a Hurricane.*"

"*Thin Lizzy.*"

"Obviously, *The Boys are Back in Town.* But I prefer *The Rocker.* Or for the musicianship alone, *Emerald.*"

Ben kept throwing out names, Zoe kept catching them. Eventually, he held up his hands in surrender.

"I'm playing a losing game, aren't I?"

"I know my music." Zoe wasn't bragging. She was an expert on the subject because it was what she loved. "Ask me about anything else, I'll fall flat on my face."

"I doubt that. You're a smart young woman, Zoe. Well spoken. Polite. If I were your father, I would be very proud."

It was like a sucker punch to her gut. Not painful as much as unexpected. As if Ben's innocently delivered words had knocked the wind out of her. *If Ben had been her father.* It was a tempting thought. A happy childhood. A scar-free psyche. Who wouldn't want those things? But changing the past—as wonderful as that would be—would completely screw up the present. Ryder wouldn't be her brother. She would never have met Dalton or Ashe. *The Ryder Hart Band* might exist, but Zoe wouldn't be a part of it. Rewriting the first part of her life would mean the best part would disappear.

"Are you okay?" A concerned frown on his face, Ben covered Zoe's hand with his. "The color drained from your face."

Zoe wasn't surprised, but she didn't want to burden Ben with a pile of her *what ifs.*

"It's probably the light," Zoe assured him, clearing her throat with a gulp of lemonade. "I have a naturally pale complexion."

"This wasn't the light."

"Okay. You got me. If you were my father, Smith would be my brother. No offense, but I prefer things the way they are."

Zoe hadn't pulled the words out of thin air. It was the truth. Smith was another big reason she wouldn't change the past. If she had been given a different path, Smith wouldn't be on it. Or if he were, he would be there in a different role. *Her brother?* Zoe barely contained a shudder. *Hell, no.*

"Smith would agree." Ben seemed happy with Zoe's explanation. There was a moment's hesitation before his next words. "I've never worried too much about Smith. He's always had a good head on his shoulders. It helped that he was my son, not my daughter. And before you give me hell, I know that's sexist."

"You called that one right." Despite her tone, Zoe was willing to give Ben a pass. She knew what he meant. As a woman, she didn't like it. But as a sister with a protective brother, she understood.

"I do have a point. This is my roundabout way of getting there." With his thumbnail, Ben scraped at the label on his beer. "Smith wouldn't want me to say this, but what is he going to do?"

Run screaming in the opposite direction? That would be Zoe's choice. She wasn't accustomed to fatherly wisdom. The whole thing made her nervous.

"Relax," Ben smiled as if he could read her mind. "All I want to say is thank you for making my son happy."

"Smith didn't need me. He's always been that way."

"True."

"I didn't have anything to do with—"

"Yes, you did."

Zoe searched for an argument but didn't have one. "I suppose he makes me happy too."

"Now, was that so hard?" Ben teased, the twinkle in his green eyes reminding Zoe of Smith. "Happy isn't always easy, Zoe. However, if you have it? Don't take it for granted because all the money and fame in the world isn't a substitute."

A little body ran from the house, her dark pigtails bouncing with her every step. Spying Ben, her face lit with joy, her legs scurrying to cover the distance across the porch.

"Grandpa!"

Laughing, Ben easily caught the miniature missile in his arms.

"Careful, Sara. One of these days Grandpa might miss."

"Never." The girl snuggled close for a second, her face wreathed in a big smile. Just as quickly, she was on her feet tugging at Ben's hand. "Grandma needs you in the garden."

Ben let Sara pull him to his feet. "We can't make Grandma wait, can we?" On his way, he turned to Zoe. "Enjoy the quiet for a little while longer. Around here, it never lasts for long."

It seemed for as long as Zoe could remember, she had either been running *from* one thing or running *toward* another. Her life was filled with work, work, and more work. When she did take the time to play, she played hard. Skiing, biking, deep-sea diving. Her mind and body were stuck on one speed—fast. And she liked it that way.

Things were different with Smith. Zoe wasn't worried about rushing to the next thing. The activity in her brain didn't exactly slow down. More like it mellowed. Instead of jumping three steps ahead, she was focused on the here and now. The only other time that happened was when Zoe was on stage.

Gently, Zoe rocked back and forth. When Ryder met Quinn, he said that she helped put things into perspective. Was that what Smith had done for her? Had he given her a different view of how her life could be if she were willing to open her heart?

Holy crap. *Open her heart*? Where had that thought come from? Was she falling in love with Smith? Or had she already fallen? And how the hell was she supposed to know? Witnessing Ryder, Dalton, and Ashe as they found love hadn't given Zoe any clue on how to recognize the emotion.

Zoe knew one thing. The idea of love didn't frighten her. However, because she hadn't thought that it would ever happen to her, she wasn't prepared. On top of that, she had no idea how it worked. Was she supposed to keep her feelings to herself or blurt them out in a rush of verbal diarrhea? Wasn't that a lovely image?

The smart thing would be to wait until Smith said it first. That was assuming he felt the same. What *if* he told Zoe he loved her? Would that be the catalyst she needed? Would she magically know that, yes, she was without a doubt in love? And why in God's name was she asking herself so many questions?

So much for her brain slowing down.

"Dad said I could find you out here."

Zoe looked up. *Smith*. His green eyes and warm smile set her heart racing. At the same time, a sense of calm washed over her. Fast and slow wrapped into one big, sexy package.

"I needed some air. Your father was kind enough to keep me company. And teach me how to brush a horse."

With a smile, Smith took the rocker next to hers, matching her rhythm. He didn't speak, and Zoe felt no need to fill the silence. Having him next to her felt good—right.

Reaching out, Zoe placed her hand over Smith's where it rested on the arm of the chair. He made a slight adjustment until their palms met, his fingers threading through hers.

"It looks like everybody is staying for dinner."

Zoe wasn't surprised. "That's a lot of mouths to feed. I hope your mother doesn't run out of food."

"No chance of that happening. She keeps a supply of casseroles and desserts in the freezer for occasions just like this. Mom loves having her family around. But these days, one meal is her limit."

"I thought the do-it-yourself sandwich bar was genius."

"After all the years of feeding this brood, Mom has dozens of time—and labor—saving tricks. Plus, she refuses to clean up after us. Ethan and Tim are currently on dishwashing duty." Smith squeezed her hand. "I was thinking about you."

"That's always nice to hear." Better than nice. Zoe had Smith on the brain; it was only fair that she had wormed her way into his. "Any particular reason?"

"I brought you here to rest. If you aren't used to it, a big family can make that difficult. They're a good bunch." Zoe shrugged.

"A bit overwhelming, but nothing I can't handle—with an occasional break."

"Good to know. I have a present for you."

"Really?" Zoe felt a burst of pleased anticipation. She wasn't immune to the lure of a good gift—unless there were strings attached. She wasn't worried about that with Smith.

"I've been working on it for a while."

"Well?" Zoe asked impatiently.

"Later." Smith laughed when he saw Zoe's frown. "After everybody leaves. It's something I want to share only with you."

"We're alone now."

There was a warm intensity in Smith's eyes that left Zoe breathless. His gaze never leaving hers, he kissed the back of her hand. "Later."

A present. Not a declaration of love, Zoe thought. That was a relief. She might not know a lot about it, but she knew one thing. Love wasn't a room filled with flowers or shiny, expensive gifts. Two words came to mind. To Zoe, they said it all.

Honest and heartfelt. Zoe relaxed. Lifting her glass, she took a sip of lemonade, a smile forming on her lips. Who knew? Maybe she had this love thing figured out after all.

Chapter Nineteen

EET ME IN *the barn*.

Left on her pillow, it wasn't the longest letter Zoe had received from Smith, but there was something to be said about short, sweet, and to the point. She folded the paper, slipping it into her suitcase for safekeeping.

Realizing what she had done, Zoe laughed. When had she become such a romantic sap? A few written words—without as much as a signature—and she saved it like a silly schoolgirl. Or a rabid fan. Since she was neither, Zoe chalked it up to habit. The letters he sent her were in a drawer in Los Angeles. Sappy or not, she would put this note with them. Nobody had to know.

Carefully, Zoe opened the bedroom door, checking the hallway. Blissful silence greeted her ears. Smith's siblings and their families had cleared out about an hour ago with a not-so-gentle push from Mama Carson. Between the hugs, kisses, and clinging grandchildren, the exodus had taken almost an hour.

Zoe had to give the group credit. After a day of food, laughter, and games, they left the house the way they found it. Dishes done. Floors swept. Cushions straight on every piece of furniture. In other words, they left it the way Nellie liked her home. Neat as a pin. Zoe thought it said a lot about their respect and love for the woman who raised them.

Soon after the last taillight disappeared from view, Ben and Nellie retired for the evening. Zoe had looked around for Smith, but he was nowhere to be found. Deciding he knew where to find her, she took a quick shower. Smith's note was waiting on her pillow when she returned to her room.

In deference to the night air, Zoe wore a light sweater over a loose-fitting, ankle-length dress. Her hair hung in a loose braid down her back, the tennis shoes that she had slipped into making no sound as she tiptoed down the stairs.

Sneaking around—even when it wasn't necessary—felt oddly exciting. It was certainly a new experience.

Zoe had toed the line when she was in foster care. She was always home well before curfew and wouldn't have considered leaving without permission after the lights were out and everybody was in bed. There were times when she desperately longed to play the teenage rebel, but Zoe didn't want to take any chances. The home she lived in was better than most. And close enough for Ryder to visit. If she caused trouble, that might have changed.

Until Zoe turned eighteen and no longer under the care of the state, she never put a foot out of place. After that—when she had joined the band—she spent the first year under the eagle eye of her brother. Ryder gradually eased up, but by then, Zoe was either too busy, too tired, or not interested. It turned out that the idea of being a wild child sounded more fun than the reality.

As Zoe approached the barn, she could see a sliver of light under the door. Before she could push, it opened, Smith standing on the other side.

"You found my note."

"I did." Smith twirled Zoe into his arms. She laughed, grasping his shoulders for balance.

"Not my most eloquent work."

"No." Zoe didn't mention that she found his words worthy enough to save.

Slowly, Smith backed Zoe away from the door, shutting it with a firm push. "I've wanted to do this for hours."

"Dance me around an empty barn?" Zoe looked at the deserted stall. "Where's Tammy Sue?"

"Enjoying the night air. I'll let her back in when we leave." Smith kissed the corner of Zoe's mouth. "And no, as much as I enjoy having you in my arms, I want a kiss, not a dance."

Happy to oblige, Zoe sighed when Smith's lips covered hers. She found that there were so many kinds of kisses. This one started sweet, heating quickly until she clung to Smith.

"What about my present?" Zoe moaned. Smith lowered her onto a blanket-covered pile of fresh-smelling hay.

His hand sliding up her leg, Smith whispered, "Who said this isn't it?"

It wasn't what Zoe had expected. She had pictured a box wrapped in pretty paper. But she had no objection to unwrapping Smith instead. His package was worth the effort.

"I need you, Zoe."

"Then take me."

Zoe tossed her arms over her head. It was the closest thing to surrender as she would ever come. Only for Smith. Nobody else could make her lose control. He touched her as if she were all he could ever want. Special. That was how Zoe felt as she soared upward, her eyes wide open. She watched the path of Smith's hands. The way he kissed her breasts. Tasted her skin. The look of pleasure on his face was so beautiful she felt like weeping.

When their bodies were joined, Zoe gripped Smith's waist, urging him on. Higher. Higher. Together. Smith was in the driver's seat, but Zoe was with him every step of the way. Her limbs held him close. And when they peaked, their cries of release melded into one.

"Don't you dare move," Zoe warned. Her arms felt like rubber, but she wasn't letting Smith go.

"I couldn't if I wanted to. I'm worn out." Somehow, Smith found the energy to shift his weight off Zoe, tucking her close to his side.

"Cold?"

"Nope. I'm perfect."

"Mmm." Smith's lips touched the top of her head. "You certainly are."

"I've never had sex in a barn."

"Obviously."

"Hey." Zoe bit Smith's chest—just enough to show she meant business. "Smug is not a good look for you, buster."

"According to *G.Q.*, I look good in everything."

"Seriously? You're quoting a magazine puff piece?"

"Just saying," Smith chuckled. Showing impressive speed, he grabbed Zoe's hand before she administered a pinch to his butt. Keeping hold, he placed her hand on his chest. "Did you want to know how many times I've done it in a barn?"

"No!" Zoe paused. "Maybe. Okay, yes. But if it was in *this* barn, leave that part out."

"Not this barn or any other. There was one time in a gazebo. But that's not the same thing."

"Yet you felt the need to throw it out there." Hiding her smile, Zoe shook her head.

"I apologize. It slipped out." Smith reached behind Zoe, coming back with her dress. "Ready for your present?"

"Another one?" Sitting up, Zoe pulled the dress over her head. "What did I do to deserve such an embarrassment of riches?"

"The first gift was as much for me as you." Smith slipped on his jeans. Leaving them unbuttoned, he stood. "Now that I think about it, the second gift is also for both of us."

"You're going to sing for me?" Zoe asked when Smith returned with his guitar. This would be a first. Excited, she sat up straight, crossing her legs.

Smith nodded. "I've been tinkering with this song for a while. I think it's finally ready for its debut."

As she did with any song the first time she heard it, Zoe closed her eyes. All it took was the first three chords. A shiver ran down her spine. It didn't happen often, but when it did, she knew when she heard something special. The music gave her a chill. However, it was Smith's voice that pulled her into a different world. Deep and slightly smoky, his words weaved a spell. It was obviously meant to be sung as a duet, but he expertly navigated both parts. A man's desire. A woman's need.

It wasn't a gentle song to be hummed in the shower or played at a high school prom. The song took the listener on a hard-driving journey that never let up. Her eyes shut, Zoe felt the beat pulsing in her veins. Hot to the point of boiling. Like sex, it built to a bursting crescendo leaving her limp. Unlike sex, when the music ended, she felt unsettled instead of satisfied.

Raising her eyelids, Zoe looked at Smith, her breath catching in her throat. His eyes blazed emerald, his chest heaving as if he had run for miles. There was an air of expectancy surrounding him as he waited for Zoe's reaction.

"It's wonderful." Zoe knew the word was weak, but she had taken the same emotional journey as Smith. She was trying hard to find her bearings.

"It started out as something different. Less…"

"Devastating?"

"You felt it too? Thank God." With a deep breath, Smith set aside the guitar. "I thought it would be more of a conventional love song. This is what came out instead. Knowing you? Knowing *us*? I shouldn't have been surprised."

A love song? Zoe's head fell forward. Well, she wanted honest and heartfelt. She hadn't expected it to be couched in a song that nearly ripped her guts out. Maybe the best song she had ever heard. Knowing that she was the inspiration was humbling. And freaking amazing.

"I want to say thank you, but it doesn't seem like enough."

"It's a duet."

Zoe felt a chill. In an instant, her blood went from hot to cold. She knew what Smith wanted. With a sharp shake of her head, she stopped him before he could ask.

"No."

"That's it? I write you a song—a song for us to sing together—and all you can say is no?"

"No, thank you." Zoe wanted to look away, but she held her gaze steady. "I don't sing lead. You knew that."

"Why?"

"It's not my thing." Needing something to do with her hands, Zoe used her fingers to comb out her hair. "There are at least a dozen artists who would jump at the chance to sing with you."

"You really want me to sing *your* song with somebody else?" Smith asked.

It was the last thing Zoe wanted. The thought of it made her sick to her stomach. The words refused to come out, so she raised her chin and nodded.

"Bullshit." Smith shoved his arms into the sleeves of his shirt with more force than necessary. "I can't make you sing the fucking song. But don't compound your stupidity with a bald-faced lie."

"Stupidity?" Zoe jumped to her feet. Anger felt so much better than despair. "Fuck you, Smith."

"Looks like that's all I'm good for."

"That's not fair. I didn't ask you to write that song." Zoe stuffed her feet into her shoes. "You didn't get your way so now you're angry? Boo hoo."

"I'm not crying. I'm flat-out pissed."

"Join the club."

Zoe banged her way out of the barn, marching across the yard. Smith was a few steps behind.

"This conversation isn't over, Zoe."

"What's left to say?" Remembering Smith's parents, Zoe held back from slamming the door. "The conversation is over. And so are we."

"What?" Smith barked.

"Quiet." Zoe rounded on him. "You'll wake Nellie and Ben."

Steam practically came from Smith's ears, but he heeded Zoe's warning, lowering his voice. "You can't break up with me over a song."

"We're musicians. I can't think of a better reason."

"Is this because of Ryder?"

"What?" Zoe's feet faulted briefly halfway up the stairs, her shoulders stiff. The reasons were her own and none of Smith's business. She refused to let him bring her brother into the argument. Especially when he had hit too close to home. "Don't be ridiculous."

Smith hurried after her like a bloodhound who had found the scent of his prey.

"Do you honestly think Ryder would want your misplaced guilt to keep you from singing?" Smith put out his arm blocking Zoe from entering her bedroom. "Unless he's behind it?"

The first wave of Zoe's heat was rapidly passing. She didn't have the energy to tug at Smith's arm—not that it would have done her any good. His muscles were like bands of steel. She didn't have the physical strength to fight him and her brain power waned fast.

"Please move."

Smith wasn't ready to let the subject drop. "Why didn't I think of this before? Ryder. He's the face of the group. It's *The Ryder Hart Band*. A man with that kind of ego wouldn't want to share the singing spotlight."

"You have no idea what you're talking about." Zoe crossed her arms, her feet planted firmly. "Ryder isn't like that."

"No? Seems like I've solved the mystery. Big brother is jealous that little sister's voice would blast him off the stage."

Zoe almost fell for it. *Almost.* The glint in Smith's eyes alerted her to his game. He was using Ryder to provoke her into spilling her guts. If he had caught her before the heat in her blood had cooled, she might have given him what he wanted. Instead, Zoe's temper was heading toward frigid. When that happened, she stopped talking. Stopped fighting. Stopped. Period.

"Get out of my way, Smith."

Smith wasn't a fool. He could read the situation. With a sigh, he dropped his arm. "Goddamn it, Zoe. Don't do this."

"I didn't do anything. You did," Zoe said, her voice controlled and neutral.

Without a look, she walked through the door, shutting it with a quiet click. It wasn't an act. Ice had entered her bloodstream, and headed straight to her heart.

Zoe was tired. Not like after she had met her mother. That had been the culmination of a week of worry and stress. An ending to a story that began shortly after she was born. With a weary sigh, Zoe dropped onto the bed. Kicking off her shoes, she took the pillow, hugging it close.

It was easier to be honest with herself when Smith wasn't nearby. The truth? Zoe wasn't angry with him. *She* had ruined everything by overreacting. The problem was, she didn't know what else to do. Not now. Maybe not ever.

Touching her lips, Zoe traced the outline of her bottom lip, wondering if she had kissed Smith for the last time. Was it over? It was obvious that he didn't want it to be. All Zoe had to do was go to him and… What? Give him an explanation she didn't have? How could she make Smith understand something she didn't really understand herself?

Rolling to her back, Zoe looked around the room. Just that morning it had seemed like a wonderfully comfortable sanctuary. A place where she could rest. Heal. Now all she wanted was to get away. As quickly as possible.

Zoe grabbed her phone. It didn't take long to find what she was looking for. After a few taps on the keypad, she waited.

"Hello? Yes. I need a car and a driver." Zoe wasn't familiar with the area. Besides, she felt in no condition to drive herself. "It's the Carson farm just outside of South Ridge, Alabama. I don't have an address. Not a problem? Good. How soon can somebody get here?"

Three hours. Not exactly a fast escape, Zoe thought. The bright spot was that everybody would still be in bed when the car arrived. Opening the dresser drawer, Zoe removed her clothes. Anticipating a longer stay, she had emptied her suitcases earlier that day. If she had only known, she could have saved herself the trouble. As she moved to the closet, her own words mocked her.

I never run from anything.

"This isn't running," Zoe said to the empty room. "It's strategically regrouping. There's a big difference."

The difference was minor. Zoe preferred her way of looking at it. That way she could pretend—for a little while—that she wasn't lying to herself.

Packing didn't take long. After years of spending so much time on the road, she had a foolproof method. Her suitcases were filled and sitting by the door in no time. *Now, what?* Zoe paced. But that gave her too much time to think. For an instant, she considered leaving on foot, quickly quashing the idea for several reasons. It would be foolish to go off in the dark down a strange road. She might miss the hired car, or it might drive right past. Then there were clothes. She wasn't leaving them, and there were too many to lug with her. Zoe was stuck until her ride arrived.

Too keyed up to stay in her room, Zoe slipped into her jacket and shoes. A few at a time, she quietly moved her luggage down the stairs to the porch.

It took three trips—holding her breath the entire time for worry somebody would hear her. Finally, Zoe closed the front door. She stood at the top of the steps, filling her lungs with the cool, clean night air. When something brushed against her leg, she let out a yelp—and jumped a foot. A small whine alerted her to the culprit.

"Al." Relieved, Zoe sat on the top step, her arm around the dog. "I thought you slept in the mud room."

Al looked at her with dark, soulful eyes. He butted his nose against Zoe's chin—a doggy greeting she supposed. Then lay down, his head in her lap.

"I appreciate the company," Zoe said, giving his tummy a scratch. The deep sigh told her that her efforts were a hit.

Like brushing the horse, Zoe found it calming to have Al by her side. He didn't want answers or expect her to be something she didn't know how to be. It didn't take a lot to make him happy. A full stomach, a gentle touch, and a little kindness. If only humans were that easy to please.

"Want to go for a walk?"

Apparently, Zoe said the magic word. Al was down the steps, tail wagging, before she could get to her feet. With her companion, she wandered around, not going far from the lit area that surrounded the house. Her mind wasn't clear, but the chaos had settled to a dull roar. What was it about this place? It made her think of the book *Lost Horizon*. Was Alabama the equivalent of Shangri-La? A place where troubles melt like lemon drops?

"Nope. That's *The Wizard of Oz*," Zoe informed an attentive Al. "One of the drawbacks of a head filled with books and music is that they become jumbled now and then. Judy Garland and James Hilton? Not quite in the same ballpark."

As Zoe stopped to admire the moonlit night, her phone buzzed.

"Car is ten minutes out." Surprised, she looked at the time. "I'll be."

Zoe patted Al's head. "You helped me pass the time, my friend. I wish I had a bone or something equally tasty. I guess a thank you will have to do."

Al's tongue swiped Zoe's hand. "Since you're such a gentleman, I will take that as a *you're welcome.*"

Zoe had always had good timing. The hired car was pulling to a stop just as she rounded the corner of the house.

"Ms. Hart?"

"That's right."

The driver tipped his hat, handing Zoe his identification.

"My luggage is on the porch."

"Running?"

Zoe sighed, her eyes closing briefly. *So damn close.* Composing her expression, she turned to face Smith.

"No."

"What do you call slipping away in the middle of the night?"

The driver put the last suitcase in the trunk. "All set, Ms. Hart."

"Thank you." Zoe met Smith's gaze. "I'll see you in London."

When she would have gotten in the car, Smith put a hand on Zoe's arms. "How can you be so calm?"

"Would you rather fight?"

"Hell, yes." Smith's grip tightened for a brief second before dropping away. "Yell at me. Tell me I'm an asshole. Tell me—" He shot her a look filled with anger and frustration. "Tell me anything. But don't leave. Or wait until daylight. I'll drive you to Birmingham."

Two hours in a confined space? With Smith. No! Zoe wasn't up to his questions or the bite of his disappointment when she had no answers.

"Goodbye, Smith."

"Goodbye? Is that what you really mean?"

"For now."

Zoe slid into the backseat.

"Here." Smith handed her an envelope. Manila, not blue. "I wrote you a letter. Two, actually."

"When?" Zoe traced her name, the single word in Smith's familiar handwriting.

"One last week. One tonight."

Frowning, Zoe kept her eyes on the envelope. "Why didn't you mail them? The one from a week ago?"

"I don't know. Maybe I was afraid you wouldn't write back."

As she reached for the door, Zoe looked at Smith one more time. "I would have," she said. "I always will."

Zoe shut the door before Smith could respond. However, the flash of surprise in his eyes had her lips curving with bittersweet regret.

The car pulled away. Zoe didn't look back, but she could picture Smith and Al standing together, watching her disappear into the night. For several miles, Zoe stared at the envelope. She couldn't chuck it out the window. Nor was she keen on opening it. Two letters. The first one shouldn't be too bad. Right?

Zoe tore the seal, dumping the contents onto the seat. Instead of two, three items fell onto the leather upholstery. She recognized the folded stationery immediately. The third piece of paper was larger, but she knew what it was before she looked.

Neat, hand-drawn lines covered the surface. Black dots—some with tales, some without, were everywhere. To the untrained eye, the placement of the dots might have seemed random. To Zoe, they were a perfectly formed masterpiece. The song Smith had written for her. There was no copyright or proof of ownership. Not even his scrawled signature.

With a less than steady hand, Zoe set the song aside. She hovered over the letters, trying to decide which to choose. Two pages or one? It seemed logical that last week Smith would have had more to say. Tonight's note probably contained an angry rant and a screw you.

Hoping she was right, Zoe picked up the longer letter.

Dear Zoe,

It's been three days

Zoe let out a relieved sigh.

I'm still kicking myself for letting you go without finding out what was wrong. I know what you're thinking. I could have asked, but there was no guarantee you would have answered. FYI? Stubbornness is not a virtue.

Zoe smiled.

I should have pushed even knowing you would push back. Was I right to give you space? Are you okay? Would you tell me if you weren't? Probably not. You want to stand on your own two feet. I applaud you for it.

That said, there is no shame in asking for help. Forget that. You don't have to ask. Simply hold out your hand. I will always take it.

Her eyes burning, Zoe blinked. Damn the man. First, he jabs at her for her stubbornness. Then, he turns around and says something so lovely she wanted to cry.

Call me. Text me. Write me a letter. Please. I need to know how you're doing.

So ends the emotionally charged part of our program. We have almost a month until London. This is a formal invitation to join me for a week of fun and relaxation in South Ridge, Alabama. Did I mention the sex? No? Relaxation. Sex. I consider them to be the same thing.

Why South Ridge when you have your choice of vacation locations? Point of interest number one—and first on any list worth its salt—I'll be there.

Smith went on to tell her about his family and their farm. Some things Zoe learned during her brief stay. There was more. Interesting, amusing little stories that had her chuckling. Smith painted a vivid picture with his words. Because she had met the cast of characters, Zoe could picture them all.

Setting aside the letter, Zoe felt a pang of regret. More like an entire truckload. Ben and Nellie had welcomed her with open arms, and she repaid them by taking off without saying goodbye.

Maybe a letter? *And* a phone call. Smith's parents deserved *at least* that much consideration.

Zoe's gaze fell on the last piece of paper. *Oh, what the hell.* There wasn't much Smith could say that she hadn't already said to herself. She hoped.

Zoe,

Just her name. It seemed she no longer rated *Dear Zoe*. One word in and she felt her stomach begin to knot.

I'm not going to rail at you in a letter.

That was encouraging.

I wrote the song for you. Only you. If you don't want to record it with me, then it will never be heard. Frame it. Tear it up. Burn the fucker. I don't care.

Does this sound like a guilt trip? I suppose it is. That wasn't my point, so I'll call it a bonus. The song was a message. In case you missed it, here it is.

It's a love song. I. Love. You. I guess I was crazy to think that was a good thing. I'm not sorry. If you are? Too damn bad. I have the right to feel the way I feel.

I hope we can hash this out in the morning. If you're reading this letter, I guess that wasn't possible. The next move is up to you. Understand this. I don't care if you never sing to anybody. Not even me. That was never what this was about.

Next stop, London.

Smith

Zoe stared at the letter, rereading it again and again. *I. Love You.* That was the part she kept going back to. Reaching out, she picked up the sheet music. Of course, it was a love song. *Her* love song.

To herself, Zoe read the music, her foot tapping out the beat. Gradually, she added the lyrics. Again and again. Just like Smith's letter. Time passed without notice. By the time the car had reached the airport, she had her song memorized.

With care, Zoe returned the song and the letters to the envelope. The plane was fueled and ready to fly her to Los Angeles. She slipped on her sunglasses before stepping onto the tarmac. Smith was right, she thought, the song still in her head. The next step was up to her. The question was, did she have the strength to take it.

Chapter Twenty

"RYDER? Are you busy?"

Ryder motioned Zoe into his office. He and Quinn hadn't settled on a permanent residence. Right now, they were living in a luxury downtown hotel. They planned on settling someplace permanently—someday. For the time being, they enjoyed the luxury of room service and a maid who changed the sheets every day and delivered clean towels whenever needed.

"Why am I doing paperwork and paying bills when we pay a business manager?"

"For the same reason, I do. It's our money. If we don't keep an eye on it, nobody will." Zoe took a seat on the sofa. "You told me that. Remember?"

"I wonder who told me?" Ryder leaned back, his fingers drumming on the desk.

"You read it in a book."

"Damn books. Serves me right. If I were content with my tenth-grade education, I wouldn't be smart enough to care about what happened to my money."

Ryder loved to joke about his lack of formal schooling. In truth, he read more—with a mind-boggling diversity of subjects—than most college graduates.

"I need to talk."

"It's about time." Ryder shut his laptop, giving Zoe his undivided attention. "You've been moping around ever since you got home. I wanted to kick you in the ass days ago."

"Why didn't you?" Zoe asked. She took a seat on the sofa.

"Quinn wouldn't let me."

"It's gotten that bad?" There hadn't been much for Zoe to laugh about lately. A joke at Ryder's expense was just what she needed. "Quinn has you that far under her thumb?"

"About some things," Ryder admitted freely. "She reminded me that you would come to me when you were ready."

"She was right."

"She usually is." Ryder swiveled from side to side, waiting for her to speak.

Zoe had given this a lot of thought. The arguments she had with herself had been epic. Finally coming to a decision, she approached Ryder. Now that she was here, it was harder than she anticipated. And that was saying something.

After seven days of no-holds-barred self-evaluation, Zoe had come to a conclusion about herself. Her childhood had screwed her up more than she wanted to admit. She loved to sing. She hadn't realized how much until faced with the prospect of never singing the song Smith had written for her. Damn the man. He hit too close to the truth.

"I want to apologize," Zoe blurted out.

"What is it you think you've done?"

"How long have you tried to get me to sing lead on a song?"

Ryder snorted. "Forever?"

"Close enough. Promise you won't hate me?"

"Zoe." Ryder walked across the room, joining her on the sofa. "What is this about?"

"You're the lead singer. Period."

"No," Ryder corrected. "I'm the lead singer. There's always been room for you. Or Dalton. Or Ashe. I stopped suggesting it to them a long time ago because I was tired of hearing them laugh their asses off. You just snarl and leave the room."

"I don't snarl." Actually, that was exactly what she did. "I think I've changed my mind."

"That's terrific." Genuinely happy, Ryder gave her a quick hug. "What changed your mind? And what about that apology you mentioned?"

Zoe sighed. The apology thing just slipped out. Nerves. She debated glossing over it. But that would be a lie by omission. There were some things Zoe was willing to keep from her brother—if she thought it would save him from some unnecessary pain. Not this time.

"You took care of me. Kept me safe." Zoe looked into her brother's eyes, wanting desperately for him to understand. "I wanted to do the same for you, but I couldn't. You didn't need me the way I needed you. So…"

"Son of a bitch." It was said under his breath, the vehemence made Zoe wince. "You think I *needed* to be the group's exclusive lead singer because our father abused me and not you? That's crazy, Zoe."

When Ryder jumped to his feet, Zoe followed. "No. I mean maybe."

"You pity me." Zoe had expected anger. The sadness in Ryder's expressive blue eyes cut her to the quick. "Of all the things you could have told me? I think that hurts the most."

"Never." Fiercely, Zoe grabbed Ryder's shoulders, giving him a shake. "You are the least pitiable man I have ever known. You're brave. Strong. I am floored by your capacity for love and compassion. We were misfits. You, me, Dalton, and Ashe. We became a group, but you made a family."

That brought Ryder up short. Covering his face with his hands, he shook his head. "I want to be angry. Then you go and say something like that."

"If it helps, I didn't do it on purpose. Honestly, Ryder. I've been happy playing guitar and singing backup. Until recently, I didn't think I wanted more than that."

Ryder leaned against his desk, his arms crossed. "What changed?"

"You did. Or rather, you found a sense of peace that you've never had before. Another reason for me to like Quinn." Zoe paced, aware that Ryder was waiting for her to finish. "Whatever was holding me back, isn't anymore. I hope that makes sense because I don't have anything else."

"I read a psychology book."

"Of course, you did," Zoe said, tongue in cheek.

"If that was your attempt to tease a smile out of me? Stop."

Zoe sobered. "Too soon?"

"Yes."

"I took care of you the only way I knew how. Subconsciously, I think you were doing the same for me."

"*Are* you angry? Disappointed?" Zoe couldn't stand the idea of either.

"A little of both. But I'll get over it."

"They really messed us up." It seemed like just when Zoe thought they had dealt with every shadow from their past, another one reared its ugly head.

Ryder opened his arms. Gratefully, Zoe walked into them. As always, a hug from her brother was like a soothing balm.

"What happened to us can't be erased, Zoe. We've refused to let it define us. There are a lot of people who would be living in a rubber room, curled into a ball."

"Not the Hart kids."

"That's right. We learned early that life can be a mother you-know-what. Instead of giving in, we gave life a full-on kick in the nuts."

"Yes, we did." Zoe liked the way Ryder put it. Feeling better, she moved to the mini-bar, grabbing two bottles of water. "For future reference? I'm not five years old. You can say *fucker*. I've heard worse."

Ryder accepted the water. "Not from me."

"Fair enough."

"Are you ready to step up to the mike? I'll enjoy a break or two. Or three."

Zoe smiled. "One. To start."

Taking a seat, Ryder's expression became quizzical. "Tell me. What was the catalyst of this sudden epiphany?"

"Smith Carson." When Ryder didn't respond—except to narrow his eyes—Zoe raised an eyebrow. "You have Quinn. Dalton has Colleen. Ashe has Belle. Don't I deserve my own somebody?"

"You're in love with Smith?"

Zoe didn't care for the tone of Ryder's voice. "You sound surprised."

"Nobody is good enough for you, Zoe. However, I don't have to live with the man—thank God. Does Smith make you happy?"

"Yes."

"Does he treat you right?"

"Always."

"Then I'll get used to him."

"Gee, thanks, big brother."

"Don't mention it," Ryder said with a wave of his hand as if Zoe's words hadn't been heavily laced with sarcasm. "Now that we've settled that. If you're going to do this, you might as well make your debut in London. Do you have a song in mind?"

"As a matter of fact, I do." Zoe took the sheet music from her bag.

Ryder looked it over. "Smith wrote this?"

Anxious for Ryder's opinion, Zoe nodded. "For me."

"Huh." Tossing the paper onto his desk.

"Well," Zoe demanded.

"We need to work on the arrangement. If you want to debut it in London, we need to hit the rehearsal studio."

"You like it." Zoe knew it was a good song, but Ryder's approval was the cherry on her already scrumptious sundae.

"If that song doesn't go multi-platinum—at the very least—then there is no justice. Zoe," Ryder grinned. "That S.O.B. wrote you a hit."

ZOE LOOKED AT herself in the mirror. She had gone through this pre-concert routine more times than she could count. The only thing that changed was her outfit and the way she chose to wear her hair. Tonight, she wore a dress. The vivid blue material hugged her body like a glove showing off her subtle curves while the hem stopped at mid-thigh, highlighting her long legs. As for her hair. Tonight, Zoe left it hanging in a straight, silky shot down her back. Two thin braids framed her face, a string of genuine diamonds weaved into each one.

There was a brief knock on her dressing room door. It opened before Zoe could give permission.

"Want to talk?" Quinn asked, leaning in.

"No." Without glancing up, Zoe zipped her feet into a pair of black ankle boots with an intricate series of crisscrossing silver straps and buckles.

"Want to get drunk?"

Zoe laughed. "Tempting. But since I'm about to face a sold-out Wembley Stadium, that's a hell no."

"Want me to get the hell out of here and leave you alone?"

Not that long ago, Zoe's answer would have been a resounding *yes*. It seemed those days were over. She shook her head.

"No. Stay. Please."

Quinn closed the door behind her. Dressed in black leather leggings and a white silk shirt, she looked exactly like what she was. A kickass photographer. The glow of happiness had to do with her rock star fiancé.

By now, Quinn knew Zoe pretty well. She took a seat and waited for Zoe to speak. Or not. Either way, it was nice to have some company.

"This could go horribly wrong." Zoe knew better than to expend energy before a concert. The butterflies in her stomach would burn off as soon as she hit the stage.

"Do you want my opinion?"

Zoe nodded. To keep her hands busy, she fiddled with the large gold hoops that dangled from her earlobes.

"Smith will come through. Great song. Happy ending."

"He told me the next move was mine."

"And you've made it."

"That doesn't mean he'll like it. What if Smith has changed his mind?" That particular scenario had plagued Zoe's sleep for the past two weeks.

"He hasn't." Quinn's confidence made Zoe feel a little better. Not great, but better. "Are you nervous about singing for the first time in front of an audience?"

"Not a bit. Ryder, Dalton, and Ashe are three of the toughest critics around. If they weren't certain I could pull this off, they wouldn't let me anywhere near a microphone."

Zoe wasn't putting on a brave face for Quinn's benefit. Playing lead guitar, she was used to getting attention on stage. Tonight, she would step into a different kind of spotlight. It felt right. A year—even six months ago—she wasn't ready. Now, she was. The fluttering in her stomach had nothing to do with singing. Her butterflies had Smith written all over them.

There was a rap on the door. "Five minutes, Ms. Hart."

From her bag, Quinn grabbed her ever-present camera, snapping a quick picture of Zoe. "You look gorgeous. I swear, if Smith Carson screws this up, I'll kick his ass."

"Thanks," Zoe said. "But if this whole thing goes south, I'll have nobody to blame but myself."

"WHERE ARE YOU going?" Randy chased Smith down the steps. "Your dressing room is in the other direction."

"I don't feel like sticking around." Using the towel that was draped around his neck, Smith wiped the sweat from his face. "I'll shower back at the hotel."

"Wait."

Smith was tired of waiting. For three weeks, he waited to hear from

Zoe. After arriving in London, he waited for her to get in touch. Up until show time, he waited for some kind of message. A word. Anything to let him know she had made up her mind—one way or the other.

Smith had completed his part of the evening's entertainment. The crowd was happy even if he wasn't. Zoe knew where he could be found. He was through waiting.

"Damn it." Rather than try to keep up, Randy stopped. Raising his voice, he yelled, "Get your ass back to your dressing room."

"What did you say?" Smith was in the mood for a fight. Randy's size and bulk made him the perfect target.

"There's a letter waiting on your dressing table. From Zoe."

Unclenching his fists, Smith smacked his assistant on the back. "Why the hell didn't you say so?"

"If you had gone to your dressing room in the first place, I wouldn't have needed to." Realizing he was talking to himself, Randy took a seat on the stairs. Ever since Smith returned from Alabama, he had acted like a bear with a sore tooth. Randy couldn't take much more of it. Crossing his fingers, he raised his eyes upward and said a prayer for love.

OUT OF BREATH, Smith tore down the corridor, ignoring the speculative looks sent his way. He fumbled with the key to his dressing room door, cursing the inconvenience. Finally, he was inside.

The letter wasn't hard to find. The white envelope was propped against the mirror. Without preamble, Smith tore it open.

I hope this isn't the last letter that I write to you. I know that it's the most important.

Three words. I refuse to put them on paper before I say them to your face. I want to see your eyes. I hope to hear you say them back. Will you? If the answer is yes, Randy knows what to do. If not? I don't want to think about that possibility.

With all my heart, thank you for your patience, dear, dear, Smith. Only you can say if it's been worth it.

Zoe

Smith looked at the clock. Almost two hours until Zoe would be finished. Unbuttoning his shirt, he tossed it on the floor followed by the rest of his clothes. Whistling, he gave the letter one more glance before he entered the bathroom. It appeared he would be taking his shower here after all.

THE STAGE WENT dark, inciting the crowd to grow louder—if that was possible. The moment was for effect. Ryder had thanked everyone for coming. However, there wasn't a person in the stadium who believed for a second that the show was over. Standing. Cheering. Clapping. Nobody made a move toward the exits. They knew what was coming and they knew the role they were supposed to play. Adding to the noise, the crowd began to stomp their feet.

"Are you ready?" Ryder asked Zoe, exchanging one guitar for another that waited just off stage.

"That depends on Smith."

"He's here." Ashe downed a bottle of water, pouring the last bit over his head.

"Where?" Zoe looked around. "I don't see him."

"On the other side of the stage. I caught sight of him just before the lights went out."

Zoe felt her stomach settle. There was nothing left for her to do. She had made her move. The rest was up to Smith.

Taking a deep breath, she met the gaze of her friends. Ryder first. Then Ashe. Finally Dalton. Her bandmates. Her family. If she fell on her face, Zoe knew they would pick her up. They were ready. All they needed was her signal.

Zoe nodded. "Let's do this."

On cue, the spotlight came on, following the band as they took their places. Fans in the audience had seen this year's tour enough times to know what was coming. Ryder would step to the front—as he always did—and *The Ryder Hart Band* would play their encore. When Zoe moved to the microphone—breaking protocol—an anticipation-filled buzz filled the already raucous stadium.

"Hello, London! My name is Zoe Hart."

Zoe's voice was clear and strong. She didn't have long to wait for the audience to yell hello in return. She grinned when the wave of their response nearly knocked her back a step. Knowing it wasn't possible amidst the noise, she would have sworn she heard Ryder's laugh. Looking to her right, she caught his smiling wink. There was nothing she couldn't do when her brother had her back.

"As most of you know, I play a little guitar." There was another roar. "Tonight, with your permission, I would like to try something new. We have a new song—written by a friend of mine. It's called *The Only Chance I Wanted*. Since he wrote it for me, it seems only right for me to sing lead. However," Zoe yelled over the wildly enthusiastic shouts of encouragement, "I can't do it alone. Smith? Will you join me?"

Eyes glued to the light spot at the edge of the stage, Zoe's heartbeat drowned out the craziness going on around her. Though only seconds passed, the wait seemed like it took an eternity. Zoe locked her knees in case her shaky legs decided to give out. As Smith stepped onto the stage, Zoe didn't feel the stage shake. She didn't hear the screams. The flashes of camera lights didn't register.

Smith—tall, handsome, his eyes locked with hers—took Zoe's hand. Leaning close, he raised his voice just enough so she could hear. "Breathe."

Zoe nodded. The music started. Smith took his microphone. And together, they brought the house down. Everything slowed down. They were making a memory—for the audience—but mostly for each other. Anybody lucky enough to be there that night had no idea what they were witnessing. It wasn't just the debut duet between two superstars. It was a love story playing out before their very eyes.

When the last note faded, Zoe lowered her microphone. Smith did the same. They bowed—again and again. Waving, they acknowledged their fans. If the lights hadn't dimmed to black, it could have gone on all night.

Before Zoe could fully catch her breath, Smith pulled her off the stage.

"Slow down," she laughed, jumping to avoid a pile of cables. "These boots were not made for running."

Without breaking stride, Smith lifted Zoe into his arms. He deftly weaved through the stagehands and miscellaneous bodies that littered the backstage area. Some people stopped to gape, others were too focused on their jobs to pay attention to a couple of crazy musicians.

Randy waited by the dressing room door, opening it as they arrived.

"Nobody gets in." Smith slow down. "If I hear so much as a knock, you're fired. Understood?"

"Understood, boss."

"You can put me down now," Zoe said when they were alone.

"No. I don't think I can."

Smith kissed Zoe. It was a combination of leftover adrenaline, frustration, need, and love. Now that she knew how the emotion felt, she had no problem recognizing it. Her hands clasped Smith's head, never wanting to let him go.

"You did it." Breathing heavily, Smith broke off the kiss. His green eyes blazed with heated satisfaction.

"*We* did it." Zoe slid to her feet. Smoothing the hair from Smith's forehead, she found she couldn't stop grinning. "I was so afraid you weren't going to join me on that stage."

"How could I not? You were giving me what I wanted most."

"Me singing?"

Smith shook his head. "Your heart."

"I love you." Zoe didn't wonder that the words came easily. There was no need for hesitation when something was so perfectly right.

"Now, I ask you. Was that so hard?"

Zoe laughed, throwing herself into Smith's waiting arms. The journey had been brutal. Now that she was at the finish line? It was the easiest thing Zoe had ever done.

Epilogue

GOLD HAIR GLINTED in the late spring Alabama sun. With joyful abandon, she ran through the field toward the person she loved most. Smith held out his arms. Awkward yet adorable, the puppy jumped without the least bit of worry. Implicit trust. It was a beautiful sight to behold.

"She has you wrapped around her little paw," Zoe said from her seat beneath the old cedar tree.

"It's your fault." Smith pet the puppy, concentrating on the spot she liked best, behind her right ear. With a final pat, he put her down so she could explore the new territory.

Zoe had arranged for the puppy to be waiting when they arrived at the Carson farm. Love at first sight. It went both ways. For the last three days, man and dog had been practically inseparable.

"It's a good thing I'm not the jealous type."

"Marigold loves you too." Smith joined Zoe on the blanket, pulling her close. He picked a small, purple wild flower that grew randomly all over the hill, tucking it into her hair. "Not quite as much, but it is love."

Yes, Zoe thought with a sigh, her head resting on Smith's shoulder. It was definitely love. He understood that the tiny flower meant more to her than dozens of store-bought roses ever could. The feelings she had for Smith grew with each passing day. There was no limit. Which was fine with Zoe. She finally found her happiness. Bigger. Better. Never ending. Only a fool would argue with that. And Zoe Hart was no fool.

"I had a phone call from Ryder before we left the house."

Zoe didn't question why Ryder had called Smith instead of her. Her man was part of their circle. Fully accepted by everybody—including her brother.

"They're still coming, aren't they?"

"The plans haven't changed."

The entire gang—Ryder, Quinn, Dalton, Colleen, Ashe, and Belle— were due to arrive the day after tomorrow. It wasn't their first visit. In the past six months, the farm had become a favorite destination. Smith's parents had welcomed Zoe's family with open arms. And to her amazement, her city boys took to country life like ducks to water. They couldn't wait to rise with the sun, and help with the chores. Zoe would never have guessed it possible.

"What did Ryder want?"

"*The Only Chance I Wanted* has been certified diamond."

Ten million units sold. Zoe couldn't believe it. The demand had been so great, she and Smith had agreed to record the song in London a few days after debuting it on stage. Zoe knew it had hit written all over it, but they never anticipated the popularity of the single. There was a full album planned for sometime next year. Not that they were in a hurry. Right now, they were too busy enjoying some well-deserved time off.

"You're going to be a very rich man."

"I already am." Smith rolled to his side until he and Zoe were face to face. "That song is worth a lot more than money."

Knowing what he meant, Zoe shook her head. "I like the song. I *love* you. Always."

"Forever," Smith said, the love he felt for her evident in his emerald green eyes. Gently, he kissed Zoe's lips, lingering long enough to take her breath away.

Always and forever. It was the sweetest music Zoe had ever heard.

Coming Soon

Coming In February
WITH ONE MORE LOOK AT YOU

◆

A Brand New Series Coming in 2017

ONE STRIKE AWAY
For a Little While (Book One)
For Your Eyes Only (Book Two)
For the First Time (Book Three)

After the Rain

(One Pass Away Book One)

Prologue

*L*OGAN. LOGAN. LOGAN.

Logan Price closed his eyes, taking it all in.

"Hear that, kid?" Starting quarterback Gaige Benson slapped him on the back. "Two games under your belt and you're a star. Now let's go out there and add super to the front of it."

The announcer for the team set them in motion down the tunnel with his familiar introduction.

"And now, let's hear it for your division champion *SEATTLE KNIGHTS*."

The roar of the crowd. There was nothing like it. A packed stadium. Fans chanting his name. Few people would ever experience what it was like to take the field in a professional football game.

Logan Price had been working for this his entire life. He could still remember in exact detail the first game he ever saw. Too small to climb onto the stool in his father's bar by himself, his old man had lifted him onto the seat.

Stay and be quiet.

Not an easy order to follow for an active, inquisitive little boy. One look at the game and for once, Logan had no problem following his father's command. The old TV transported him to a foreign world filled with bright lights and shiny helmeted warriors. Logan didn't know what he was watching. He did know he wanted to be one of those men.

A Sunday afternoon in rural Oklahoma. *Lefty's Pub* was filled with after-church drinkers who figured they had done their duty to God and family. The rest of the day was their time. A beer. Or two. Or six. Cronies who understood a man's need to unwind before the start of another workweek.

And football.

If the Friday night high school game was their true religion, the Sunday afternoon games were a close second. As Oklahoma boys, they hated anything Texas. The men of Denville gathered every week to root for whichever team was playing the Dallas Cowboys.

No matter how the games ended. Whether the crowd was happy or disgruntled. It meant more drinking. Hours later, husbands, boyfriends, and sons would stumble out, pile into beat-up trucks, and weave their way home to frustrated wives, girlfriends, and mothers.

As he grew older, Logan's view changed. He moved from the stool to behind the bar. And he promised himself one thing. He would never become one of those men. He wouldn't spend the week at a job he hated. His home wouldn't be a semi-wide trailer filled with hand-me-down furniture and a wife to whom he couldn't face going home.

His Sundays were going to be spent playing football, not watching it.

"Ready to take down this vaunted Arizona defense?" Gaige yelled at him, butting helmets.

Vaunted. Good word, Logan thought. His QB liked to use what his granny called highfalutin talk. Must have been that Ivy League education. He knew that Gaige Benson didn't grow up with a silver spoon in his mouth. He came from the mean streets of Brooklyn. He had the scars to prove it.

Like Logan, Gaige had vowed to get out of the life into which he was born. In the process, he polished himself up like a new penny. He took advantage of his full-ride scholarship to Yale. He didn't spend all his time on the football field. Fancy vocabulary. Fancy clothes. Fancy women. They were all part of the package Gaige purposefully fashioned for himself.

Seventeen years after clawing his way out of the tenement that he grew up in, very little of that borough-rat remained. Until game time. No one was tougher than Gaige Benson. Three-time league MVP. Considered one of the best ever to play the game. No one stood in his way when he was playing the game. He had the scars to prove it.

"Gather round."

Knights head coach Harry Coleman gathered the team close. He had to yell over the crowd, but he had the voice to do it. Booming was putting it mildly. The first time Logan heard it, he stood right beside the man. The ringing in his ears didn't go away for three days.

"Divisional game. If I have to say any more than that, you shouldn't be out here. Go kick some ass."

The defense took the field to start the game. Arizona had a rookie quarterback drafted in the second round from a small college in the Midwest. The only reason he was out there was because the regular starter suffered a concussion in last week's game and the regular backup had food poisoning. Thrown into action at the last minute, Logan swore he could see the guy's hands shaking before he took the first snap. When the ball went sailing between his legs, Logan shook his head.

The moment was too big for some people. For Logan, it wasn't big enough. He aimed for the biggest stage of all. The Super Bowl. It wasn't a matter of *if* he would get there, but when.

"Three and out." Gaige grinned, pulling on his helmet. "Come on, kid. Let's go show them how it's done."

Logan ran onto the field. *Kid.* He shook his head, grinning. From the first day of training camp, Gaige had hung that moniker on him. Ironic since he was almost twenty-five, a good two years older than most of the other rookies. However, he supposed when someone had been in the league as long as Gaige, all the new guys seemed like kids.

"We're starting on the ground," Gaige instructed them in the huddle. "Sweep out left. Basic. Got it?"

Lining up as he had a thousand other times, Logan checked the defense. He knew he was fast. One of the fastest in the game. What set him apart was his anticipation. He had the uncanny ability to read the guy covering him. He knew when to fake left or when to fake right. Stutter step or flat out, in your face, catch me if you can.

His speed got him out of Denville, Oklahoma. His brains and determination got him to the NFL.

The sounds of the game were as familiar to Logan as the back of his own hand. The call from scrimmage. Each quarterback had his own unique cadence. Gaige was a master of mixing his up. Study him all you want. Good luck figuring it out. His teammates knew. A signal just before they broke the huddle.

Pay attention, you were golden. Slack off even once? Gaige could ream a guy out with the best of them. And he had no problem doing it in the middle of the game.

An entire YouTube channel had been devoted to Gaige and his rants.

They were as legendary as the man himself. With a ball in his hand, he was cool as ice. The rest of the time, watch out.

No one would ever accuse Logan of lacking focus. Today was no exception. They were driving down the field. First and ten from the Arizona twenty-yard line. He already had three carries of thirty-five yards. It was going to be a good day.

"Ready to take it in?" Gaige asked.

"Always."

"Then show them what you've got."

A quick snap later, Gaige handed the ball to Logan. The offensive line created a seam. Not a big one. Just big enough. Using the push of his powerful legs, Logan surged through. One more step. They wouldn't catch him. No one could.

Like everything connected with the game, Logan heard the snap of the bone with total clarity. The agony that surged through his body was so intense he almost passed out. In the next few minutes, he was going to wish he had.

"Get back." Logan heard Gaige through the haze of pain. "Goddamn it. Move the hell off."

The three-hundred-and-fifty-pound linebacker didn't get off by standing. He rolled. Crushing Logan's broken leg as he went. He would never know if the move had been deliberate. Now, it was the last thing on his mind. He only cared about two things. How bad was the injury and when would he be able to play again.

"Hold on, kid." Gaige took his hand. "They're bringing the stretcher."

The team doctor checked his eyes. Logan knew he was asked some questions. What they were and how he answered, he would never remember. By the time they carted him off the field, Logan knew the break was bad.

"Gaige." Logan reached for him.

"I'm here, kid."

"Is it over?"

"The game?" Gaige walked with him, his head bent toward Logan. "No. But I promise we're going to win the bastard."

They loaded him onto the open cart. They had him secured and the vehicle rolled away before Logan had his answer. He wasn't wondering about the game. It was his career.

To no one in particular, he whispered the question again.

"Is it over?"

Chapter One

*L*OGAN SAT UP in bed, his body covered with a fine coating of sweat. He glanced at the clock. Three in the fucking morning. On the one night he managed to get to bed at a reasonable hour, he was plagued by the nightmare that had haunted his dreams for the past two years.

Running his hand through his long, damp hair, Logan fell back onto the mattress. His sheets were as wet as he was. With a grimace, he rolled onto the floor. Flexing his stiff knee, he stripped the bed, tossing everything onto a pile of dirty clothes he planned on taking to the laundromat on his day off.

There was an alternative. He could always take Linda Sue Hemmings up on her offer. She would do his laundry anytime. Payment. On-call stud service whenever her husband Darryl was out of town on business. As much as Logan hated folding socks, he decided the price was too high. He had lost a lot in the last few years. He still held onto his dignity. Just barely.

Still groggy, Logan shuffled to the bathroom. Flipping on the light, he grimaced at what the mirror reflected.

Too many late nights followed by not enough sleep. As patterns went, it wasn't a healthy one. Perpetually bloodshot eyes. Dark circles on his dark circles. He needed a haircut. Logan ran his hand over his face. Even more, he needed a shave.

He had to hand it to himself. When he let himself go, he went all the way. All he had to do was stop showering. If he wasn't worried about driving the customers away with his smell, he might have considered it.

The old plumbing rattled with protest when he turned on the faucet. It wasn't a bad place. There were worse. Logan splashed some cold water on his face. He didn't bother with a towel. It would dry soon enough on its own.

He had two choices.

Toss and turn for a couple of hours on the unmade bed – he really needed to get more than one set of sheets.

Or lose himself with an old friend.

Sleep wasn't coming which made the choice an easy one.

Logan pulled on a pair of old shorts, a faded t-shirt and sweatshirt that was too ratty to be called anything as fashionable as a hoodie. After lacing up his sneakers, he hit the road. When he was a kid, he ran for the fun of it. In high school and college, it strengthened his legs and improved his stamina. Now, the only thing it accomplished was getting him a reputation as that half-crazy Price boy. Running the deserted streets at all hours? Maybe his head had been permanently injured along with his leg.

Logan jogged past *Lefty's Pub*. The place where he spent most evenings tending bar. The day he left for college he swore to anyone who would listen that he had served his last beer. Eight years later, here he was, washing glasses and putting up with not so subtle jabs about how the mighty had fallen.

Coming back to Denville was more of an adjustment than Logan anticipated. He expected the cracks about his failed NFL career. Any kind of success tended to breed a certain amount of jealousy and resentment. There were those who reveled in his injury.

Logan Price always thought too much of himself. Denville wasn't good enough for the high school's star running back. He forgot all about us when he made it big.

The sound of his feet pounding on the unpaved side street couldn't keep the usual thoughts from creeping back. Some of what those people said was true. He had been full of himself. At seventeen, one wasn't written up in national magazines without it going to his head.

Logan never tried to hide his plans. A full-ride scholarship to the college of his choice. Then the pros. MVP awards. Super Bowl rings. The cocky attitude of a teenager wasn't any easier to take than if he had been an adult. Most of Denville embraced their golden boy.

After All these Years

(One Pass Away Book Two)

Prologue

SEAN MᶜBRIDE WOKE up with a smile on his face. It happened a lot lately. And he thoroughly approved.

He stretched his long, athletic body. Some mornings every inch of him ached. Such was the life of a professional football player. Everything was about preparing for the game. Focus. Concentration. The goal was to be ready for game day.

He had to hold it together for sixty minutes. Pull out a win any way possible. Sacrifice his body to the football Gods and pray he walked away healthy enough to do it all again next week.

Sean dreaded the day after the game. The adrenaline had long ago worn off and he felt all of his thirty years. There were degrees of bad. Sometimes he shuffled to the shower, the aches and pains palpable, but mercifully bearable.

Then there were the bad days. After a day of three-hundred-pound defensive backs using him as their own personal punching bag, he didn't get out of bed—he crawled.

Bruised from top to bottom, his joints creaked and his muscles protested like screeching banshees. Those were the times he wondered why he did it. He could have been a doctor. Or a lawyer. He could have taken his father's advice and gone into the family business. No seventeen-year-old with dreams of glory in the NFL wanted to think about becoming a butcher. But damn. Cutting meat sounded good on those mornings.

This was a good Monday. His body felt lithe—limber. The bruises were there. That was part of his life. However, yesterday had been one of those rare games when every moment fell into place. From the kickoff to the final whistle, the outcome of the game was never in question.

Sean caught every ball thrown his way. He evaded the defense. Fast as the wind. Three touchdowns. One hundred and eighty-two total yards. A damn good day for any wide receiver. He would have had more if Coach Coleman hadn't taken him out of the game in the fourth quarter. With a big lead, there was no reason to risk injury when he wasn't needed.

The after-game celebration moved from the locker room to one of the team's favorite hangouts. Naturally the atmosphere was raucous. Cautiously so.

The Knights were having a stellar season. Ten wins, two losses. Sean and his friends had enough games under their belts to understand how quickly that could turn. Injuries tended to come in bunches. So far, they were healthy. However, that was bound to change. The hope was to get to the playoffs with all their major players on the roster.

After the game, they had a few drinks. Three was Sean's limit these days. A few years ago it was a different story. He would have closed the place down after a win. He and his bed partner of the moment would have moved on to someone's apartment, partying until dawn before going back to her place and fucking like demented rabbits. Then he would go home alone and catch a few hours sleep until it was time to grab a quick shower before heading to the Knights' headquarters to review film from the game.

Those days were over. Sean wasn't a kid anymore, high on his own press clippings and more testosterone than brains. Not that he had settled down completely. He could still party with the best of them. However, he chose his moments—ones that never took place during the season.

Women were another matter. Sean liked sex. Always had. If there were a God, he always would. While his bed partners weren't as varied, they were almost as frequent.

Sean knew players who abstained a few days before the game, saving their *juice*. He wasn't one of them. Sean had plenty of juice, thank you very much. Sex was necessary for a happy and healthy mind. For *his* happy and healthy mind.

A big plus to having sex at night was sex the next morning. It was one of his favorite things. A partner, warm and willing.

The perfect way to start the day.

Speaking of which. Smiling, Sean turned over. His hand reached out, expecting to find a soft, sweet woman. Instead, he found cold sheets. Sitting up, he looked around the room. Like the bed, empty. The bathroom door was open and the light off.

Not bothering to cover up, Sean jumped out of bed. Buck naked, he searched the house. She wasn't in the kitchen. Why would she be? She didn't cook, not even coffee. She was on a first-name basis with half the baristas in Seattle.

Was that it? Would she be back soon with two cups of steaming black caffeine and his favorite muffins? Sean was talking himself into that scenario when he saw the note.

He picked up the paper that had been propped against the lamp by the front door.

Sean.

Thank you for the past few weeks. After years of building it up in my mind, I was worried that it couldn't live up to my expectations. I should have known better. It was everything I had hoped for—and more.

We didn't make any promises. No strings were attached that need to be broken. After all these years, you can finally breathe easy. It's over. We are now friends without the expectation of benefits.

When we see each other, it will be as if it, we, never happened.

Sean read the note. Then read it again.

What the fuck? What was in those drinks?

Sean searched his memory for some kind of clue. The bar. His teammates. Then she was there. They laughed. Everything was smooth and easy. They seemed to be developing a rhythm. In his mind, they were together. Not a man and a woman—a couple.

It sounded good to him. He would have sworn she felt the same. He didn't want another woman. He wanted her. In his arms. In his life.

No expectations? Hell. He woke up with plenty of them, only to find out he was alone. Alone in bed. Alone. Period.

Sean scrubbed a hand over his face. He remembered the way she tasted. The way she melted into his arms. The curves of her luscious body pressed against his. Her sighs. His belief he would never get enough of her.

Crumpling the note into a ball, Sean tossed it across the room. Suddenly he felt every ache. His legs felt like lead. Slowly, he shuffled toward the bathroom. He needed a shower. Long and hot. Determined not to look at the bed, Sean's peripheral vision wouldn't let him off the hook that easily. It captured everything. The rumpled sheet. The pillow still holding the imprint of her head. A slash of red on the floor.

Frowning, Sean picked up the scrap of silk. So small he wondered why she had bothered. The image of her standing in nothing but her heels and the panties popped into his head. Unconsciously, his body tightened with desire.

Right, that was why.

Sean ran the smooth material over his cheek, feeling it catch on his morning stubble. He breathed deeply. He smelled vanilla and spice. Her essence. He would never forget it. As long as he lived, he would be able to close his eyes and conjure up her scent. Her taste.

His eyes popped open. *Friends? Nothing more? Bullshit!*

Keeping the panties in his hand, Sean headed for the shower. This wasn't over. Not by a long shot. It was just the beginning.

After the Fire
(One Pass Away Book Three)

Prologue

*S*HE HAD ONCE asked him if he believed in a higher power.

God? Buddha? Fairies dancing around a blazing fire late at night? Something. Anything bigger than us.

Gaige Benson hadn't known what to say. Not then. But as he stood in the empty open-air stadium—the stars lighting the evening sky—he knew the answer.

Football was his religion. The field he played on and the building surrounding it, his cathedral. If a higher power had a hand in it, then his answer was yes.

He believed.

Walking to the center of the field, Gaige took it all in. He found football at the age of thirteen. A boy who saw his future mapped out. Working in a factory. Drinking away his salary. Divorce. Doling out child support without maintaining a relationship with his children. A weekend father, who half the time didn't bother to show up.

The first time Gaige picked up a football, he felt a connection. The first time he threw it, it wobbled with the grace of a drunk leaving his favorite watering hole on a Saturday night. But it didn't matter. He threw the ball again. And again. Until he taught himself to make it spin in a perfect spiral.

At the time, Gaige didn't know his talent could be useful. Where he came from, Brooklyn kids didn't dream of bigger or better. Most of them didn't dream at all. Gaige was no different.

One day he was passing a playground when a football landed at his feet. The boys on the field yelled for him to toss it back. Without thinking, Gaige sent it sailing, a perfect strike. Then kept walking. He was wary of the man who ran after him. Strangers were the enemy—according to his father. They either wanted money or accused you of something you hadn't done.

Gaige took everything his father said with a big grain of salt. Don Benson didn't have a dime to his name. Why would anyone expect to get money from him? And if a man accused his father of something, chances were he was guilty.

But Gaige was a cautious boy. He fought when necessary and ran when he had no choice. The man trying to get his attention was big. His dark complexion didn't worry Gaige. In his experience, a man was either good or bad. The color of his skin had nothing to do with it.

It turned out that this man wasn't simply good. He was the best thing that ever happened to Gaige.

Terrance Aldridge coached the local Pop Warner football team. A boy with an arm like Gaige's shouldn't let his talent go to waste. Gaige listened. Play football? On a field? With other boys? Was such a thing possible? He didn't know if it were a scam—nor did he care. If there were the slightest chance, he would take it.

The only obstacle was getting a parent's permission. Terrance gave him the papers to be signed, telling Gaige to have his folks call him if they had any questions. Gaige didn't laugh aloud, but he wanted to. His mother never asked questions. Unless they were directed at his father. Wynona Benson hadn't made a move in fifteen years unless she received permission first.

His father was another matter. His word was law. Don Benson could do no wrong. If he drank too much and staggered home two days late, it was his right. If he backhanded his wife—just because—whose business was it? He earned the money. He made the rules. End of discussion.

Gaige hadn't asked his father because he knew what the answer would be. No! Not because he thought there was anything wrong with football. He watched it every Sunday—after laying down a bet that he never won. No, he wouldn't let Gaige play because he was a mean bastard who wanted everyone to be as miserable as he was.

Gaige got around it easily enough. He forged his father's signature. It wasn't the first time and it wouldn't be the last. There was no reason to think anyone would find out. His parents didn't care how he spent his days as long as the police didn't come knocking on the door.

He could steal. Lie. Cheat. Hell, his father wouldn't bat an eye at murder. *Do what you want as long as you don't get caught.* The mantra at the Benson house.

Gaige had no intention of his father finding out. He tried out for the team and made it. The money for equipment was another matter. Gaige didn't steal. Or cheat. Lying was a necessary evil. He would have done almost anything to play but it looked like his first and only dream would die before it had a chance.

Luckily, Terrance was able to dip into a discretionary fund to help boys like Gaige. It rankled to take charity. Especially when the other boys on the team had families to pay their way.

"Don't let it stop you, Gaige," Terrance told him. "Remember. And one day, when you have the means, pay it forward, son."

Twenty-five years later, Gaige hadn't forgotten that kindness and generosity. When he saw someone in need, he did something about it. Over the years, the *Gaige Benson Foundation* paid out millions of dollars to charities and individuals. He had filled the board with people he trusted and could count on to distribute the funds judiciously and without prejudice. The first man he had recruited was the man to whom Gaige owed everything— Terrance Aldridge. Friend. Father figure. Teacher.

"Hey, Gaige." Logan Price called out from high in the stands. "You coming? The guys are waiting to go to dinner."

"Five minutes."

Closing his eyes, Gaige breathed in the air. February in Texas. Tomorrow he would play in his first—and last Super Bowl. Win or lose, he was hanging up his cleats. He was thirty-eight years old. He had more money than he would ever need. He had won every award from Rookie of the Year to league MVP—four times.

This season he put everything on the line to get here—including the possibility that he had lost the only woman he had ever loved.

Gaige Benson was known for his razor-sharp focus. Any distractions off the field were left there as soon as the first whistle blew. It wouldn't be any different tomorrow. Nothing would get in the way.

His gaze drifted to the section where she would be sitting. If she showed up. Gaige planned on going out a winner. But what about the day after? Or the day after that? His future stretched out in front of him. He had plans in place. There were hundreds of options for him to consider.

Do you believe in a higher power?

Her voice and that question had haunted Gaige for almost sixteen years. If there were a God, he prayed the woman he loved would find it in her heart to forgive him. He had a lot of years left. He didn't want to spend them alone.

In his lifetime, Gaige Benson had dreamt of only two things. Playing football. And loving Violet Reed.

Dreaming With a Broken Heart

(Hollywood Legends Book One

Prologue

T HE ROOM WAS dark. Too dark for Garrett's liking. A little stuffy, a slight antiseptic smell with an overlay of sex. That's what you got from a cheap motel and furtive lovemaking. Odors and memories you'd just as soon forget.

The sounds from behind the closed bathroom door indicated his partner was trying to remove all traces of their recent activities. It shouldn't hurt. This wasn't the first time, and damn his weak resolve, it wouldn't be the last.

If he smoked, he would have something to do with his hands. Watching his father struggle with lung cancer put the fear of God in him and his brothers at an early age. All four of them had their vices; smoking wasn't one of them.

Get up. Get dressed. For once, be the first to leave. Even if he could find the balls to walk out on her, he couldn't leave her alone at this time of night. In this part of town.

God, it was like a furnace in here. Despite having the AC wall unit on high, Garrett knew it must be hotter in here than outside. The sheet riding low on his hips was too much. Damn modesty. The room was too dark to see anything; if she didn't like seeing his naked body, she could turn away. Garrett whipped off the coarse cotton material at the same moment the bathroom door opened.

"You don't have to go," Garrett said to the shadowed figure.

"Yes, I do."

She always made sure the light was off. Her silhouette showed a tall woman, thin. Too thin. Even by L.A. standards. She was gaining weight — slowly. Garrett could attest to that. He knew it was a struggle. One she fought every day.

Garrett felt the anger drain from his body — his heart melt. Her demands were not capricious whims. They weren't her attempt to gain the upper hand. Her goal was not to manipulate. She had her reasons. They were real. Legitimate.

"It's still early."

Garrett kept his voice low and even. Shouting didn't help. She never fought back. Retreat. That was her coping mechanism. The last time he blew up it was two weeks before she would take his calls.

"I…" she cleared her voice. "His flight gets in at midnight."

"Don't be there."

"You know how he gets."

Garrett knew all right. She was devoted to a man who treated her like crap, forgot her existence ninety percent of the time, yet expected her to be there when he decided to come home. His fists clenched the mattress. It was the only thing preventing him from grabbing her, begging her to stay. *For once, pick me.*

"I don't know when I can see you again."

I don't know if I ever want to see you again. Garrett thought the words. He would never verbalize them. She was his drug of choice. Weeks passed. The need for her grew. Outwardly, his life looked smooth as glass. Inside, the itch grew.

Garrett became an expert at compartmentalizing. His work never suffered. His family never suspected. No one had the slightest clue about what was raging inside of him. *She* knew. Because she shared his unbreakable habit. Enablers. That's what they were. It was sick. Sometimes, like tonight, he hated himself. He wished he could hate her. Then, maybe, he could walk away.

"I'll be out of town for the next month."

Garrett wished he could see her face. Was she sorry he'd be gone? Relieved? Would she miss him half as much as he was going to miss her?

"Take care."

Garrett waited a second, letting the motel room door close behind her. Jumping up, rushing to the window, he pulled back the thin, dingy curtain. He never walked her to the taxi. Even the minutest chance of them being seen was too much.

The ritual of watching until she was safely inside the vehicle, seat belt on, doors locked, was something he never ignored. Nothing bad would happen to her when he was around. It was when he wasn't there that trouble found her. One more frustration. It wasn't his place to protect her. Knowing that drove him crazy.

Garrett grabbed his jeans from a nearby chair, pulling them on. Unlike her, he wouldn't clean up before he left. He would carry the smell of her with him — let it fill the interior of his car. Tomorrow he would pretend it was still there.

Damn it. Enough. He deserved more than this. They both did. One month. When he got back, one way or another, things were going to change.

Chapter One

HOLLYWOOD. DREAMS FULFILLED. Dreams crushed. It happened every day. Wide-eyed kids still came hoping to be a star. More often than not, they went back home — a nobody. Iowa, Nebraska, Texas, Georgia. Insert state here. Small town, big city. It didn't matter. The movie industry seemed vast from the outside. In truth, it was the most insular of worlds. Making it took determination, perseverance, and a whole lot of luck. Talent was so far down the list it wasn't funny.

Connections. That was what got you through the door. If you had a recognizable name, the door swung wide, the smiles welcoming. If you couldn't pull your weight once you were inside, no one hesitated to kick you out. That famous name only got you so far. The rest was on your shoulders.

Sink or swim. No life preservers were thrown your way. If anything, you were fitted with cement shoes. The only thing this town loved more than a winner was the child of a Hollywood legend falling flat on his face.

Garrett Landis felt the weight of those expectations every time he stepped on a movie set. His father set the bar so high none of his sons was expected to reach his lofty heights. The fact that all four seemed well on their way to not only matching Caleb Landis' achievements, but surpassing them, caused quite a stir.

Resentment simmered under the surface of hearty backslapping and insincere ass kissing. Their father taught his boys many things. In this business, never turn your back on friend or foe. Treat everyone with respect, from the lowliest crew member to the head of the studio. The most important thing? In this business, trust no one — except brothers. Eight years after making his first low-budget independent film, Garrett followed those rules without question. The Gospel according to Caleb Landis. His father's words were his bible. His brothers were his rock.

Wyatt, the oldest, followed directly in their father's footsteps. He was a hard-ass, bottom-line producer. Nathaniel, Garrett's fraternal twin, was the daredevil of the bunch. He was the most in-demand stuntman in Hollywood. Baby brother Colton was blessed with movie star looks. His charisma leaped off the screen, pulling in even the most cynical audience member. Or so one critic wrote after seeing Colt's first movie. Individually, each Landis brother was formidable. Together, they dominated almost every branch of the industry.

"How can we be behind schedule when we haven't shot a single frame?"

"Welcome to the glamorous world of moviemaking."

Garrett grinned when he answered his assistant director, Hamish Floyd. This was their fourth collaboration. The first two made a nice profit. Number three broke box office records. Expectations for *Exile* went through the roof the second Garrett's name became attached. With Wyatt behind the scenes, the movie's success was practically guaranteed.

Garrett didn't believe in sure things. He worked hard on every project, no matter the size. Bigger budget, more potential headaches. That included a prima donna leading lady who couldn't get her ass on set at the designated hour. Garrett refused to start leaking money on day one.

"You want me to coax America's sweetheart of the week out of her trailer?"

"You'd never get past her PA," Garrett told Hamish. "Lynne Cornish thinks one hit movie and a few magazine covers give her the right to make her own rules. She's going to find out on this movie set, there is only one set of rules — mine."

"She has a contract."

"Wyatt's standard contract. She signed it. Her mistake if her lawyers didn't read the fine print."

Contracts were fluid. *Before* they were finalized. Each actor, depending on their box office leverage, could get their people to make demands, tweak the perks. The basics were non-negotiable. Under no circumstance, barring personal injury, a death in the family, or a genuine nervous breakdown, was an actor allowed to delay production. Once, you were warned. Twice, bye-bye. As far as Garrett's big brother was concerned, potential loss of a lead actor was the reason they paid huge insurance premiums. It hadn't happened to Garrett. Not yet. There was always a first time.

Tim Bodine, Lynne Cornish's PA, waylaid Garrett before he was halfway to her trailer.

"Lynne isn't feeling well."

"She was fine an hour ago."

When she was flirting with every man on the set. Apparently, Ms. Cornish could drag herself to any early breakfast if adoring men were present. She found out quickly that Garrett wasn't among them. Whether her sudden *illness* was a result of a hurt ego or plain laziness, he didn't give a damn. Starting right now, Lynne Cornish needed to know who was boss.

"Does she need a doctor?"

"Nooo." Tim drew out the word.

The PA's lack of concern only ratcheted up Garrett's annoyance.

"Five minutes."

"What?" Tim yelled at Garrett's retreating figure. When there was no response, the man hurried to catch up. "She can't make it in five minutes. Lynne doesn't think today will work for her. At all."

Garrett rounded on the smaller man. He topped him by at least eight inches. Tim was slight, Garrett muscular. Yet that wasn't what had the PA stepping back several feet. It was the look in Garrett's steely eyes.

This man exuded confidence. Strength, both physical and psychological, radiated from his core. You didn't mess with Garrett Landis. Not if you had half a brain.

"She was looking a little better when I left her trailer," Tim said, clearing his throat. "She wanted to speak with you. *Privately.*"

Well, shit. Garrett didn't see that coming. Lynne made it clear, early on –she was interested. He made it equally clear he wasn't. End of story. They would have a friendly, professional relationship. Finding out his beautiful leading lady was angling for more didn't hold the thrill it once had. It made Garrett… tired. His personal life was full of enough turmoil — he didn't need the added drama of an on-set romance.

"I don't have the time, or inclination, Tim."

To Garrett's surprise, the PA blushed. In Hollywood, that ability was knocked out of a person fast.

"I can't guarantee anything."

"Then Lynne will be out of a job. How long do you think you'll last after that?"

Tim Bodine looked like a smart man. One capable of cajoling his uncooperative employer. Garrett didn't care what it took to get his star in front of the camera as long as it happened. Immediately.

"Five minutes?" Tim asked, a little panicked.

"I'll give you ten."

Garrett wondered if it was too late to get out of feature films. Animation. That sounded good. No location shoots. Voice-over actors happy to skip wardrobe fittings and hours in the makeup chair. A little direction on his part. Mostly setting the scene. One or two takes. Right now, it sounded like heaven.

"What's the word?" Hamish asked him.

"Bitch?"

"Any chance she'll be joining us in the near future?"

"Your guess is as good as mine."

Garrett looked around. They were ready to go. Cameras primed, leading man looking as impatient as Garrett felt. At least he'd lucked out with Paul McNally. He was a professional through and through. No power plays. No outlandish demands. There was no propositioning the director. Paul's first job was a small part in a Caleb Landis production. He was a great actor. More importantly, he was a friend. Garrett felt lucky to work with him.

"Once again, you've lived up to your reputation," Hamish said with admiration. "You really are a miracle worker."

Garrett looked over his shoulder. Lynne Cornish. In full costume and makeup. A little pouty. He could work with that. It complimented the scene.

"Tell them five."

"We're shooting in five minutes, people," Hamish called out Garrett's directions. "Pee now or forever hold it."

Garrett moved over to camera A, checking the shot. Perfect. This was his world. He knew what he was doing. No one questioned his authority or failed to jump at his command. Unlike his personal life, his professional life stayed on a clear path.

Dreaming With My Eyes Wide Open

(Hollywood Legends Book Two)

Prologue

$\mathcal{N}$ ATE LANDIS NEVER thought much about the way he looked. Women seemed to like his face. That was genetics. He was the son of Hollywood royalty. Alone, they turned heads. Together, they dazzled. It made sense that they would pass some of that on.

Nate took it in stride. He was strong. Healthy. His body was trained to do what he wanted it to do, under what could only be called extreme situations. He ate right, worked hard, and played harder.

At some point, his lifestyle would catch up with him. Age would take care of that. Right now, he was in his prime. If he wanted to scale a mountain, that's what he did. Jump from a plane? A piece of cake. Race car driving. Deep sea diving. You name it; Nate was the first one in line.

When he was three years old, his mother called him her little daredevil. Fearless, she swore he gave her wrinkles for worrying what he would get into next. Nate would always laugh, peering closely at Callie Flynn's flawless complexion. What wrinkles? In her fifties, she was, and would always be, one of the movie industry's great beauties. Nothing he or his brothers did could alter that.

As Nate stepped to the edge of the cliff, he didn't think about the two-hundred-foot drop. He'd jumped from higher than this. It was what he did. And he did it better than anyone else. For some reason, today he thought about his mother.

Callie never discouraged him from pursuing danger, even though Nate knew she wished he had chosen a safer way to make a living. She didn't say so, but he knew she worried about his safety. It didn't stop him — he seldom thought about it. Until today. As he waited for the director to signal the camera was rolling, for the first time Nate let himself worry about his mother's reaction if something happened to him.

He shook off the morbid thought. Now wasn't the time. He needed to focus. Ninety-nine percent of the time, if something went wrong, it was due to a loss of focus. Nate took a deep breath. He cleared his mind. Three flashes of light. That was his signal. He squared his shoulders, coiled his body. And jumped.

Nate Landis was a stuntman. Some might say it was his calling. If a director needed it done big and done right, that person called him. Nate loved his job.

He let his body relax as he sailed through the air. The count in his head was precise. If he pulled the ripcord too soon, the shot would be ruined. Too late, he risked ending up a pile of broken bones.

Nate planned every stunt. He worked out the timing, the logistics, and the angles. He never let anyone perform a stunt unless he tested it. Over and over again. He refused to rush. Anxious directors. Bottom-line producers. Some tried to push him into cutting corners.

Few things made Nate lose his temper. His brother Garrett claimed Nate had the longest, slowest burning fuse in history. But he had his hot buttons. Endangering himself and his crew was one of them. Last year, a director, trying to save time, ran a stunt when Nate was away from the set. Poorly conceived and executed, two stuntmen went to the hospital with second-degree burns.

Todd Winesap went to the hospital with a broken jaw and a tarnished reputation.

It took a lot to make Nate mad. But watch out when it happened.

Nate ran the count through his head. Eight, nine, ten. He gave the cord a firm, steady pull. Smooth as glass, the chute opened. Even so, he traveled at a high speed. The parachute was safety measure number one. Number two was the large, air-filled target waiting below.

Having done this stunt hundreds of times, Nate knew what to expect and how it should feel. And he knew when something was wrong.

The air bag, that Nate had personally supervised the placement of, wasn't where it was supposed to be. He didn't have the time to wonder how that had happened. If he didn't act fast, he wouldn't be around to beat the shit out of the asshole responsible.

Grabbing the guide strings, Nate pulled a hard right with all his considerable strength — and prayed.

Chapter One

HOLLYWOOD WAS AN unforgiving town with a long memory. Drugs could be forgiven. Drunk driving. Spousal abuse. Those things could be forgiven. In the movie industry, your worth was measured by one thing — box office returns. Three strikes, you're out.

Early in his career, Caleb Landis knew the meaning of holding on by his fingertips. He was young, inexperienced, and hungry. That meant working all the angles. No one opened any doors for a dirt-poor would-be producer. That was fine with him. He had no problem barreling his way in. His take no prisoners attitude earned him respect. And enemies.

Hard work. Long hours. Sacrifice. Eventually, it paid off. Caleb's career spanned over four decades. He had money and power. The shelves of his office were lined with every award the industry could give him.

When a movie had the name Landis attached to it, the world knew they were getting quality.

Sitting back, Caleb looked around the table with pride. His family. That was his greatest accomplishment. The fame and money meant nothing compared to the joy of knowing the most important people in the world surrounded him. The people he loved. The people who loved him.

It all started and ended with his Callie.

Screen goddess to the world. To him, protector of his heart.

He had no doubt the first time he saw her. He knew she was the woman he wanted to spend his life with. She was the only woman he would ever love. Their life hadn't been the fairy tale some people made it out to be.

They had their ups and downs. But through it all, one thing never changed. Their unshakable love.

His beautiful wife had given him four strong, healthy sons. Men a father could be proud of.

Wyatt was the oldest. Like Caleb, a producer. The difference was *he* trusted his gut. If a project felt right, he fought until he got it made. Wyatt was a thinker. His first concern was the bottom line. They had squared off more than once about artistry versus the almighty dollar.

The end was always the same. He and Wyatt were different enough that butting heads was inevitable. They had enough similarities to put those differences aside. The most important thing was the movie. Together they made art — and money.

Caleb's gaze moved to the other side of the table. The laugh he heard was a deeper version of his sweet Callie's. It made him smile. Colton. The youngest of his four boys. He was the only one to follow his mother's lead, stepping in front of the camera to make his mark. And what a mark it was going to be.

Colt had a face the camera loved. The first offer to put him in the movies came when he was only a year old. The offers kept coming. Callie didn't want any of her sons to be *child stars*. Caleb agreed.

Growing up was hard enough. In Beverly Hills, the temptations were magnified. Caleb and Callie did their best to give their children as normal a childhood as possible. Family dinners. Game night. Backyard barbecues. If that childhood included trips to Cannes and vacations on private yachts, so what? This was their version of normal. It wasn't perfect. But then, what was?

Colton was one of the biggest movie stars in the world. In public, that meant screaming fans and preferential treatment. At dinner with his family, he was expected to set the table and dry the dishes. It was true when he was ten. It was true now, even if his last movie *did* break box office records.

Then there was Garrett. Caleb sat back smiling when he heard his middle son complaining to his mother.

"What is the world coming to when a man's family takes sides against him?"

"First, Jade is your family. And ours." Callie patted Jade's hand. "Second. She's right. You're wrong. End of discussion."

"Hey." Garrett looked at the two women. His mother on his right. The love of his life on his left. There was no rock. No hard place. With a snap of his fingers, there would be a thousand men lined up to take his place. He was no fool. He knew he had it good. "I give up," he said, wisely conceding the point.

Dazzled by Jade's smile, Garrett melted. He tucked a lock of her long, silky red hair behind her ear. The unconsciously intimate gesture had his parents smiling with approval.

"A wise decision, son." Caleb nodded at Garrett with a wink. "When you realize your lady is the brains in the relationship, the sailing will be much smoother."

"Where are you on *Exile?*"

Garrett and Jade were just back from Vancouver where he had finished principal shooting on his current film. His last project had garnered him an Oscar nomination for best director. Caleb believed this one would win his son the statue.

"I'm in the studio next week. The soundtrack needs some tweaking, but the composer assures me it will be ready."

"It better be," Wyatt added. "The Los Angeles Philharmonic doesn't come cheap. You have them for a week. That's all the budget will allow. After that, I'll take it out of your salary."

"It's my own fault for working with family," Garrett sighed. "I could knock any other producer on his ass if he talked to me like that. Mommy would have a fit if I bruised her baby's face."

"Jade, you're marrying an idiot."

"Pardon my French in advance, Mom." Garrett gave Wyatt the finger, and then added, "Fuck you, Wyatt."

"Nice mouth, brother. You might think about washing it out with soap before kissing your woman." Out of Callie's sight, Wyatt flipped Garrett the bird.

"I just brushed. How about kissing me instead?"

"Nate!"

Callie was across the room in a flash. Instead of jumping into his arms, as was her custom, she held back. She knew the doctor said Nate's ribs were healed, but she was his mother. The thought of causing him the slightest pain was unthinkable.

"Where's your sling?"

"Gone for good. Thank God."

Nate's left arm was still in a cast. With little effort, he used his right to swing Callie in a circle. The comforting scent of roses and vanilla drifted around him. As always, it took him back to his childhood when she would tuck him in at night. Burying his face in her hair, he breathed deeply.

Mother. Love. Safety. From the time he was born, she had steered him with a gentle yet firm hand. There was a fine line between controlling and supportive. Callie Flynn showed her sons by example that a woman could thrill the world with her acting and still be the best mother anyone could ask for. Nate affectionately kissed the top of her head. What would he have done without this woman?

"We didn't think you were going to make it." Callie took his good hand, leading him to the table. "Sit. I'll get you a plate. I swear, since the accident you've wasted away to nothing."

Colt snorted in disbelief. "How can you tell? The man is a freaking brick wall."

"Callie's right." Jade smiled at Nate. "You look thinner."

"I knew the woman couldn't keep her eyes off me. Tell me you've finally realized you picked the wrong brother."

"One more word and I'll forget you're my twin." Garrett turned to Jade. "I always felt sorry for him. I got the looks, the brains, and the charm. And Nate got the…? What did Nate get?"

"The ability to kick your ass?" Nate flexed his impressive biceps. "And more women than even Colton could handle."

"Hey," Colt interjected. "That's my reputation as a man-whore you're besmirching. What would the tabloids say if word got out that my brother was getting more women than I was?"

"Don't listen to him, Colt." Garrett loved jabbing at his twin. Just as Nate loved returning the favor. The sport never grew old. "He overcompensated for his shortcomings by living in the gym. I suppose some women find brawn over brains attractive."

"More than a few."

"Enough." Callie chuckled. She had heard this banter for years. "You," she said to Nate, "stop talking — eat. And you," she looked at Garrett. "Leave your brother in peace for five minutes."

Thanking her with a smile, Nate took the plate from his mother. It overflowed with roast beef, mashed potatoes, fresh green beans, all drowned in rich, brown gravy. Adding three fresh baked rolls from the basket on the table, Nate was a happy man.

The truth was, since the accident on the movie set last month, he hadn't been himself. It would be different if he could work. Keeping busy was the best way to calm his mind and body. Unfortunately, the injuries he had sustained kept him sidelined.

Too much time on his hands. Too much time to think about what had gone wrong. The botched stunt could have ended in tragedy. Thanks to his quick reflexes, physical strength, and determination not to end up in a heap of mangled bones, Nate walked away with a few cracked ribs and a broken arm. The only reason he stayed the night in the hospital was to appease his mother. The doctor assured her Nate didn't have a concussion. Callie didn't want to take any chances. One night of observation was a small price to pay for his mother's peace of mind.

It didn't hurt that his nurse was a curvy brunette with warm, soft hands.

"I know that smile." Wyatt shook his head. "Which conquest are you thinking about now?"

"You wouldn't give me such a hard time if you were getting laid more often." Remembering where he was, Nate gave his mother a repentant grin. "Sorry."

"Your brother's love life is his own business," Callie said firmly.

"Thank you." Wyatt gave Nate a *take that* glare.

"Though…"

"Ah, crap." Wyatt's head fell forward, his chin hitting his chest.

"Come on, Wyatt," Garrett laughed with delight. "Every man lives to have his mother discuss his sex life."

Dreaming of Your Love

(Hollywood Legends Book Three

Prologue

*L*IGHTS FLASHED FROM every direction. It blinded and dazzled all at once.

Screams drowned out every other sound. This was Los Angeles. Busy streets in every direction. Jet patterns overhead. The excited—in some cases rabid—fans that surrounded the roped-off red carpet made it seem like nothing existed but them and the bright lights.

It shouldn't have been a pleasant experience. Alighting from the over-the-top luxury of a Rolls Royce into chaos and mayhem? No normal human being would willingly seek out such an experience.

However, Colton Landis was not a normal human being. He was an actor.

Colt turned his world-famous megawatt smile on the crowd, eliciting another deafening burst of heartfelt screams.

"We need to get inside, Colt. The movie starts in ten minutes."

"Relax, Deb."

Colt's publicist had been with him for five years. Deb Kline knew how to spin a press release like nobody else. They saw eye to eye on most things. Except how much he should expose himself to his fans. If she had her way, he would zip from point A to point B as quickly as humanly possible.

In this case, point A was the limo, and point B was Grauman's Chinese Theater.

"I'll relax when you are safely inside. Have you forgotten Dallas already?"

"Dallas was an anomaly."

Colt continued to wave and smile. Deb wanted him to curb his accessibility. She had always been cautious, but after a fan somehow breached security during a press conference to announce his next movie, she was particularly leery of events like this one.

"Colt."

"Don't go over there, Colt."

Deb knew the second Colt observed the waving autograph books, her words fell on deaf ears. He believed in giving his fans what they wanted. It was one of the things that made Colton Landis a huge movie star. He genuinely loved his fans. He loved meeting them, speaking with them, having his picture taken with them. Most of her clients searched for any reason to avoid these moments. Not Colt. He didn't have a public persona and a private one. What you saw was what you got—twenty-four hours a day, seven days a week.

Colt made her job as a publicist a dream. Keeping him safe was a nightmare.

He refused to have a bodyguard. Part of it was ego—and he had plenty of that. Many of his parts portrayed him as a big, macho, tough guy. How would it look if he had a bigger, more macho, tough guy constantly shadowing him? Not great for his reputation. He would look weak. And in Hollywood, perception was everything.

It was a valid argument. Not so valid? Colt believed that, for the most part, his fans were harmless. Not that he was a naïve Pollyanna. There was no need for Deb to point out the entertainment world's tragic examples of the heinous acts obsessive fans could commit.

Colt lived the life. He grew up watching his superstar mother traverse that fine line between making herself accessible to fans and maintaining some much-needed privacy.

However, he didn't have a family to consider. No wife. No children. His life was his own. A bodyguard would mean he was giving in. Turning his life over to fear instead of embracing every single moment of his fairytale existence.

"Ten minutes."

Deb didn't know if Colt heard her over the screams. Nor did she care. She was getting him into that theater if it meant grabbing his ear and dragging him along like an errant five-year-old. And wouldn't that make a great picture in *People* magazine? Okay. No ears. *Ugh. This man was going to make her old before her time.*

Colt held a woman's phone at arm's length, including himself in a selfie of her and her three friends.

"I love you, Colton."

Colt couldn't single out the speaker. The cry came from every direction. He waved and called out, "I love you, too."

He signed a few more autographs, moving along the line. Deb was right. He needed to get inside. It wasn't fair to keep everyone waiting. Ten more, he promised himself. It killed him to see the expressions on the faces of the fans who were left out.

"Thanks. See you soon," Colt called out to the crowd.

Handing her signed book to a dreamy-eyed woman, Colt gave the crowd a final wave.

"Ready?" Deb tried to maintain the *stern teacher* expression she had spent twenty years cultivating.

Colt had a way of making her professional mask slip. Thank goodness she was old enough to be his youngish grandmother. While his charm was undeniable, her age and experience allowed her to put the sexual pull that radiated around him into perspective.

Until he turned his smile on her. Full blast.

"Am I that big of a pain in the ass?"

There it was. That naughty twinkle in his deep blue eyes that made the world swoon. On screen, it was irresistible. Paired with dark hair and a tall, muscular frame, was it any wonder the camera loved him?

Reluctantly, Deb returned his smile.

Colt was her client. He was also her friend. She knew he wasn't trying to be difficult. He was being himself. For a man who was adored by millions, catered to on a daily basis, and could buy and sell two or three third-world nations without raising a sweat, Colton Landis was surprisingly down to Earth. And hard-headed. And opinionated.

On top of that? On occasions such as this one, a major pain in the ass.

Still, if she were honest, there wasn't a single thing about him that she would change. As movie stars went—hell, as human beings went—Colton Landis was a joy to be around. Not that she would ever tell him that. The last thing he needed was another person extolling his endless virtues. Colt hated that kind of treatment. One of the reasons they worked so well together was because Deb didn't kowtow.

Deb was about to hit him with one of the nifty sarcastic one-liners he loved, when a scream came from the crowd. Not a *we love you* cry, but one of terror. Before she could react, Deb saw a man jump over the velvet rope. He carried a knife.

Colt pushed her to the side, effectively putting himself between her and the attacker. *He isn't after me*, Deb wanted to protest. But everything happened so fast, she didn't have time.

In the blink of an eye, the man raised the knife and stabbed Colt.

If I Loved You
(Harper Falls Book One)

Prologue

*I*T WAS SOMETHING out of a fairy tale.

Thousands of flickering lights dazzled her senses, almost as much as the tall, wickedly handsome man who so expertly danced her onto the shadowed balcony. The music that filtered from the nearby ballroom only added to the already magical atmosphere.

Women dreamed their whole lives of a moment like this — a prelude to a happily-ever-after ending. Ever so briefly, she let herself drift into that fantasy as if she was one of those women. For a moment, she let herself pretend that her childhood had been filled with the kind of whimsicality that allowed those fantasies to carry over into adulthood.

But no, she wasn't a romantic, hopeless or otherwise. She didn't want a prince to sweep her into his arms and carry her away on his faithful steed. She was more than capable of rescuing herself. She preferred it that way.

The stars were in the sky, not in her eyes.

"I'm glad you asked me to dance," her partner whispered, pulling her closer.

Suddenly, she was nervous. The champagne she downed earlier had completely worn off. No more floating on a cloud of false courage. If she was going to do this, she was going to have to do it on her own.

"Jack," she said. Damn, it was hard to sound seductive when your voice squeaked. "Jack." That was better, lower, and slightly husky. She'd read somewhere that guys liked husky voices.

"Rose."

"Yes?"

"Nothing, I just thought we were saying each other's names." He put his lips next to her ear. "I like the way you say mine."

"Jack." Good Lord, she had to stop repeating his name. "I need a favor, Jack. A big one." Or should she say, she hoped he *had* a big one. Rose groaned to herself. At least she hadn't said that aloud.

"I'll help if I can."

"You're the only one who *can* help." She took another deep breath. "I need you to take me home and screw my brains out."

www.ingramcontent.com/pod-product-compliance
Lightning Source LLC
Chambersburg PA
CBHW071140170626
46809CB00002B/704